I0745753

Jack's
HEART

Wyoming Wildflowers Series

Wyoming Wildflowers: The Beginning (Snowberry) – a prequel

Almost A Bride (Indian Paintbrush)*

Match Made in Wyoming (Fireweed)*

My Heart Remembers (Bur Marigold)*

Jack's Heart (Yellow Monkeyflower)

Wyoming Wildflowers Trilogy Boxed Set, 3 Books in 1

* Included in Boxed Set

Jack's Heart

Wyoming Wildflowers Book Four

Patricia McLinn

Jack's Heart

Patricia McLinn

Copyright Patricia McLinnn

www.PatriciaMcLinn.com

Dear Readers: If you encounter typos or errors in this book, please send them to me at: Patricia@PatriciaMcLinn.com. Even with many layers of editing, mistakes can slip through, alas. But, together, we can eradicate the nasty nuisances. Thank you! - Patricia McLinn

All rights reserved.

ISBN-13: 978-1-939215-44-4

PROLOGUE

It hadn't been her best decision.

And that was saying something, considering some of the not-so-great decisions she'd made.

Including getting pregnant by a guy she now acknowledged she'd known in her bones wasn't the guy for her.

Including heading as far away as possible from her family in Gloucester, Massachusetts.

Every last one of them would have rallied around her. Which was precisely why she'd gone to Port Orchard, Washington. She'd gotten into this on her own, she needed to handle it on her own.

Valerie Trimarco, woman in charge.

Right.

Although, she had done okay in Port Orchard these past months. She'd supported herself, made some good friends, had everything arranged for the birth.

Every detail lined up and ready to go.

Right up until this overwhelming need to have the baby in Gloucester — to be *home* — swamped every island of sense she possessed. All thoughts of handling things on her own or even with the help of her friends disappeared. All she could think of was getting home. *Home.*

So she'd packed her car and headed for Massachusetts.

That still wasn't such an awful decision. After all, the airlines limited flying this close to the due date. Besides, she liked driving alone. And her car was reliable and sturdy.

However, even reliable and sturdy cars eventually run out of gas if they're kept running.

Running the engine for brief periods of warmth had seemed reasonable once the car got stuck in the snow-clogged ditch.

Of course it wouldn't have gotten stuck if she hadn't had to swerve to avoid that cow when she came around the curve in the road.

On the other hand, she wouldn't have been on this cow-infested road if she hadn't had to keep changing her route because of the snow storm sweeping down from the northwest. From the last report she'd heard, I-94 should be closed right about now.

So she'd made the right decision to take I-90 out of Billings, even though it had soon become clear the storm would hit her before she got far enough east to get ahead of it.

She'd adjusted again, planning to reach Buffalo, Wyoming, then swing south by way of I-25 to connect with I-80 , which also ran east-west, but — she hoped — far enough south to miss the storm.

That was not to be, either.

She'd caught a radio report about a backup before Buffalo from an accident that had spread lumber across the highway. By the time it could be cleaned up, the storm would have arrived and no one would be going anywhere.

So she'd created her own detour, taking a road south. When it ran out, she turned east. That road gave up, too, so she picked up another heading south. And did another east-south combo before she reached this one. She'd been heading east a while, so she really should have reached I-25 … if it hadn't been for that cow.

And the ditch.

Her phone repeatedly reported "no service."

Pushing was out of the question, considering her condition, but she'd tried rocking the car out of the ditch like the trained-to-drive in snow New Englander she was. Alas, no amount of rocking helped when the nose of your station wagon was sucking in mud and snow.

Then the wind picked up, blowing around curtains of snow. Not light and airy sheers, either. More like heavy velvet.

This was not good.

A sound and a shadow — later, she never could remember which caught her attention first — jerked her head toward the window of the driver's door.

It looked like a brown blanket hanging beside the window with — was that a boot?

Another sound came, this one like a voice, though she couldn't make out words.

Then, at the very top of the field of vision allowed by the window, she saw a pair of eyes. She blinked, then squinted, finally making sense of what she was seeing.

It was a man on a horseback. He'd bent nearly double, apparently to look into the window. He had a scarf muffling the lower part of his face, and the top part covered by a cowboy hat secured with a second scarf tied around it, leaving only the eyes.

"Ma'am? You okay?" He shouted it this time, and she realized it was what he'd said before.

She pressed the button to lower the window a few inches. At least there was enough juice left for that. She hoped there'd be enough to raise it again, because it was going to get very cold in the car very fast with the window even partially open.

"Where am I?"

"Ma'am?"

"Don't look at me like I've lost my marbles." Though that was mostly an assumption, since all she had to judge by were his eyes. "I know I'm somewhere in Wyoming, and I should be real close to I-25."

He'd tugged his hat even lower after her first words. "You're on the Slash-C Ranch, and you're about six miles from the Interstate."

"Hah! I knew I was getting close."

"But you've been running parallel to it for however long you've been on this road."

"Damn." She must have gotten her souths and easts confused at some point. A mini-contraction playfully stabbed her. "Damn, damn, *DAMN!*"

She panted as the contraction ebbed, knowing it wasn't anywhere near to the worst, since she'd already had a few of those.

"Ma'am, are you okay?" he asked again.

"Depends on what you mean by okay."

She had the impression of a frown from under the brim of the cowboy hat. "Pardon?"

"If you mean do I have any broken bones or other injuries, no. If you mean am I as well off as the cow I swerved to miss that ambled off looking for more grass to eat, no again. I admit this wasn't my best decision, coming off the Interstate to try to beat the weather, but it really shouldn't have turned out this bad."

"You're not hurt and your vehicle still runs—"

"I'm not hurt, but I am in pain. And my vehicle as you call it won't run long because it's about out of gas."

"I'll ride back and get you some gas—"

"You missed the part about me being in pain. I—"

She broke off, because this contraction was not a mini and it wasn't playful. She concentrated on trying to remember her training, trying not to tense up, trying to keep the hiss through her teeth a hiss and not a scream.

"Ma'am? *Ma'am?*"

Now she'd done it. She'd rattled the cowboy.

The contraction eased, not quite passing, however.

"I'm in labor," she said with uncharacteristic brevity.

His head ducked lower, apparently for a better look into the car window. "Shit."

"That about covers it. And I'm no expert, but I think this kid's eager to see the world. Like her mother. So that's probably a good sign we'll get along, and this motherhood thing should—"

She quit because the cowboy was leaving. Without even getting off his horse. He'd turned the horse and started back along the side of her station wagon toward the road. She stuck her head out the window and saw the swish of the horse's tail as it stepped up the embankment toward the road.

She couldn't believe it.

But she could. Because it was exactly the kind of outcome that resulted from too many of her decisions. Still, you'd think the guy would have at least said something—

A sound from the passenger side of the car yanked her head around to it.

Over the top of the shade to her favorite lamp, which had survived the slide into the ditch because the passenger seat was packed as tightly as the rest of the car, she realized there was something outside that frosted window.

Two somethings. The cowboy and horse shape had separated into two separate shapes. The cowboy shape was looping the reins around the passenger door handle.

He hadn't left her.

Her eyes felt hot, but tears didn't form.

He hadn't left *them.*

Then he shouted something through the closed window she didn't hear. She closed her window before opening the passenger window, because she wasn't a complete idiot, and if there was only enough juice for one move she wanted it to be to *close* a window. This way if it stopped working after she opened the passenger window there'd only be one window letting a blizzard in.

He shouted again.

"Wait a second," she snapped. Then the window was down.

"I said release the tailgate. And—"

"Why?"

"—Put this window back up so it doesn't let more cold in."

"I know. Why do you think —?"

But the cowboy shape was moving, leaving the horse shape by the passenger door.

She raised the window, but that didn't help much with keeping the outside out, because in another moment he had the tailgate open.

"What are you—?"

"Quiet," he ordered. "Working."

"Like you can't talk and work at the same ti—"

Another contraction cut her off. This one was different. She couldn't say it hurt more, because they all hurt. But it seemed more *serious*. She wanted to pull her knees up, but the steering wheel prevented it. She concentrated on breathing. *Focus. Focus. Focus …*

What was that sound?

As the contraction relented, she recognized she'd been hearing the sound for a while.

The cowboy was moving her things around on the cargo deck of the old station wagon.

"Hey, what are you doing?"

He didn't respond.

She started to turn to see what he was doing, thought better of it, and tilted the rear view mirror.

She could only see to the back in part of the mirror's view. In the rest, he'd piled her belongings up to the roof.

"I won't be able to drive," she protested. "You're blocking all my sight lines." Even family who gave her grief for being impulsive, emotional, and having wanderlust acknowledged she was a great driver. A little fast, maybe, but safe.

In the mirror, she saw a portion of his cowboy hat come up, as if he might be looking toward her. "You're not driving anywhere anytime soon."

"Couldn't you get a tow truck?"

"I've radioed the home ranch. They're coming."

"Good. That's good. Then we can wait." She didn't feel one bit guilty for roping him into that *we* waiting. Even being here with her had to be better than riding around in a snowstorm. Except … "I don't know where you'll sit, though."

"Making room back here."

"You're going to sit back there?" That didn't seem very sociable.

"Both of us."

At the moment, with the cold streaming in from the open tailgate, the prospect of being near some body heat had appeal. "Will there be room?"

"Yeah." He sounded grim. "Got any more blankets?"

"There's a box—"

"Got that. Need more for — this will do."

She saw a flash of scarlet in the mirror, tried to twist around again, found that still wasn't a good idea. "Hey, was that my cape?"

"Dunno."

"Long, hooded, cashmere, lined with satin, my favorite piece of clothing ever."

He wasn't listening. Because partway through her description, he'd backed out of the tailgate and dropped it closed behind him.

How hard was it to recognize a cape? Didn't take a fashion expert for heaven's sake, so—

Her door opened abruptly.

"What were you doing with my cape?" she demanded.

"Put your arms around my neck."

"What?"

"Put your arms around my neck."

"I heard you," she said a little testily, but she figured she was entitled. "Let's try *why?*"

"So I can carry you to the back."

"Carry me? *Carry* me? Do you have any idea how heavy I am?"

"Less than a bale of hay."

That stopped her, because she had no idea how much a bale of hay weighed. And while she was stopped, he scooped her up.

Out of self-preservation she put her arms around his neck. She figured if he started to drop her she could hold onto his neck long enough to soften her landing.

"And you're having to carry me through snow," she added.

"Been in snow before."

His breath puffed warm across the slice of her cheek exposed between her pulled-down knit cap and the scarf wrapped up around her chin and mouth.

"Why are you doing this? I was fine where I was." Sort of.

"More room."

The wind had strengthened. If his mouth hadn't been practically in her ear she might not have heard his low voice through all the layers of cloth.

"Doesn't take that much room to wait. You said somebody's coming from this ranch of yours so—"

"Not mine. I'm foreman. Not owner."

"Ownership is not real important to me at the moment."

He grunted. Might have been part of a chuckle. Might have been in pain from trying to support her elephant-like body.

He turned the corner to the back of the car, and the going got a bit easier, apparently because he'd tamped down the snow during his box-rearranging. He set her on her feet, and lifted the tailgate.

He'd created a sort of elliptical nest in the middle, cushioning the deck with blankets and—

"My cape!" She snatched the nearest section of fabric and reeled it in, bundling the fabric in her arms.

He moved as if he intended to lift her again. She evaded it by swinging her arm away, and nearly lost her balance on the snowpack underfoot. She saved herself by sitting — hard — on the edge of the tailgate.

"Can you get in by yourself?" he asked doubtfully.

"Yes."

And she did. By inching herself backward like a panting, heaving cross between a crab and a rhinoceros. Each time she moved backward she scrunched up the blankets a bit, and he pulled them down.

As soon as she got far enough in that — with her knees bent — the tailgate could be closed without performing a double footectomy, she flopped back, trying to replenish her oxygen. The wadded up fabric of the cape sat on her chest. She watched it rise and fall with each breath.

She supposed she should be grateful she hadn't had another contraction during these maneuvers.

"Okay?"

Her eyes flicked to him. He'd come up beside her without her even noticing his movement. In other words, he'd climbed in like it was the easiest thing in the world. Damn him. "You're kidding, right?"

He made that sound again, and since he was no longer carrying her, she had to conclude it had more to do with amusement than pain.

"I'm gonna radio again."

In the time she took two breaths, he was out and had dropped the tailgate down, cutting off the wind.

She started trying to fold the cape to put it somewhere safe. But the voluminous flow of fabric made it more than a little tricky while she was lying down and with barely enough room to stretch her arms.

She could just make out his voice over the wind, which probably meant he was shouting into the radio. She listened harder, trying to assess his tone.

Neutral. Matter-of-fact.

Then she felt the serious pain edging back in. Sliding in inexorably, like an oil slick being brought to shore by the tide.

She fisted her hands in the cape's material.

Each swell, rising a little higher, carrying the black, foul-smelling blob of pain a little closer until—

"How're you doing?" he said from someplace close by. He had to be, right? She couldn't hear him that clearly if he were outside, but she hadn't heard him get in— Oh, hell, who cared?

"The contractions are coming— Oh … Oh, God!" Pain swallowed the universe and her along with it. There was nothing but pain. There would never be anything but pain.

It receded, but she knew that was just a ploy so it could hurt more the next time. Higher and closer with every swell. She knew the ocean's ways. This was an ocean of pain.

But at least, for now, it let her see what was around her. She looked up into the cowboy's face.

He was partially kneeling beside her, his hat was gone. He had light brown hair with a weird dent in it. And eyes somewhere between blue and gray.

"My cousin has gray eyes," she said between pants. Why was she panting like she'd run ten miles?

He frowned. "That so?"

"That's so. Eleanor Thatcher — McRae. Can't forget the McRae becau—"

She screamed. Not like at a scary part in a movie scream, where you follow up with a nervous laugh. But a scream like when the pain that swallowed you had all its knives out slicing every little bit of you.

When she reached the border between the ocean of pain where she would never leave and the world that other people inhabited, she realized the cowboy had his hand on her forehead, stroking back her hair.

"You're going to have that baby soon."

"Can't. Water hasn't—" She panted the words out. She didn't have her breath back from the pain or the scream or both. "—broken."

"Sometimes doesn't happen until after. We're going to deliver it here."

"Here? Don't be silly. We can't—"

"We can."

He said it so simply, she began to believe. "Have you delivered a baby before?"

"Yes."

She looked up into his eyes. They were very calm. Yet, sad. So sad. Why would he be so sad? Because she was going to die? But he'd said he'd delivered babies before, so… "Oh, shit, you mean *cows!*"

"Cows and horses and sheep and dogs."

She gestured to herself. "Human!" Then at her abdomen, "Human baby!"

"It's all nature."

"I don't think so. I'm not—"

"You're going to have this baby. Here. And soon. And nobody else is going to get here before you do. It's you and me."

She locked eyes with him and opened her mouth to point out again what a stupid, horrible, bad, bad, *bad* idea this was. His calm, sad eyes stared back at her.

She said, "You and me."

"Right. I'm going to need some room. So—" He hooked her under her arms and slid her more toward the front of the car. She was sitting up more than she had been, which was slightly more comfortable. Like being on a bed of pins instead of needles.

He spread the cape over her, then started backing up.

"Where are you going?" She didn't sound panicked, because she didn't panic. She was up for anything. Ready for any adventure. Yes, sir. That was her.

"We gotta get you out of these pants. Fast." He opened the tailgate and stepped out, having to remain bent over so he didn't hit his head. He started on her shoes, but left her socks on.

"Won't be hard. I haven't worn anything but elastic for months. Never thought I'd miss zippers, but — Wait. Wait!" He'd started to tug on the bottom of the pant legs, which were cooperating like they thought they were going to get some action.

"Contraction?"

"No." The pants were gone. He draped the side of the cape over her, moving more things around. Making room for where he'd have to be when she— "This is going to happen. This is really going to happen. Here. Now."

"Yes."

"And you're going to use my cape."

"Yes."

She loved that cape. This kid better be worth it. And if anyone else ever said anything like that about her precious baby she would scoop their heart out with her fingernails. "Oh, God, at least tell me your name."

"Jack, Ma'am. Jack Ralston."

"I'm Valerie. Valerie Trimarco. Or Val. Lots of people call me Val."

"Ma'am." He crawled back in beside her, tugging the tailgate closed after him. The wind howled at having its fun thwarted.

"If you call me Ma'am one more time, I swear I will not try to muffle my screams one little bit."

His mouth quirked. "Okay, Valerie."

"Okay. As long as we understand each other." For no reason other than the reasons that had been staring her in the face for hours, some of them for months, her eyes welled with tears. And then the well ran over. "Oh, God, Jack Ralston, what are we going to do?"

He leaned over her, looking her straight in the eyes. "We're going to have this baby, Ma— Val. You and me."

"You and me," she repeated.

"And everything's going to be okay."

CHAPTER ONE

Present Day

"And everything was okay, because you came into the world, bright and beautiful and healthy and screaming," Val said, concluding the expurgated version of her birth that Addison Rose Trimarco loved to hear.

And now everything was going to be okay with this, too.

It was a good idea. A great idea. Her followers would go nuts for it. That's why she was back in Wyoming for the first time in three and a half years.

"Now, it's time for you to go to sleep."

"Say it, Mommy."

"See you later—"

"Allie-gator." They finished together.

As her daughter giggled, she stroked her hair back from her forehead. "Sleep tight, Addie."

"No bites," Addie ordered. She'd shortened the traditional don't-let-the-bed-bugs-bite goodnight wish into a command to the universe that matched her spirit.

Then she closed her eyes and went to sleep.

That still astonished Val.

For the first two-and-a-half years of her life, Addie had been what could be kindly called an erratic sleeper.

That's how the blog, then the podcasts had started. With her own sleep echoing her daughter's disjointed patterns, Val had found herself awake and longing for connection at the oddest times and often with only snatches of moments to try to fill the craving.

So, rather than harass family and friends who didn't keep Baby Hours, she'd blogged. And she'd discovered a community of other mothers feeling as if they'd been unplugged from the universe. She gave them a voice through "Mommy: The Truth Zone" and they gave her astonishing loyalty. Everything blossomed from that. She made a living now at something she loved.

Nearly as miraculous, Addison had gone to sleep one night almost a year ago at a normal time, and that was that.

Val slipped out of the cottage's solitary bedroom. The double bed had already been there. Her kind hosts had added the youth bed for Addie.

In the living room, Val picked up her keyboard, plugged it in to the travel monitor, and started typing about the miracle of Addie going to sleep. Remembering the years of sleepless or fragmented nights and days, she hoped her earlier travails — and their eventual end — would give someone out there tonight the knowledge that they weren't alone. That there might be a full night's sleep somewhere in their future.

It was strange not to be telling her readers about what she'd been doing today.

But that would ruin the surprise.

So it had to wait until tomorrow, when she would finally thank Jack Ralston.

Really thank him. With a surprise party to celebrate what he'd done for her and Addie, joined by the people who knew him here in Knighton, Wyoming.

And then she'd share the party and the thanks and how wonderful he'd been with all her followers for the first time.

She should have done this years ago.

Well, okay, not at first. Because at that point in her life taking a shower had been an accomplishment that left those Mount Everest-climbing folks in the dust. A surprise thank-you party in Wyoming? No way.

Even when Addie started sleeping, it had taken a while to rebuild her own energy. Plus, there was the issue of when. On Addie's birthday, as a sort of anniversary? Couple problems with that. She had first-hand experience of Wyoming in January. Also, shouldn't Addie get to have fun on her birthday with her friends? And then there was the fact that Val's family and friends in Gloucester would shoot her for depriving them of celebrating that day with Addie.

With the birthday out, that left too many other choices, none better than another. She'd dithered along, pretending she was waiting for the perfect moment when she'd just been procrastinating.

Until opportunity knocked on her door — or dropped into her inbox, depending on how you looked at it — and refused to go away.

Fate had said *now*. So, here she was.

Everyone had been incredibly supportive and helpful here in little Knighton, Wyoming. Particularly the family that owned the Slash-C Ranch where he worked. Not even at her most optimistic could she have dreamed up better people. They were all in on the surprise. Excited about it. Had not only made it possible, but fun.

That left Jack Ralston.

Everything was going to be okay.

More than okay. Great. Terrific. Super.

****

"Jack's right behind me," Matty Brennan Currick announced as she pushed open the door. "He thinks we've got something to go over for the Slash-C. Dave's with him to prevent any last-minute snafus. All set, Valerie?"

"All set," she lied.

Oh, the arrangements were all made. Everyone who should be here was. The food was ready. The banner hung over the Café's counter. The camcorder was already running to make sure she caught everything.

So, yes, all the *stuff* was ready. It was *her* that wasn't ready.

Especially her stomach. Which had chosen this moment to imitate those old barnstorming airplanes doing loop-de-loops. Great timing.

Everything would be okay.

So why were her hands slick on the video camera? Why was its "anti-tremor" software working overtime?

Donna Currick placed a hand on her arm, and said quietly, "It'll be fine, dear."

Matty Brennan Currick had answered the phone when Val called the Slash-C out of the blue nearly three months ago now with her story about the foreman of the ranch the Currick family owned. And Matty was the person Val had been communicating with regularly. The one whose enthusiasm for all this had carried Val past any and all obstacles. Matty's husband, Dave Currick, had been as nice as he could be since she and Addie arrived. So had everyone else. In these two days she'd met dozens of people, and liked every one of them.

But the one she felt the most drawn to was Donna Currick, Dave's mom and Matty's mother-in-law.

She couldn't be much younger than Val's mom, yet she felt almost like a contemporary. Though a contemporary who was really smart and saw through people like glass. Which was almost as scary as it was appealing.

"It's just… Do you think it'll be a surprise?" Val asked her now.

"Oh, yes, I'm quite sure it's a surprise."

A wryness in her tone caught Val's attention, but there was no time to pursue it. Matty, still stationed by the door, stage-whispered a stern, "Shh!"

Matty backed up to join the group by the counter, leaving Val's camera a clear view of the entryway.

The door pushed open, Dave's easy voice carrying in ahead of him. "…a couple more factors to consider before we place the order. Go on, Jack. Matty'll have us a booth by now and we can…"

He kept talking, but Val didn't hear the words.

Jack Ralston.

Jack.

Last night, she'd worried that she wouldn't recognize him. It had been years, after all. Not to mention that, at the beginning, he'd mostly had on coat, hat, and mufflers. And by the end, she'd had other things on her mind.

She recognized him.

Recognized the way he moved, even with the sunlight from outside back-lighting him. Which made no sense, because she'd hardly seen him walking at all.

And now he wasn't moving, either.

He'd stopped dead in the doorway.

His eyes — oh, yes she remembered his eyes — scanned the group and stopped on her.

"Surprise!" rose as a roar around her.

It startled her into breathing again with an indrawn *uhh*, which was when she realized she hadn't been breathing for some unspecified amount of time.

Then her breathing stopped again.

Jack didn't so much jolt, as recoil for a fraction of an instant.

Surprise. It must be the surprise.

Immediately, his hand came up and she thought he was going to take his hat off. She prayed fast and fervently that he would smile. That everything would be okay. That this wasn't a stupid, stupid, stupid idea.

Because in that first instant she'd seen something in his eyes…

He tugged the hat lower, hiding more of his face.

He didn't smile.

Dave Currick clapped a hand on his back in would-be congratulations, but Val didn't miss that it was mostly a push forward, bringing Jack inside the door. The door swung closed behind them, and while her eyes adjusted, Jack Ralston became a still, shadowy figure.

A ragged chorus of "For He's a Jolly Good Fellow" started from the back of the room in a key so low James Earl Jones would have had trouble matching it. As it wrapped up, individual voices rose.

"…when Val called and said she wanted to honor you…"

"…didn't know anything about what a hero you were…"

"…thank you for what you did…"

"…her blog. Can't say I follow it, but my granddaughter says…"

"…so exciting to have her here…"

"…course we know, and now the whole world will…"

"…can't hide your light under a barrel this time…"

"…you should have heard Lisa when we told her about Valerie Trimarco being here, and what she wanted to do for you…"

Through the camera lens, Val watched Jack take a long stride forward, hat still masking his eyes.

Was he coming to greet her? Maybe she should put the camera down. Though the thought of it made her feel like a soldier considering climbing out of a foxhole and right into enemy fire. But if she ignored him, if he went past her, that would be awkward, too. Did she turn to follow him with the camera? Stick out a hand and say *you probably don't remember me, but I'll never forget you?* Or—

He didn't walk past her. He didn't greet her, either.

Next thing she saw through the lens was a tan blur, then the camera was gone from in front of her face, gone from her hands. Gone.

She had an unobstructed view of Jack Ralston's back as he headed out the café's door.

****

People closed ranks around her. Someone took her arm. Someone else put a hand on her shoulder.

"Dave, you go after him," Matty said.

"Me? What about Dad?"

"Your mother's better at that sort of thing. Donna will you—?"

"Let me," Val said. Immediately followed by a prayer that they'd say no. Why had she —?

"Good idea, dear," said Donna. "I'll look after Addie."

She opened her mouth to withdraw the offer, to argue that Addie would be getting restless, to find some reason to get out of this.

Addie cuddled deeper against Donna's shoulder, and the older woman used her free hand to give Val a nudge. "Go on, or you'll lose him."

She went.

Squinting against the bright sunlight outside the café, Val spotted him crossing the empty street diagonally. He was heading toward a long low building made out of logs and with a wooden sidewalk in front of it. His head was bent and he was fiddling with her camera as he walked. That must be what had slowed him up enough to keep his long gait from taking him out of sight.

"Hey!"

He didn't turn at her shout, even though she'd kept her tone relatively restrained and friendly, considering he'd absconded with her camera and clearly was doing something to it. She sprinted after him, catching up just before he would have taken the two steps that led up to a wooden sidewalk. Close up, she saw that only the front of the building was made of logs — or made to look like logs — and it appeared fairly new. Signs for a dentist, a real estate broker, and the lawyer who was friends with the Curricks marked the row of doors.

"Jack. Jack Ralston."

He didn't stop until she grasped his shirt sleeve's turned back cuff. Even then he simply turned and looked at her.

"I'm Val. Val Trimarco. Three-and-a-half years ago, you helped me, uh …. You delivered my baby. In the back of my station wagon?"

He said nothing.

This was worse than just about anything she could have imagined. "You don't remember—"

"I remember."

It was too grim to carry any reassurance. "Or remember me?"

His grunt indicated he did.

"Or recognize me —

"I recognize you."

He didn't sound happy about it. She hadn't screamed *that* loudly . . . well, yes, she had. But he hadn't seemed all that upset about it, not after Baby Girl Trimarco was born, anyway. It had seemed like her coming into the world had thrown a blanket of let-bygones-be-bygones over every pain, discomfort, embarrassment, ill word, and, even, that one truly accidental connection of Val's fist to his cheekbone. She could have sworn he wasn't holding a grudge when he loaded them into the ambulance.

"Oh. Okay. Well, I came back here to Wyoming to thank you."

He grunted again.

She propped her hands on her hips, starting to get annoyed. "Can we at least sit down and talk?"

"About what?"

"About how I wanted to surprise you and—"

"Ambush."

She glared up at him. "It was not. It was supposed to be like a surprise party, honoring you. And all your friends were excited, saying how nice it was that other people would know what you'd done and what a great guy you are. They're all back there now feeling bad because you were a total—" She swallowed her first-choice word, as she had so frequently since she'd become a mother to a child who was also part parrot. "—grouch. Not to mention snatching my camera and walking off with it, which is *theft*."

He looked down at her. None of his facial muscles budged a millimeter. He might as well have the scarf back covering the lower part of his face the way it had when he'd knocked on her car window.

Although, at least then she'd been able to tell a little from his eyes.

She focused there now, and noticed the slightest deepening of the lines fanning from his blue-gray eyes. As if —

"You laugh at me, Jack Ralston, and I'll let loose a scream like you haven't heard in three and a half years."

He held up both hands in surrender, the muscles of his face relaxing, though not quite reaching a smile.

She sat on the step. "C'mon. Sit down for a minute."

She wasn't sure he was going to comply until he did. Leaving a couple feet between them.

He didn't say a word. It was going to be up to her. Considering he'd walked out, she had a hunch the planned party wasn't going to be the great ice-breaker she'd hoped it would be. She better come up with something else.

"You did a great thing that day, Jack Ralston. And I do thank you."

"Anyone would have done the same."

"No way." She looked at him. The turned-up side of his hat revealed his profile, but that gave nothing away. "I sure wouldn't have. I'd have run the other direction. If my car hadn't been stuck in that ditch, and if I hadn't been taking the situation with me no matter where I went, that's exactly what I would have done."

Without turning his head, he started to cut a look toward her. Presumably he finished it, too, but by that time, she had a hand up, shielding her eyes, gazing up and down the street.

Like there was anything to look at, since everyone was still in the café, waiting for the guest of honor or the how-stupid-can-you-get organizer of this party to return.

"Anyway, that's what I *used* to do best. Not as bad as when I was younger — remind me to tell you about my job resume sometime — because I'd gotten better about it, mostly thanks to El and The Fishwife. That's the restaurant we started. But I hadn't quite turned the corner all the way if you know what I mean. That didn't happen until Addie. Oh, did I tell you her name is Addison Rose? No longer Baby Girl Trimarco, so, see, she's made me face up to things. Deal with them. Be a grownup. I've pretty much stayed put since her. And I've been in the same job for several years now. That's new, too. Well, it's not exactly being in a job. More like I made one up."

"Yeah?"

"Yeah. I blog. About single motherhood. ... how it started, how it took off ... And some about cooking. Review products a little. Talk about real stuff. What happens every day when you're raising a child. When you're in the kitchen. What?"

"Nothing."

"Yes, there is something. I see that look."

"Personal life in public."

"Oh that. Now you sound like El. Always talking about the line between public and private. For her it's like the Grand Canyon or something. For me, it's more like a squiggle in the dust. I keep telling El, I'm not as reserved as she is. And — now what?"

But instead of repeating or explaining the look he'd given her, he said, "El. Cousin?"

"Right. My cousin, Eleanor." Sure. *That* he remembered. Even without seeing El's lush curves and intelligent face. "She's very cautious. Well, not as much as she used to be, not since she and Cahill got married and had little Sam. And now with El's brother-in-law living with them, and her mother-in-law coming over soon she's going to have less and less time to fuss at me. It's not like I don't take precautions. I do. I never show Addie on-screen. I use other names for everyone and mix up events so nobody knows exactly who did what or when. No public appearances for Addie ever. And since that little incident, I don't ever say the house is going to be empty at a certain time or anything like that."

"Incident?"

"These guys broke in. One of their girlfriends was coming to an event and was all excited about it, so she was reading the blog out loud to her boyfriend, including the part where I said nobody would be at home because Addie was going to her grandmother's where she is spoiled rotten. Which I fully admit I should not have put in the blog — the part about the house being empty — not the part about my mother spoiling her, because she does, and it's got to stop. And that's something a lot of mothers experience, so we talk about that. Especially with a family like mine. And that stuff about the *have* to spoil her because she doesn't have a dad? That's an excuse to give her more candy. Nothing like having a sugar-crazed kid after a couple hours at grandma's and—"

"Break-in."

"Oh. Right. So these two guys broke in. And I guess they thought I was going to be some rich person with lots of electronics they could fence, just because I'm on the Internet, and boy were they disappointed, because most fences won't take bouncy chairs and OshKosh B'gosh overalls. So they were resorting to stealing my TV, which has to be at least a decade old, when Cahill — that's El's husband and the greatest guy in the world — and his little brother Kiernan, though why I'd call him little, when he's six-two and a hunk and a half I don't know, but... Where was I?"

"TV."

"Right. The TV. They were detaching the TV from all the cords when Cahill and Kiernan went by and saw lights when they knew I wasn't home. Caught them red-handed coming out the door to where they'd parked their van. Kiernan snapped off a bunch of pictures for the record, then they kept them there until the police came. *Should* have made them reattach my TV and get it to work right again instead of putting them in jail for a month. Sure would have done me more good, because it took me forever to get the cords sorted out and plugged back into the right place. Well, actually, Kiernan did it. But even then it's never worked completely right since."

She paused for breath.

"You talk a lot more now."

She thought the corner of his mouth quirked, but maybe it was a tic.

"I had other things on my mind then. I was in *labor*, remember? And besides—"

"Yes."

The *yes* that confirmed he remembered stopped her. Memories splattered across her mind, like big, fat rain drops hitting a sidewalk, each an individual ping of a moment, coming faster and faster as they formed a whole. Many of the individual pings carried pricks of embarrassment or discomfort, some sharper than others, but the whole taken together formed the birth of her child, and that was a memory worth keeping.

"And besides?" he prompted.

She broke out of her memory-transfixed state with a huff of breath. "And besides, I'm a little nervous now."

"Not then?"

"No. Then I was scared witless. And practically wordless. Especially when I thought you'd taken off after I told you I was in labor."

He turned and looked at her directly for the first time, and she saw surprise in his face.

"You went around to the passenger side to tie up your horse, remember?"

"More protected."

"Was that why? Well, I had no way of knowing. I thought you'd taken off on me like — Uh, like most normal people would have done in the circumstances. Then, there you were, knocking on the passenger window and giving cranky orders, which should have warned me, since it set the tone for what followed."

Push, Val.

I am pushing.

Push harder.

This is as hard as it gets. Sorry to disappoint you, Jack. I am. I'm really sorry. After all you've done, and now I just can't. I'm always disappointing people. Leaving. Moving on when it gets tough or —

Quit crying, and push.

I can't.

That's better. You pushed when you yelled. Do it again.

I can't. I can't push. I can't have this baby. I can't.

You're having this baby. Now. Push now, Valerie Trimarco. Do it!

"Didn't take off on you," he said. A protest.

"No, you didn't." She cleared her throat without looking at him. "That's why I wanted to thank you. That's what the surprise party was for. All your friends helped and — what?"

He gave her a blank look. Not like he didn't understand, but like he'd erected a brick wall between his understanding and her.

"You flinched," she clarified.

The look stayed blank. The brick stayed solid.

"Okay," she said slowly. "Well, anyway, we all wanted to give you this party to celebrate what a great guy you were that day. And for me to thank you properly."

"You thanked me."

"Yelling out the back of an ambulance doesn't count."

The ambulance hadn't been able to get to them. They'd had to go to it.

A ranch truck driven by a kid Jack had called Bryan had arrived first. She'd held the baby, while Jack picked her up in his arms again, with as many dry covers as he could manage, and clambered into the truck's passenger seat, holding her and the baby. Bryan drove. Slower and slower, as each bump made her groan, and Jack snapped, "Ease up."

At last they were back to a main road. She thought she'd slept a bit. Next thing she knew, the truck door was open, she and Addie were being bundled onto a gurney, then into an ambulance.

Still groggy, she'd called out "Thank You." The door slammed, trapping the final "Jack" inside with her.

She thought she'd dreamt his presence in her hospital room that night, but she hadn't dreamt the two-foot-tall stuffed horse that had joined their belongings by the next morning.

No note or card or name attached. But he wasn't going to disappear that easily. She remembered the name of the ranch, and she'd intended to track it down right after she took a nap.

But then there was another feeding, and another nap. And then El was there.

And, oh, it was so good to let her cousin take care of everything to get her and Addison Rose to Gloucester, then settled in to the house. She'd let events and time roll past in a way that wasn't at all like her. She'd recognized that, but as if from a long distance, and without much caring.

It wasn't until almost a year later and almost that long of doing the blog that one of her followers said she'd probably had at least a touch of postpartum depression, not to mention a major case of sleep-deprivation.

"I wanted to thank you properly," she repeated doggedly. "Plus, it all seemed meant to be. After all this time when I should have gotten in touch with you to thank you, now all the planets were aligned and— No. I mean that's all true, but it's only part of it. It was also because you didn't desert us. Maybe that's why I hoped you'd help me with this."

He didn't give her even a *Help you with what?* Just silence.

"See, I rented out my house. It's on the beach in Gloucester — that's Massachusetts. North of Boston."

"Cape Ann."

She gawked at him for half a second, then caught herself. "Right. Didn't know if you'd remember all that. Anyway this crazy writer fell in love with it, and I told him I absolutely would not sell it to him. For one thing it's still half El's no matter what she says, and even if it weren't, it's a family house. And on top of that, it's right there on the beach, and Addie loves the beach, so no way. But then he offered to rent it. Wanted the whole summer, but I got it down to two months and then, when I asked for this astronomical rent and he said yes, what could I do?"

Apparently he had no answer for that.

"So I had to find somewhere to go. *Not* back to Mom and Dad's or Addie won't have a tooth left in her head from all the sugar, even if they are her baby teeth. And not to El and Cahill, because they should not give up good income from any of the inn's rooms just because I'm making a killing — how is that fair? And they're too damned stubborn to listen to reason about my paying rent. So, I decided to come to Wyoming. Back to where it all began. Being a mother, I mean."

He shot her a quick look, which she did not return.

"Like I told you, I write this blog. So I'm writing about the trip. Tracing back to when Addie was born. The misadventures. And the first few days. And working in the things I've learned, and the perspective I've gained — and how those first worries seem pretty small compared to now, and how that's preparing me — hah! — for future worries and issues to keep getting bigger and bigger, because eventually we'll be facing boys and piercings and driving, and all the rest. So, of course, I want to feature the man who brought Addison Rose Trimarco into the world."

"No."

"Why not? It won't be maudlin or anything. I was camping it up telling you, but the blog's not gooey sentimental. Honest."

"No."

"Don't you have more to say than 'No'?"

"Absolutely not."

"Jack—"

"I will not be part of this. In any way. Ever."

He placed the camera on the step by her hip then stood. She was sure he would walk away, all without looking at her. But after one step, he turned and faced her.

"You did the great thing that day," he said.

She looked up quickly, totally unprepared. It must have been the glare of the sun in her eyes that made them tear. "Thank you, Jack."

Thank you for saying that. Thank you for letting me rattle on. Thank you for helping bring my precious Addie into the world.

He tugged on the brim of his cowboy hat, and said, "Good-bye, Ma'am."

"Don't call me—"

But he was already going, leaving only a chuckle behind that said he'd done it on purpose.

CHAPTER TWO

Val admired the spirit of people who didn't let a hiccup like the guest of honor walking out ruin a party.

She said as much to Matty on her return to the café to find Addie happily playing with Matty and Dave's son Brennan and a little girl named Cassie Ruskoff. Brennan's younger brother Finn and Cassie's younger brother Rob played with blocks nearby. All under the watchful eye of several women, while the party went on without Jack Ralston.

"We're pretty far-flung, so no time we get together is ever wasted," Matty said, offering up a choice of a beer or a plastic cup of white wine. "Don't let it bother you."

Val took the wine and circulated. The handful of people she'd met introduced her to everyone else. Each said how glad they were she was in Knighton, and they hoped she'd stay on as planned.

Since her house was otherwise occupied, and Matty had offered her a very reasonable rate on a place to stay, that seemed a likely bet.

She chatted with Taylor Ruskoff for several minutes, watching the kids play. Taylor was the mother of Cassie and Rob as well as being the lawyer whose office was in the building where Val and Jack had sat. They were joined by Ruth Moski, who was the office manager for the town's other lawyer — Matty's husband and Donna's son, Dave Currick. If Val hadn't been raised in a family and town of vast and complex networks of interconnections, she might have been getting a headache by now.

She spotted Donna Currick standing alone, looking out the café's front window, and excused herself.

Donna smiled as she approached. Val got right to the point. "You knew this wasn't going to end well."

"Oh, I wouldn't say that. Everyone's having a great time."

Except the guest of honor.

Val adjusted her statement. "You knew how Jack would react."

"I suspected," Donna acknowledged.

"Why didn't you tell me — or tell Matty — not to do it, then? Why didn't you stop us?"

She laughed. The bright, charming laugh that had made Val like her immediately, and that now turned Ed Currick's head toward them to smile at his wife of many decades.

"Stop you and Matty? I'm not that foolish. Besides, it's important to give people every opportunity to surprise you. Maybe particularly Jack Ralston."

Val opened her mouth to ask why particularly Jack Ralston. But she saw Donna wouldn't tell her. It was one of those Delphic utterances her mother was prone to, too. Direct questions never penetrated them.

"So, Jack doesn't like surprises?" she asked instead.

Donna gave a small nod, perhaps in approval. "No, he doesn't. Though he deals well with them, extremely well, when they have to do with ranch business."

Or a strange woman giving birth in a snowstorm.

"But not— I was going to say in his personal life," Donna said with a head tilt, as if this had just occurred to her. "But I don't know that Jack has a personal life. So, let's say in his dealings with people."

Val didn't believe for an instant that that thought had just occurred to Donna Currick. The older woman was setting out a line of breadcrumbs to lead Val somewhere. Might as well see where the trail went.

"Do you know why he's that way?"

"No. Among the many things I don't know about Jack Ralston, that might be the most important. Because I don't believe any of the people here—" The graceful sweep of her arm took in all of the café. "—who work with him, respect him, like him, and have come to care about him know that."

They looked at each other a long moment.

"Perhaps," Donna said lightly, "someone from outside our little world in Knighton might be able to help him open up more."

****

Maybe Valerie Trimarco *had* been nervous.

She always talked fast, but not like she had today. Unless she'd trained herself to slow down for those videos on her blog.

He'd stumbled across the blog the first time.

Well, if Googling her name counted as stumbling.

That had been months after. At least three months. Then it had been just curiosity. Not so surprising under the circumstances. After what they'd gone through. Wanting to know for sure that the baby was okay. That she was okay.

That first video, she'd been bleary-eyed with lack of sleep, her hair wild, and sporting smudges under her eyes that might have been rubbed off mascara, the smears baseball players put on, or lack-of-sleep dark circles.

She'd looked into the camera and she'd talked. As honest, funny, and open as she'd been that day.

He hated that she opened herself up like that to anyone in the world who happened to click there. Opened herself to anyone *else*. His watching didn't count. Which was good, because he couldn't look away.

Especially not when the baby she held in her arms off camera started to fuss and she rocked it. The motion so instinctive, so simple.

Even after she said goodnight and the video ended, he kept staring at the static page, not letting himself watch it over again.

At least not until the next day.

The months that followed, he'd let it get out of hand. Watching every day. Sometimes watching and reading every scrap over and over.

Even though it was the worst time of year to be further cutting into his sleep, what with calving going full-bore. There'd been days he'd fallen asleep in the saddle, and nights he'd fallen asleep with his head on the desk beside the laptop. And other nights he'd had too much to drink, which he hadn't done since —

That's when he got himself in hand.

No reason not to check up now and then on the baby he'd helped bring into the world — and her mama — as long as it stayed within reason. Once a week. No more. And no re-watching. Ever.

He'd seen when she'd blabbed all about her house being empty. And he'd seen the ruefulness and embarrassment when she'd reported the break-in. He'd also seen the determination when she'd said, "Yeah, I hate admitting I was stupid and naïve. But it's worth admitting it if it helps one of you out there avoid this mistake."

Stupid and naïve.

That phrase had ridden with him for several days before he shook it off.

As long as he kept to his rules about how often he watched, it was okay. Nobody was going to check his computer's history. Nobody was going to know.

And her being here? She'd go now. Things would be back to normal. Back the way they should be.

The way they had to be.

****

"Jack?"

"In with Brandeis."

Dave Currick came down the line of stalls. All empty except this one, because the other horses were out in the corral. All except Brandeis.

"Why'd you bring him in here?" Dave asked, instantly concerned, but staying out of the stall so as not to crowd.

"That left hock felt hot again. Thought I'd give it another wrap."

Jack stepped out of the stall, gesturing the other man in.

Dave ran his hand down the stallion's side, easing carefully to the spot, already expertly wrapped.

"Damn," he said softly. "I should have listened to you and left it on another day at the start. Glad you caught it."

"Wasn't bad. I might be being overly cautious."

"Glad you are."

Both men eased away from the stall, leaving Brandeis as calm as when they'd arrived. Side by side they walked toward the wide doors open to the outside.

Jack stopped there. Dave Currick wouldn't have sought him out if he didn't have something to say.

Ed Currick had hired Jack. That was shortly before he officially retired from running the ranch the Currick family had owned for generations so he and his wife Donna could travel at will, while their son Dave took over. All the Curricks, including daughter Lisa, now married and living in New York City, owned a share, but Dave was officially his boss.

They had to be about the same age. Dave, having grown up on the place, knew cattle-ranching with an ease and depth Jack never expected to attain. But Dave also had a law practice. So day-to-day operations were in Jack's hands.

"That was kind of a strong reaction today at the café," Dave said mildly.

Jack said nothing.

"Has some tongues wagging," Dave added. "A few tongues you'd rather not have wagging."

Jack stifled a wince. He'd spotted Joyce Arbedick from the bank among the crowd in the cafe. She, along with the lineup of older men who frequented the cafe and were collectively known as the stool-sitters, were the biggest gossips in two counties.

"Yeah," Dave went on, "from that standpoint, it was a real good thing that Val came back in before they got too wound up, telling us all how the two of you had a real good talk, and were working things out fine."

Jack shot him a look.

Dave didn't return it as he cleared his throat. "Yeah. I thought she went a little far when she started in about how you'd taken the camera because you spotted something wrong with it and you needed better light to fix it, so that's why you took it outside.

"Still, Joyce seemed to buy it, and Hugh and the others got all interested in the technical specifications — as if those old coots are going to start putting up music videos on YouTube or something. Anyway, they forgot all about it when Val let them play with her camera.

"Some folks were considerably more skeptical. Not that I'm saying Val was lying. Precisely. But the ones who were skeptical aren't the ones you need to worry about."

Jack wasn't so sure about that. Oh, not for gossip. But maybe in other ways. After all, here was his boss, talking to him about his personal life. First time that had happened since he'd arrived at the Slash-C and it came hours after he walked into the café to see Valerie Trimarco standing in front of him.

That couldn't be a coincidence.

But no sense saying any of that. So he waited.

"She seems like a nice person. Val — Val Trimarco, I mean. That girl of her's sharp as all get-out, too. She'll be a beauty someday. Like her mom." He let that sink in a bit. As if it would be a revelation to Jack. That wild cloud of black hair, that skin, those eyes. "And apparently this blog of hers is quite the big deal. You should've heard Lisa go on and on about it when we talked to her on the phone.

"And let's face it, you delivering her baby out there in a snowstorm without any other help, that's a good story. Damned good story. Knight in shining armor and all, coming to the rescue of a damsel — at least a mother-to-be — in a whole lot of distress. Makes the Slash-C look good. Good for the image — that's what Lisa was telling Matty and my mother."

"You ordering me to be part of this as a condition of my employment at the Slash-C."

"Good God, no. Just... Thought you might reconsider."

"I've considered. The answer is no."

"Okay. It's your business, Jack. It's your business."

And Jack knew that would be the end of it from Dave Currick. He was a very good boss.

He also was now a curious boss, which wasn't good.

And the women of the Currick family were something more than curious, which was a whole lot worse.

CHAPTER THREE

"So I went after him, got my camera back, and confirmed he wanted absolutely nothing to do with being thanked or being surprised—" *Or with me,* but Val didn't say that over the phone to her cousin, Eleanor Thatcher McRae. For no reason other than common fairness, she didn't want El disliking Jack Ralston sight unseen. "— and when you put the two together — whoa, big mistake."

"Poor kid." El said.

Val spurted an abbreviated, dry chuckle. "You would never look at Jack Ralston and call him a *kid,* especially a *poor kid.*"

"Oh?"

Val knew exactly the mix of knowingness and suspicion that was in her cousin's head.

"Yes. He's a fine specimen of a man. And since I spotted Cahill for you, you know I've got a good eye."

"No one ever doubted your eye."

El's tone was mostly teasing, but Val went serious. "No. Everyone doubted my common sense and—" She talked over El's disputing noises. "—with good reason when it came to men. I picked some real doozies. But that was before Addie. I no longer look for hot bods and excitement. Now I look for entirely different qualities."

"Father material?" El said hopefully.

"They'd need top-top-top level security clearance to even consider that. First, it's more basic. Will they run if they hear a kid's voice? Do they pout if I cancel because Addie has a cold? Can they overcome their gag reflex from the smell of kid vomit."

"Nice. So where does Jack Ralston rank on the security clearances, now that you've seen him again."

"It's moot with him. He's not a candidate. Which is a good thing, because I'd bet my house he would never stop running if he thought I considered him one. No, I wanted to repay him for what he did for Addie and me. But he's not having it. So I'm wishing him well, washing my hands of him, and minding my own business."

There was a long pause. Her cousin was probably having to pick herself up off the floor from shock at Val demonstrating such good sense.

"You never gave up with me," El said slowly. Okay, she hadn't been on the floor from shock. But Val might be. The Queen of Caution should be saying, *Good, wash your hands of this man and come home.* The fact that she wasn't should be reversing the earth's rotation.

"We're related. Can't give up on family."

"It wasn't because we're related."

"Partly it was. And the other part was because we needed your head for business to get The Fishwife off the ground. I was only after you for your MBA. I had no choice."

"Yes, you did have a choice, Val," Eleanor said solemnly. "You nudged and pushed and prodded me so I'd accept Cahill being around The Fishwife, and then you were relentless in throwing us together."

"Didn't take much." She grinned at the memories. "It was like a magnet and iron, with you the iron trying futilely to withstand the magnet's pull, and Cahill the magnet knowing all along he wanted to suck you in. Fun to watch. "

"Glad you found it amusing," her cousin said dryly. "But to get back to Jack Ralston—"

"Really, El. It's fine. He doesn't want to be bothered, and I won't bother him anymore. Don't worry about that."

"I'm not worried about him. It's you—"

"Me? I'm absolutely fine. Wonderful, in fact. The rest of the people here are as welcoming as they can be. There's plenty of material for my blogs and podcasts, and Addie is having a ball."

El let another of those pauses develop. "It's not like you to give up, Val."

"I know. Can you believe I finally have the sense to know when I should?"

****

Storm sensed her first, as they came out of The Narrows to where the trail between the Slash-C and Flying W home ranches widened and flattened.

Then Jack spotted dark curls shifting and whirling in the breeze.

She was crouched down on, half sitting on a rock, using another one to steady her arms as she shot that damned camera of hers up at an angle into the crags and boulders and ridges that formed The Narrows.

She gave no sign of noticing an unknown horse and rider approaching her.

She should have, dammit. She should be aware of her surroundings, focused on potential dangers.

"What are you doing here?"

That wasn't the question he wanted to ask — in fact he didn't want to ask any questions. Didn't want to talk to her. Didn't want to see her. Sure as hell didn't want the answer to how she would look when summer sun glinted red fire off her dark hair.

"What's it look like I'm doing?" She asked that absently, not even lifting her head from the viewfinder. Which was irritating. Only because it was rude when someone was talking to you to not look at them.

But, then he was still mounted on Storm, so she'd have to crane her neck to look up.

He swung out of the saddle, keeping himself and Storm well wide of her.

Then she did lift her head and he wished she'd go back to the viewfinder. There was a lesson in being careful what you groused about ... even in your own head.

"Where's Addie?"

"With Donna Currick. She's looking after Matty and Dave's two and she volunteered to take in Addie for a few hours, too, while I work." Without taking a breath, she added, "And you have a nerve asking what I'm doing, Jack Ralston, since you erased all my Wyoming footage yesterday. Maybe — *maybe* — you had some right to wipe out the footage of you, but not everything since I came back to Wyoming."

If he'd had time, he would have erased more.

38

If he'd had the ability, he'd have erased everything back to before she'd been here the first time. He'd tried that in his mind often enough.

"Looks like I'll be doing it again. Give me the camera."

"No way."

"You're trespassing."

"No, I'm not."

"You're on Slash-C land and—"

"And you're the foreman, not the owner, and I have the owners' permission to go anywhere on the Slash-C, and to shoot anything I want. Although—is this the Slash-C? Or are we on Flying W land now? Doesn't matter. Because I also have the owner's permission to go anywhere on the Flying W and shoot anything I want. See, this time I *am* interested in ownership issues."

"Dave—"

"Dave's permission, and Ed's, and Donna's, and Matty's for the Flying W. Oh! And even Lisa's — she called while we were all visiting at the house earlier. The Slash-C home ranch they call it. When I dropped Addie off for a little play time with Dave and Matty's son. Anyway, Dave's sister Lisa called from New York while I was there, because she and her husband are coming for a visit next month. She's really excited about my blogging about giving birth to Addie here on the Slash-C, despite your lack of interest or cooperation. About my coming back to where it all began. She's even talking about designing a piece of jewelry to commemorate it. And we're going to link from her website to my blog and— What?"

Apparently his expression had stopped the flow of her words, but he had no clue how to keep the flow stopped. The flow of her words and her ideas and her energy and ... *her.*

He stood towering over her. Big and unmoved and silent. Like a mountain to her burbling stream.

"Are you going to say anything or just keep glaring at me?"

"Both."

She laughed.

The sound did something to him. He felt it, down deep.

He'd seen what burbling streams could do to mountains. Looking all small and sparking, but cutting through the outer crust like a laser until the mountain's core was exposed and raw.

Unless the mountain stayed so strong that it forced the burbling stream to change course. That's what the mountain needed to do in order to survive.

Her smile faded. "You're still glaring and you're still not saying anything."

"You said you wanted to go back to where it all began."

"Right. Right here."

"You should have gone back to wherever you met Addie's father. Or at least back to where you were when he walked out on you. I suppose that was when you told him you were pregnant."

Her face scrunched. Not like she was going to cry, but like she was absolutely determined not to cry. He felt like he'd captured a lightning bug in a jar. One of those jars with colored glass, so not only was the glow captured, but it was dulled by its prison. And you knew you were killing it, even as you marveled at the light. Maybe if you relented and put in air holes—

"Yeah, that's about when he walked out," she said, the lightning bug still making light, but growing weaker. Then she rallied. "But that wasn't when things really began for me. That was when Addie was born. He was long gone by then. But you weren't, Jack. You were there."

The lightning bug had escaped its prison, shining fiercely now. Hell, it seemed to have grown a stinger no lightning bug had ever possessed, and it sliced right into his skin.

She lifted the camera and snapped a picture.

"Dammit, I told you—"

"I didn't take a picture of you. Just your horse. What's her name?"

"Him. Storm."

"Storm. What happened to him?"

Her gesture took in a criss-cross of scars on his flank. "An idiot who shouldn't be allowed near horseflesh happened to him."

"But he's better now?"

"Yes."

"And he's yours."

She made it a statement, He said "Yes" anyway.

"Where are you from?" she asked abruptly

"Here."

She turned and tipped her head. "Really? You grew up here?"

"No."

"I didn't think so. There's a touch of a different accent. A rhythm to how you talk. I picked up a feel for voices when I worked in radio. Midwest somewhere, right? No. Mid-Atlantic."

He said nothing.

"You never talk about where you're from?"

"No."

"Is that part of the general not-talking *shtick*, or something in particular?"

"*Shtick?*"

The head tip deepened. "Sidetrack," she accused.

"What?"

"One of your tricks to avoid talking. I'd imagine it works really well, especially with people like me who talk a lot. You'd probably get away with it with me, too, if it weren't for El. See, it's like me having older siblings. I see I've confused you, but it's true. Being the youngest, I'd try some fib or some misbehavior or something and my parents would nod and say, Good try. But Anthony and Joe tried that at your age, too. Or No luck there, Valerie. We're on to that one ever since Karen used that line.

"You're in the same situation, because my cousin El is a lot like you. Well, not so much anymore, but she used to be. All closed off, and careful, and never taking a chance on people. I had to push her and push her and push her when she was falling in love with Cahill, or she would have sensibled her way right out of marrying this great guy who thinks she's the best thing ever."

She eyed him, and he forced himself to look back steadily under her scrutiny. What was going on in that head of hers?

She stood, brushing off the seat of her jeans. He tried not to watch. He tried hard. No luck. Not until he cued back in to what she was saying.

"...so you can try not talking, and you can try to sidetrack me when you do talk, but for all the jobs I had, nobody could say I gave up because it was hard. I only left after I cracked them. And I'm going to succeed with you, too."

"By cracking me?"

She grinned, but it didn't make him want to grin back. "Like a walnut shell."

"You have no right to rip apart my privacy because I helped you."

Her lips parted, but he went on.

"If you put me in this blog or whatever it is you're doing, if you use my name or my picture or describe me in any way that people could know who I am, I'll get Taylor to come after you with everything the law's got. But that won't do any good, because you would have already done it. Already have ripped everything apart. Is that the kind of person you are, Valerie Trimarco? Is that how you thank someone you say you're grateful to?"

"I think that's the most I've ever heard you say." She shook her head, but he thought it was at herself. "I don't understand why you—"

"It's not your business to understand. Tell me if you're going to do that. So I can start packing."

"Packing? Why on earth would you pack?"

"To leave. Or I can follow the old cowboy tradition."

"What tradition?"

"Sell his horse, hand out everything else, take his saddle and go. Or leave his saddle, too, if he's selling up for good."

She stared up at him. Intent. Determined to understand. And smart enough to do it. If he hadn't known it from those intense hours in the back of her old station wagon, he'd learned it from watching her on his computer screen.

That's what made her so dangerous.

"You won't leave. You've been here years."

"Curricks are good employers."

"Oh, c'mon, Jack. This means more to you than that. The ranch, the area, this place" she said, still weighing matters. Weighing him.

"It's a place to hang my hat. For now."

No longer light, no longer scoffing, she scowled at him. "This is your *home*."

He didn't respond.

"You know why I was out in that snowstorm that day you rescued me? Because I wanted — I *needed* to get home. Home to the people who love me. To the people I knew would love Addie no matter what. That's what home is."

"I wouldn't know." He regretted the words instantly. Felt only deep relief when she didn't seem to hear them.

"You wouldn't leave," she repeated, but in a different tone.

He didn't answer with words. But she clearly read the answer in his face.

"I—" She shook her head. "I will not be responsible for driving you out of your home."

"Thank you."

He'd meant it to be nothing more than a rote answer, but her dark eyes came up quickly to his face, as if she'd heard something in the two quick words.

"You're welcome, Jack."

She was watching him. And he didn't like it. "So, you're leaving?" he prodded her.

"No."

She was the Curricks' guest. How much could he push? "There's no cause for you to stay."

"I am going to take pictures of this place — no, I won't take any of you — but I have the Curricks' permission to take shots of the ranch and use them, and I'm going to. I'm also going to write about what happened here three-and-a-half years ago. It's a major event — no, it's *the* major event in my life. It's changed everything. I'll have to write around you. Though it'll be like writing around the Grand Canyon, for Pete's sake. Not to mention that if someone ever came here and started asking questions based on what I've already said about Addie and me, anyone in town could figure out it was you."

"They already know. Thanks to your ambush yesterday."

"Surprise party."

He ignored her correction. "I'm not worried about that. The people here might give me hell, but they wouldn't ever tell an outsider anything."

She tipped her head, still watching him. Far too closely. Far too intelligently for his comfort. "And I'm an outsider?"

"Yes."

"But they're the ones who got you to come to the café. They're the ones who listened to this outsider, and organized the *surprise party*."

"They didn't understand then. Didn't know what you intended."

"You mean they didn't understand how you would react, because they knew exactly what I intended."

He said nothing.

"Isn't it interesting that these people you've known for years had no idea how you would react to this. They were totally taken aback. Why is that, Jack?"

He shifted the reins in his hand, stepped to his horse's side, and mounted smoothly.

It would have been more effective if he hadn't wheeled Storm back around when another thought hit him.

She'd returned to looking through the viewfinder.

"There's no place for you to stay." It was a statement of fact, yet it came out like an accusation, and knew that wasn't entirely reasonable.

"Sure there is."

"Where?"

He thought her lips quirked. "Same place Addie and I have been staying for several days. Though now I don't need to keep the rental car hidden so the object of a surprise party wouldn't get suspicious."

"Where?" he repeated, downright grim now, because he had a bad feeling—

"The foreman's cottage at the Flying W."

He said something he shouldn't have. Said it under his breath, but she must have heard, because she looked up quickly with those brown eyes that were as deep as they were wide. Deep and wide and dangerous with intelligence and curiosity and—

He repeated the word then said in a harsh voice, "There's no story for you here, Valerie Trimarco."

He pivoted the horse, and trotted away.

CHAPTER FOUR

There's no story for you here, Valerie Trimarco.

Certainly not the kind of story she'd intended to tell her blog readers. Not with Jack refusing to cooperate.

She hadn't known precisely what that story would have been, because it would have depended on what she learned about and from the man she'd encountered when she most needed someone three and a half years ago.

But she'd had a feeling about it. A mood. A direction.

She could have accepted it if he'd told her it had been a mere bump in the road to him. Barely more memorable than any other day on the ranch. There was no reason it had to be a major event in his life, because it was in hers and Addie's.

She could have written about that. About how sometimes people pass through your life at the right time and how you take that gift and move on, and do your best to pay it forward.

Or if he'd turned out to be nothing like the knight in shining armor her memory had created.

She could have written about that, too. Could have made the point that ordinary people often rise to an occasion, then reassume their cloak of ordinariness until the next time called on for more.

Yeah, she'd had thoughts about writing about any number of scenarios. Yeah, yeah, all right, including the one where he was ecstatic to see

45

her, overcome by seeing Addie, tears streaming down his lean cheeks as he held the little girl and said he'd prayed every day that he would find them once more.

But she hadn't thought that one had a shot.

Not really. Not when she was awake.

What hadn't been included in the mental deck of scenarios that had kept shuffling through her head in the weeks before standing in the Knighton Café, watching that oddly familiar figure walk in, had been seeing the depthless dark of pain in his eyes.

She closed her eyes now, remembering the day Addie was born, remembering Jack, examining the mental recording of each moment. Not what she — or even Addie — needed from him. Not how they interacted. But just *him*.

Yes. The pain had been there then.

The recognition made her stomach drop. How had she missed it?

Maybe because it had mostly been overridden by his determination to do what he had to do, sometimes masked by the calm she'd so desperately needed, once in a while even lightened by his amusement at one of her cracks. But there, definitely there.

Didn't take off on you.

No, he didn't. He'd stuck with her. He'd given her Addie. Whole and strong and crazy-making and delightful.

There's no story for you here, Valerie Trimarco.

Did that mean there was nothing she could do to help him?

****

To the people I knew would love Addie no matter what. That's what home is.

I wouldn't know.

He'd thought he'd known. Once. Thought he'd found people who would be home to him. Family.

His mistake.

He swore under his breath, causing Storm to flicker his ears. He leaned forward and patted the powerful neck, reassuring the animal that neither word nor mood were directed at him.

He looked out over the land, noting and planning at one level of his mind, while another heard those words again in his head.

To the people I knew would love Addie no matter what. That's what home is.

I wouldn't know.

Maybe Val hadn't been all wrong. Maybe the land did mean something to him.

But people? No. There was no such thing as people who would love him no matter what. He'd learned that lesson.

****

Since Addie was still on East Coast time, they were up and over to the Slash-C ranch early by most people's standards. Still, the young man, followed by the Curricks' compact dog, who walked nearby as Val got out of the car said "Good morning," then added — without being asked — that he was sorry, she'd missed Jack. He'd already ridden out.

"Thanks, but I was looking for Matty." She smiled to soften any edge in his voice.

"Oh."

She raised her eyebrows a bit at that syllable. — What was that tone? Chagrin? Surprise? Disappointment? — Which sharpened her focus on the guy, as she opened the back door to get Addie out of her car seat. Maybe college age, a little older. And something about him... "You were at the party at the café, weren't you?"

"Yes, ma'am. Everyone was."

She smiled back at his clear pleasure. But there was something else about him… Something she associated with...

"Bryan. Right? You drove the truck. Got us to the ambulance. The day this one arrived." She hoisted Addie up on her hip, and his focus shifted to the girl. He smiled. "You were the first one to come help us."

"Yes, ma'am. Imagine you remembering that all this time later and with what you went through."

"Damsels don't forget any of our knights in shining armor, do we, Addison Rose?" She jounced the girl lightly. "We say thank you very much, and it's a pleasure to meet you officially."

"Miss Addie," he said, drawing a giggle from her. He tugged his hat brim again. "You, too, ma'am."

"But if you don't stop calling me ma'am, I'm going to have to run our knight through with his own lance. It's Val."

He grinned. "Yes, ma'a—"

"Uh-huh, you almost ruined this fine morning, Bryan. Redeem yourself by telling me where I can find Matty."

Following his directions to what he called "the house office," Val knocked on a door that opened onto the back porch of the main ranch house. The house was solid and good-sized with no pretensions. What set it apart from a lot of other houses she'd seen were, first, the setting and, second, that it was not alone.

Along with what appeared to be barns, sheds, storage buildings, corrals, and other structures whose purpose she couldn't guess, there were three buildings that looked like houses. And a fourth that appeared nearly completed.

"Come in." Matty's voice commanded from the other side of the door, and Val obeyed.

"Val, how are you. And Addie," she added, stretching out her arms, "don't you look sweet this morning."

Addie went right to her, clearly agreeing with that assessment. The two of them settled back in an oversized and well-padded leather chair behind the large desk.

"Bryan said you were in the office. I don't want to interrupt your work, Matty."

"Not a problem. Have a seat, while I cuddle your daughter." She gestured to a worn leather couch under the windows to the left of the door. Across the room another door was opened to a hallway, with a glimpse of what appeared to be a comfortable family room beyond it. "Glad you ran into Bryan to get directions. It can get confusing with all the buildings."

"It's quite a complex. I don't know what half the buildings are for. Just like the ones outside that adorable cottage you have me staying in."

Matty chuckled. "Don't let Cal hear you call it adorable or a cottage. Cal's Taylor's husband. You met him at the party, didn't you?" Barely waiting for Val's nod, she continued, "Where you're staying was the foreman's house when Cal was foreman of the Flying W. As for the buildings here, most are for ranch operations, but we have added a couple places — one for Dave's folks when they want to stay at the ranch for a while. We realized a while back that they were keeping their visits short because they worried about intruding on us in the main house and we couldn't budge them an inch about it. So we built them their own little place. Then we added another one for when more family visits. That made the foreman's house look shabby. We offered to fix it up and expand it for Jack, but he chose to live in the main house at the Flying

W, even though it's awfully solitary during the winter. We renovated the foreman's house here for even more family. And we're about finished with updating a separate ranch office, so we can use this room for a bedroom for our next production."

She patted her belly, and Addie leaned over and did the same thing. Matty grinned as she continued, "Problem is, the family keeps growing. When everyone's here, it's a madhouse. So next step will probably be taking over the bunkhouse. We rarely have anybody in it, because the permanent hands want their own place, and Jack likes to keep a close eye on the few seasonals, so they usually stay with him in the Flying W main house."

Jack chose to live in the main house at the Flying W. That's where most of Val's brain had stalled. The house she'd driven past on the way to the highway. Just down the entrance road from the cotta— foreman's house, where she and Addie were. Not far at all.

She'd thought he lived here on the Slash-C, which was the neighboring ranch, but a healthy distance away. Unlike the Flying W's main house, which was an easy walk. A stroll down the road and...

... stayed with Jack in the Flying W main house.

Other workers lived with him there.

Good. That was good. Very good.

"But here I am rattling away, and not asking what I can do for you, Val. Is it something at the Flying W? Do you need anything? Or—"

"No, no. The cot— house is perfect. We don't need a thing. I came over to say I'm sorry, Matty. After all the trouble you went to putting on Saturday's party, to have the whole thing wasted—"

"Quit. You started all this yesterday. Wasn't a lot of trouble and wasn't a waste. No party is ever wasted. " Her grin faded quickly. "And we're not licked yet. What you need is a second shot at Jack Ralston."

"I'm not sure a second chance—"

"Not a second chance, a second *shot.*" Her eyes brightened. She shifted Addie on her hip and used her other hand to pull open drawers in the big desk, checking folder labels as she kept talking. "And I might have an idea... But you've got to realize what you're going up against with some of the hard-headed men out here. Think in terms of elephant guns, not second chances."

Val grinned. "I'll introduce you to some of my family someday, Matty, and you'll know Wyoming doesn't have a monopoly on hard-headed men." Or women, for that matter. But they weren't discussing women.

The door on the far side of the room swung wide, and Dave walked in.

"Hey, Val. Good to see you." He raised an eyebrow in the direction of his wife. "If you tell me what you're looking for I might be able to help before you have to resort to the extreme measure of returning this little girl to her mother."

"Oh, good. Dave. Where's the folder with all the employees' information? You know, Social Security numbers and such. Has it already been moved?"

He went to a cabinet behind the desk, extracted a file and handed it to her. "Nothing's been moved yet. With you and Jack adding that book loft we got behind. Why do you want Social Security numbers?"

"I don't." She opened the folder one-handed. "I want — ah-hah! — birthdays. And that's what I thought. Jack's birthday is tomorrow. Tomorrow!"

Dave looked wary, which put Val on alert.

"Okay," he said slowly. "So Jack's birthday is tomorrow."

"So we give him another party. We'll have to do it in a way so he can't leave. And—"

"Matty. No."

Val was glad Dave said that.

Despite the lowered hat brim, despite seeing him only through the lens of the camera, she'd seen — or felt — something in Jack's response at the party that made her not want to put him through that again.

"Jack's made it pretty clear he doesn't want—"

"Oh, pooh," Matty interrupted. "What Jack Ralston *thinks* he doesn't want could fill a library."

"You have to respect a man's boundaries."

"No, you don't," his wife shot back. "Sometimes that's the very worst thing you can do."

Dave looked around. Possibly for reinforcements. "What do you think, Val?"

She looked at them, now standing side by side behind the desk, touching along their arms and sides, probably unconsciously, yet in a silent declaration that their differences on this or any other topic didn't detract one iota from the fact that they were a team. Always.

It reminded her of her cousin El and El's husband Cahill. Reminded her so much of them that it closed up her throat with emotion for a moment.

Was that missing El and Cahill? Or was it sorrow that she had nothing like they and this couple she'd just met so clearly had.

She swallowed, forcing her throat open. "I don't think another surprise party would be good. But I agree with Matty in another way. If we respect his boundaries, Jack will stay inside them."

"Exactly. Even worse, he'll keep building them higher and higher and higher. You know he's done that, Dave. You've mentioned it." She turned to Val. "So, what are you going to do?"

Ah. So Matty, like her mother-in-law had gone from *we* to *her* doing something. She should push it right back into *we*. Right now. Make it clear she certainly wished Jack Ralston all the best, would forever be grateful to him. But, really, she had no personal stake in what he did or how he lived, even if he did look bleak when people threw a surprise party in his honor.

She'd make that clear right now.

Put her foot down.

Step away from all of this.

"I have an idea," she said.

Chapter Five

In town to pick up what she needed to implement her plan, Val stopped at the Café for lunch.

She barely got in the door when two women descended on her, or more accurately on Addie. Both stretched their arms out. The older woman won, because she was closer, while the waitress had to come around the counter.

Val and Addie had met both of them at the surprise party. The older woman was Ruth Moski, office manager for Dave's law practice. The waitress' name was Rainie.

"Nice party," said one of the men sitting at the counter.

Val turned to him, recognizing Ruth's husband, Hugh. Another of the party attendees. "Glad you enjoyed it."

"Everybody did."

"Everybody?"

"Oh, you can't let Jack Ralston get you down. If you judged by him, there hasn't been a good party in this neck of the woods since he arrived. Besides, he used to be worse," Hugh Moski said matter-of-factly.

"Worse?"

"Yeah. Didn't react at all. Didn't show a thing. You know those movies the kids liked so much for a while? People not really alive?"

"Vampire movies?" *Jack as a vampire?* She wanted to giggle. Who'd ever seen a vampire with a suntan?

"Nah. The other kind. Walked funny."

"Zombies."

"That's it. Jack would get that way early on. Staring off like he was looking at something far, far off. Like he didn't see anything here and now."

"Why?"

Hugh shrugged. "Nobody knows as far as I've heard."

"And if Hugh'd heard, everybody would know," said his wife.

"Had his heart broken's what I say," Rainie contributed.

"Can't argue with that," Ruth agreed. Then added less agreeably to Rainie, "Oh, all right, you can hold her, though why you can't just hold your own, I don't know."

Rainie grinned as she took Addie into her arms. "They're too big, and you should talk. What about all your grandchildren?"

Ruth snorted. "All too big and too old. I'd be starting to think about great-grandchildren if that Zoe of ours ever found a man worth putting up with."

"Have you introduced her to Jack?" Rainie asked.

Val felt herself stiffen. She fought to hold on to her half grin.

Ruth glanced at her then said, "Like each other fine as friends, but no spark. Gotta have that spark."

"Don't know how anybody'd have a chance to spark with Jack Ralston. I know some have tried without the least bit of success. Course their sparking opportunities were awfully limited. He's either not around or he's working."

Although Ruth didn't look at her this time, Val felt as if the gray-haired woman was addressing her. "That's true enough. Anybody needs help, he's right there. Anybody offering fun, he's gone."

She grabbed the opening to change the subject. "Speaking of fun, have you heard Lisa Currick and Shane Garrison are due in town in mid-July. Sure am looking forward to meeting them."

"Of course we know," Ruth said.

"Oh, you'll like them for sure, Val," Rainie said. "Especially Shane. Told Lisa early on that if it weren't for three kids and having a few years on him, I'd have done my best to cut her out."

That drew a few chuckles from the men seated at the counter. Rainie informed them they were getting no more coffee out of her, which led to wider discussion of a legend from the previous century of how a woman in a nearby county had disposed of her ungrateful husband with poisoned coffee.

After Addie repeated one of the storytellers' phrases about "dead as a doornail," Val escorted her to a booth along the far side of the building and got down to the serious business of lunch.

****

"Here, hold Addie."

Jack recoiled. First, from the shock of finding Val and her daughter in the kitchen of the Flying W's main house when he entered it after a long day of work. Then, from the words ordering him to hold the girl. And finally from something else he wasn't going to consider.

"I don't know how to hold a kid."

But he hadn't recoiled fast enough or far enough. So he already was holding her. Val had thrust the girl at him, and what choice did he have? Drop the kid?

It was like holding an oversized watermelon with arms and legs. Thank heavens for the arms, because he had his hands under them, and they kept his suddenly-damp hands from slipping loose. Another thank heavens was that right now she wasn't using the legs for anything but dangling. Didn't take any experience with kids to know that her swinging those legs around could quickly destabilize this situation.

He raised his gaze from his survey of her limbs and encountered the wide, concentrated, dark-eyed stare of her mother in miniature.

No. That wasn't quite right... But he didn't have time to consider the differences. Not now. Not with them here. Not with his peripheral vision catching Val turning toward him.

"You don't know how to hold her? Are you kidding?"

He risked diverting his attention long enough for a glance over Addie's shoulder to her mother. She was opening the oven door, using a mitt to pull out a rack. "No."

"Well, you should be, because where Addison Rose Trimarco is concerned, you set the standard."

His gaze had gone back to Addie's eyes. It wasn't Val's stare. There were similarities, sure. But it was like a different light shining through a piece of stained glass. Both results were beautiful, yet different. Individual.

At this moment the light shining through Addie's wide, dark eyes held bright, frank questioning.

"What?" he mumbled.

"You set the standard," Val repeated. "You were the first one to ever hold her. So you're the one she measures everyone else against. I was terrified when you first handed her to me that she'd demand to go back to you."

"Yeah, right."

Addie must have heard something in his dry tone she liked, because she chortled.

"She agrees," Val claimed, turning back to open the oven door. "Don't you, Addie?

"Jack," the little girl said, as if that were an answer. She also started squirming. The watermelon with arms and legs had suddenly become a cross between a jellyfish and an octopus.

"She's moving."

"Hold her tighter."

Addie squawked a protest. Val looked around, still bent over the open oven and with her head down. "Closer to you," she instructed, "not tighter around."

He loosened his hands' grip and she nearly squirted out. Instinctively, he hauled her back in. One arm slid under her butt and the other spread wide across her back, giving up the distance his first hold had offered.

"You got it," Val said, turning back to the oven. "She's tired. Needs a little rest, don't you, Addie?"

"No." But she settled her bottom more comfortably against his forearm, and rested against his chest with a quick huff of contentment.

He was sweating.

Were they nuts? They were. Had to be. The pair of them. He'd nearly dropped the kid. If Addie hadn't realized it, she needed better instincts for self-preservation or she wouldn't last very long.

A catalog of potential dangers flashed through his mind. Look at this kitchen, with an oven and knives and things that could fall off the counter. Then outside with the vehicles, animals, tools of a ranch. And nature. Good Lord, he'd have to spend every second—

No. No, it wasn't his job. Not only that, he hadn't asked them to come here and didn't want them here. If there was any looking out to be done, it was Valerie Trimarco's job to do it. But it wouldn't come to that, because they were getting out of here. Right away. Going to be gone. So it didn't matter how many dozens of ways for a not-yet four-year-old to get hurt on a ranch came to him in a blink. And it didn't matter what percentage of them might also apply to her mother.

…Who was pulling a pan out of the oven now with a contented smile.

"What are you doing here?" he demanded.

"Baking."

"I can see that." And smell it. And feel the mouth-watering response. "Why here?"

"Matty said the stove at the foreman's co— house isn't to be trusted."

First he'd heard of that. And even if it were true, why here, why not at the Slash-C with her great good friend Matty Currick?

Before he could ask, Addie tilted her head back and up. "Everything'd be okay, Jack. Everything okay." She smiled at him before dropping her head back against his shoulder and seeming to burrow into him.

At first he thought — stupidly — that he'd somehow gotten grit in his eyes, the way you could moving the herd or roping a horse or placing irrigation pipe or haying or any of another two-dozen tasks. Except they were all outside, and he was standing in the kitchen, where nothing resembling a cloud of dust happened to blowing through at the moment.

Not dust. He hadn't shed tears since— No. He wasn't going to let them go now. What he could do — had to do — was get these two dangerous females off the Flying W and Slash-C. Get them far away. For good. And fast.

Addie stiffened abruptly. As he looked down to see why, her head snapped up, driving his lower jaw up into a collision with his upper jaw.

"Down!" she demanded. "Down! Bownies done!"

With the oven door now closed, he complied.

"They're too hot, Addie. We have to wait for them to cool." Val shot him a look. "What's wrong? Are you okay? Oh, God, you got the chin-clip, didn't you? I'm so sorry. Was your tongue —?"

"Fine. I'm fine," he said.

Her brown eyes studied him, the sharp light of her intelligence streaming through the stained glass, making it so entirely different from Addie's looks that in that moment he couldn't believe he'd seen any similarity.

She saw too much, too clearly. He almost turned and walked out to avoid it. Then he remembered he had the perfect excuse for any signs of something stinging his eyes.

"Well," she said slowly, "you will be fine. As soon as you experience the magical cure of Trimarco brownies. Because who makes the best brownies in the world?"

Addie piped right up with, "We do!"

****

A man with a child, especially a big, strong man being gentle and kind to a child, always filled Val's heart.

Make it her child they were being gentle and kind to and the emotion swelled enough to burst any dam.

She'd been touched many times by the men in her family interacting with their own babies and each other's. It always made her smile with warmth and delight.

Not now.

She couldn't catch her breath, wondered if the yawning in her gut might swallow her whole.

So, why was this so different?

It hit her like a punch expelling all the oxygen out of her. When her dad settled a grandchild on his lap, when one of her brothers or brothers-in-law consoled a child of his own or not his own, when Cahill held his son or her daughter high above his head to draw cascades of giggles, there was always, always a thread of joy in the connection.

In Jack there was no joy. There was sorrow. Sorrow and loss.

She pivoted away, sucking in her breath.

"Now these have to cool while Addie and I clean up. Because it's not nice to leave messes behind, is it, Addison Rose?"

"No messes," she agreed emphatically, though Val knew a pair of dusty brown outlines on the refrigerator door perfectly matched her daughter's handprints.

"Why don't you sit down and keep us company while we clean up?" she invited Jack.

He stepped back. Not yet turning and fleeing, but definitely retreating to the threshold of the coat hook-lined area by the back door. "I, uh, I gotta go. Gotta get back out."

"What did you come in for then? Must have been some reason."

He looked around, clearly seeking a reason that wouldn't keep him here any longer.

"Needed my slicker," he said, snatching that article from a hook. "Gotta get back to work now."

Then he did turn and flee. Back outside into a hot, cloudless blue sky. Just the thing to require a slicker.

Val didn't know whether to laugh or cry.

****

Spurred once more by Addie, Val got up even earlier Tuesday than the day before.

That was bad and good.

The bad was that she'd gotten very little sleep. She blamed the amount of sugar she'd consumed during the prep and taste-testings of the brownies. Odd that it hadn't affected Addie, but it had to be the sugar. Couldn't be the thoughts whirling through her head.

The good was that if she'd arrived any later at the house, Jack would have been gone.

As it was, she caught him about to push open the screen door on his way out.

He stepped back. The movement was controlled. So was his expression. So controlled that she had an urge to do something wild to shake him out of his control.

"Where's Addie?" he asked.

Choosing to interpret that as an invitation, she opened the screen door and stepped past him. She figured it was fifty-fifty whether he followed her into the kitchen or walked out.

When he came back along the hall and took one step into the kitchen, she said, "Playdate. Taylor and Cal. Well, not with them. With Cassie. Taylor picked her up on her way into her office practically at dawn, and she'll drop her off at lunch."

He ignored those details. Smart man, since she was babbling. He said, "What's that?"

She regarded the plate as if giving his question serious consideration. "Don't want to jump to any conclusions here, but it looks a lot like brownies to me." She placed the plate on the counter. "We frosted them last night."

"What're they for?" He leaned against the counter on the opposite side of the kitchen from her.

"They're for eating. By you and whomever you might choose to give them to. To celebrate your birthday. You took off so fast yesterday—"

"How the hell do you know—? Matty." He grumbled a curse word under his breath that seemed harsh considering he was talking about his employer's wife. And the woman whose house he was living in.

"Yup." She peeled back clear wrap from the pyramided brownies, and planted the solitary candle she'd gotten from Matty in the center of the middle one. "Your birth date's on your employment form. You wouldn't let me thank you properly, so we made you birthday brownies."

"Quit thanking me," he grumbled, with another muttered curse.

She stroked a match along the rough side of its box, lit the candle, then turned to him, holding out the plate. "Make a wish, and blow out your candle."

"I don't do candles. Don't do wishes. Don't do birthdays. And I don't do parties," he finished pointedly.

"Do you do human contact?"

"No."

The calmness of that drove her to "Don't you have *any* attachments?"

"No."

"Have you *ever* had any? Ah, yes, I see you have."

"I didn't say—"

"Didn't need to. So you've had attachments." She narrowed her eyes at him. "Romantic attachments. And now you're going to tell me one ended badly, aren't you? The last one, probably, and that's what's made you try to resign from the human race. But why only look at the end?

"Lots of people focus on the pain of the endings, but, think about it, that's only a small part. The beginning and the middle count just as much. So your girlfriend ended it. That's not the end of the world. You still had the beginning and middle. You had good times, you and your girlfriend."

He straightened from the counter. "Sometimes the finish wipes out everything before it."

"Ah. A serious relationship. Married?"

"No."

"Engaged, then. So what happened? You backed out? Got cold feet?" *She wised up in time, huh?* was on the tip of her tongue. The sort of line she'd have tossed at her brothers, her cousins, her friends. But with them she'd have known the story behind the story. She'd have known how deep the hurt went and whether that sort of treatment would ease or exacerbate.

"No."

She looked up at him and almost shivered. The pain was there, near to the surface now.

She stretched her hand toward him. "Jack?"

"No," he said again, this time telling her not to push, not to ask more, not to touch.

Even she respected the expression that accompanied the word. At least for now. Besides, it was intriguing that he'd said that much. Looked like it had surprised him nearly as much as it had surprised her.

She ducked her head, blowing out the well-burnt candle, before saying lightly, "But you didn't come out of it with any wedding cake to put under your pillow."

He stared at her.

"Never mind, it's an old custom. Not one I suppose you would have followed at any weddings you went to." She saw his words forming. "You're telling me you don't go to weddings? No, of course not. What am I thinking? Mr. Party Animal at a wedding? Crazy, I know. Okay, okay, but surely you've had a birthday cake before. Maybe not birthday brownies, but a cake. Candles. Making a wish."

"No—" Then his face changed, denying his denial. Only to be replaced by a wall of rock.

"What is it, Jack? What did you just remember?"

"I have work to do. That's what I remembered."

He walked out.

****

The longest day of the year, but that was only judging by the span from sunrise to sunset.

Longest daylight meant the longest hours outside, but there were many days when the wonders of electricity extended his work day well after the last of twilight, sometimes into the next day and the next night, especially during calving season.

So he couldn't claim to be close to the most tired he'd ever been when he returned to the house and stumbled upstairs to the shower, where he stood with the lukewarm water sluicing down on him for several minutes before he started actively trying to remove the dirt. Later, he knotted a

60

towel around his hips, then went to the kitchen looking for a gallon of something to chug.

Nothing alcoholic. He'd gone through that phase early on. Hadn't managed to kill himself quick that way, and doing it slow with booze didn't appeal. He found a container of iced tea in the fridge, tipped it back for a good, long time, then lowered it.

That's when he saw the plate of brownies sitting on the counter.

Val must have put that clear wrap back over them. She'd left the half burnt candle in the middle one.

He was pulling the wrap up before he thought about it. Took one from the near edge of the plate, nowhere near the one with the candle.

Four candles, Jacky. Four candles for our four-year-old boy.

The plastic he'd been pulling jerked, spattering a few crumbs on the counter. Just an accident. Not because he thought he heard voices in his head. He closed his eyes as he bit into the chocolate, taking it into his mouth, the sweetness melting there.

That was a mistake.

Blow out the candles, then we'll cut the cake. Blow hard!

Good job, son! You got them all!

Happy Birthday, Jacky!

Closing his eyes had been the mistake. He opened them, staring around at the familiar, old-fashioned kitchen.

The voices, the hugs, the smiles. Maybe they weren't real. Otherwise he'd have remembered before now.

Not like that other birthday.

That had been real. No question. Eyes opened or closed, those memories came. The Happy Birthday banner. The crowd. The singing. Her kisses.

And then … all that followed.

He dropped the half-eaten brownie, and banged out the back door, trying to even his breathing.

The air felt pleasantly cool after the day in the sun. He pulled it in, long and slow, the way he'd trained himself to do. Breath by breath. Minute by minute.

He saw a light from the old foreman's house. Val and Addie.

Seemed close enough that he should be able to go down the back steps, walk across a bit, and be right there.

But that was an illusion. A trick of Wyoming's air.

Not as close as they looked. Not nearly as close. In fact, Val — and Addie — were as far away from him as it was humanly possible to be. With their brownies and birthday candles. Sunny smiles and chubby fingers ... heated eyes and perfect curves.

God help him, he wasn't thinking about her as the mother of a cute kid. Wasn't thinking about her ability to bake treats that melted in his mouth.

He was thinking about wanting *her* to melt. To turn to molten sweetness all around him. To let him sink into her slowly, so very slowly. Until it couldn't be slow anymore, but had to be fast and hard and —

He caught the towel inches short of turning him into a flasher. The knot must have worked loose when he walked to the kitchen, then out here... Along with some other motion that had pushed at it.

He gripped the towel, and went inside.

He had another long day's work ahead of him tomorrow. Longer and harder than today if he had any hope of not thinking about his neighbors down the road in the old foreman's house.

On his way back in he saw what he'd missed before. A few brownies in a separately plastic-wrapped square.

A note beside them said:

Jack—

Addie was worried that you couldn't eat your brownies while you're out working, so we wrapped this for you to take with.

—Val

He ignored them. Plate, packet, and note.

Went to bed and kept ignoring them.

Through a mostly sleepless night he ignored them.

He got up in the pre-dawn, walked out without breakfast and got in the truck while still ignoring the brownies.

Sat behind the steering wheel without turning over the engine, noticing despite himself that no light showed at the foreman's house this early. Which meant she was still in bed, warm and soft under the covers, her hair wild on the pillow, her skin—.

He swore. Slapped one hand on the steering wheel. Got out and marched back into the kitchen.

Flipped the note over, wrote "Help yourself" in big letters, counting on the youthful appetites of Bryan and the other worker staying in the house at the moment.

Took three brownies from the plate. Put one in his mouth, added two more to the stash in his hand to replace it. Started back out. At the last second, he pivoted, snatched up the plastic-wrapped square and headed back to the truck, where he tossed in a utility bag that went from saddlebags to truck, depending on his day.

Swearing to himself — at himself — around the scent and taste of a chocolate Trimarco brownie melting in his mouth.

Chapter Six

Jack thought he'd pulled it off.

He'd been checking the progress on construction of the new ranch office at the Slash-C when Ed came in with a large padded envelope addressed to Addison Rose Trimarco and asked if he'd drop it off, "Since you'll be right there."

To say no, he'd have to explain that he'd intended to make a significant detour to bypass going past the Flying W home ranch on his way to doctor a group of yearling steers pastured north of the cluster of buildings that included the foreman's house. Ed would justifiably want to know why on earth he'd do that.

So he'd been stuck with saying yes.

He'd let out a breath when he didn't see anyone outside the foreman's house. But the news wasn't all good, because that little rental car of hers was sitting beside the place.

He killed the truck's engine and coasted in near the barn, was careful not to slam the door, then was damned near stealthy as he propped the envelope beside the back door where they'd see it next time they went out. He hadn't let his boot heels make as much as a single *thunk* against the wood floor of the back porch.

He'd passed her car and much of the open space between the house and barn and was congratulating himself for pulling it off when he heard the door open behind him. The front door.

Damn. He'd made a tactical error by automatically going to the back door, because that had left him with a whole lot more territory to cover than she'd had, slicing through the inside of the small house.

Along with the door opening, he heard her saying something, presumably to Addie, since it was about "not without shoes."

The door creaked more, but her "Thanks, Jack!" was clear.

"Welcome." He didn't turn. He kept going, stretching his stride.

"Hold up. Addie wants to thank you."

Another minute, minute-and-a-half at most, and he'd have been in the barn. Out of sight. Even now, he could pretend he hadn't heard...

He slowed. Stopped. But he didn't turn around.

Across the corral fence, which stretched closest to the house here, Storm looked at him with interest, then shifted his attention beyond Jack and nickered a welcome to the two females heading their way.

Traitor.

He reached for the animal's halter, adjusting a strap that didn't need adjusting.

"I got a present," Addie called out, her voice coming closer with each syllable. "Uncle Anthony sent me present."

"And you want to thank Jack for delivering it right to our door, don't you?"

"Yeah. Thank you, Jack."

He should be thanking them for the brownies. That would be the polite thing. Even if he hadn't asked for them. Even if he hadn't wanted them. Even if he'd given them away.

Most of them.

But before he formed any words, Addie, with her thank-you duty done, said with much greater enthusiasm, "Didja see it, Jack? Didja see?"

To anyone else he'd have said no, since he hadn't poked into an envelope not addressed to him.

Instead, he slowly turned toward Addie and her mother.

Addie wore a bright green t-shirt marked with a light brown blob. The oversized shirt revealed the tips of her fingers and the hem of her denim pants.

Val wore a smile. For a slice of second, Jack imagined what it would be like if that's all she wore.

"It's from my uncle."

At Addie's voice, Jack shook his head to dislodge the imagining.

"Yes it is," the little girl said. "See? See?"

She grabbed the material, stretching it wide, which made the white letters on it impossible to read.

"How'd you open it so fast?"

Addie frowned fiercely at the change of subject, but Val chuckled. "She is the fastest opener in the West, East, and all points in between. You should see her Christmas morning. It's like a package-opening tornado hits. She spotted you through the kitchen window while I was getting her a drink of water. She was down and to the back door so fast I thought for sure you'd seen her. Then she had the package opened before I shut the back door. Addie, honey, ease up on stretching your new shirt so wide. It makes it hard to see what's on it."

The girl's hold eased and the blob now revealed itself as being a cartoonish rendering of a calf.

The front read:

"You think roping a calf's tough?"

Val gestured and Addie obeyed, turning her back, while twisting mightily to look at him over her shoulder, grinning wide.

"See what it says? See?"

It said:

"Try a lobster!"

Drooping somewhere down the back of her thigh was a reddish blob that might have been a lobster with a rope around it.

"Could you rope a lobster, Jack? Could you?"

He sucked the insides of his cheeks in between his back teeth. She was serious, so that's how he'd answer.

"I never have. Suppose if I needed to, I'd manage."

She nodded, as if to say, *I knew it.* "Uncle Anthony can't. He catches 'em in pots. That's gotta be easier than ropes. I love lobster. It's 'licious. Do you love lobster?"

"Can't say. Never eaten it."

Her eyes widened with surprise and a dismay that touched him. "But … But you gotta eat lobster."

"Maybe someday."

"You come see us at home and eat lobster," Addie invited.

Before he had to respond to that, her attention shifted to the corral. More specifically to the horse inside the corral, who'd ambled a couple feet away when he released the halter, moving along the fence line to nibble on what appeared to be a particularly tasty weed.

"Hi, Storm!"

Addie's shifted attention left a spreading silence.

"Uh, thanks again for bringing the envelope over, when I know you have a million better things to do," Val said, talking fast. "I told my brother we're at the Flying W now, but he only half listens to me at best. He was too preoccupied with his notion that his niece is becoming too enamored with the Western life. You know how it is with siblings."

"No." Surprised by his own voice, he looked at her. Then he wanted to kick himself for that, too. What? Did he think she was a ventriloquist with her hand up the back of his shirt? …. *Her fingers stretching up, her palm warm and seeking against his skin* — no, not a good image to let loose in his head.

"No other kids in your family?"

He was so grateful for her question breaking that image of her hand on his bare back that he said again, "No."

If she'd said something then, he could have resisted adding more. But she was silent.

Her silence created an irresistible vacuum, pulling words from him. "No family." No, no, no, what was he doing? He wasn't going to say — "Orphaned young."

"Oh, Jack." Emotion filled her eyes immediately. It wasn't the pity he used to see when he was young and would tell people. It was like she was trying to put herself into his shoes, the way preachers always said you should. Looking into the openness and warmth of her eyes he could almost think she had.

"Don't feel sorry for me," he said roughly, even though he didn't think she was doing that, not exactly. "I was one of the lucky ones. Real lucky. Fostered long-term by reliable people. Passed away a few years back, only a month apart."

"But… What happened to your parents?"

Odd. He hardly thought of them anymore. Felt like he hadn't known them. Not like the Bazerocks— He chopped off that thought with brusque words. "Killed in a car accident when I was four. I came through with scratches. Not a lot of relatives. None could take on—"

He'd caught movement out of the corner of his eye. Before his mind put all the pieces together, his muscles reacted. If he also welcomed the interruption, he couldn't be blamed for that.

He stooped, stretched out one arm, curled it around Addie's solid little body, and swept her back to the fence.

She'd simply ducked between the two lowest rails and stepped inside the corral. Now she was still inside, but not heading toward the open space in the middle where Storm might inadvertently hurt her.

Val gasped. But she didn't let that slow her any, either, as she tugged her daughter back outside the fence through the same gap the girl had exploited.

"Addison Rose Trimarco. What did I say I about fences?"

"To stay outside them," the girl said.

"Did you?"

She considered a moment. Jack was pretty sure she was weighing whether or not to fib. "No."

"No," confirmed her mother. She huffed out a breath that sounded shaky, though her words hadn't been.

He shot a look at her and saw pale skin and huge eyes. She'd acted, now she was imagining horrors that had been avoided.

"You know why there's a fence there?" he asked Addie, drawing her attention, giving her mother a chance to recover her equilibrium.

"No."

"To keep Storm inside, so he doesn't roam around and get lost or get someplace where he'd get hurt. And it's to keep you outside, so you don't go someplace where you'd get hurt."

"Storm wouldn't hurt me."

"Probably not on purpose, but he's so big it's not fair to expect him to not hurt you by accident. And sometimes, he gets upset about other things and wouldn't be paying attention that you're there at all. So, you stay on your side of the fence, and he stays on his side, and everybody's good."

"Vegas goes on Storm's side," she said referring to the Curricks mixed breed dog.

"Yup, He does. Can you run as fast as Vegas?"

She wanted to say yes. It was there in her face. But she was Val's daughter, so she was honest. "No." Then she rallied, which was also proof she was Val's daughter. "You go on Storm's side, and you couldn't catch Vegas."

"True. But I've spent more years than you are old learning about horses."

"I can learn."

"Yes, you can. You're a very smart girl. And the first lesson is to stay on this side of the fence. When I'm sure you know that lesson, you can move on to the next one."

Her lower lip came out. She looked up at him through her lashes, gauging if that was weakening him.

As soon as she decided it wasn't, she raised her head and looked at him straight-on. Then she said, "Okay."

If she'd been older he'd wonder if that was a fake-out. But his gut said it was genuine.

That was a problem. Because there'd be consequences.

A pickup beeped as it came into view from the direction of the highway, approaching sedately.

"Brennan!" the girl shouted.

"Addie, you stay here," Val said immediately. "You stay right here until the truck stops and I say okay."

It was a Slash-C truck. In fact, Matty's truck. But driven by Donna, he saw after another moment. And yes, with one of the child seats in back occupied. Addie had nailed it.

She bounced in place while Donna brought Matty's truck to a halt in front of the foreman's house. Donna waved as she got out of the truck, then immediately opened the back door to extricate Brennan. Vegas bounded out, making a beeline for Storm.

"Mo-om," pleaded Addie.

"Okay. But don't bother Mrs. Currick."

Addie shot across to the truck, telling about the envelope from her uncle long before the truck's occupants could hear her. Especially because Vegas yipped joyfully as he now danced along beside her.

He watched her while his thoughts darkened. Donna could have brought the damned envelope to the Flying W. She must have known she was coming over here. And he'd bet a month's pay she'd told Ed to give him that task. She was as bad as her daughter-in-law, interfering with his life. All he wanted was to be left in peace, stay away from this mother and daughter until they went back East where they belonged, and get his life back to —

"You do know what you did, don't you?" Val asked from beside him, still watching her daughter.

"I didn't do anything," he snapped, thinking of Donna Currick.

"What you said to Addie," Val clarified.

Oh. "If she learns the first lesson not to go through fences—"

"And she will. Now."

"—I'm honor-bound to figure out a second lesson, and be the one to teach it to her."

From the corner of his eye, he saw her nod. That corner of his eye must have been real sharp, because it also saw the hint of a smile. Then her eyes went wide and she jolted.

They both turned toward the corral.

"She poked me with her nose." The surprise in Val's voice blended with a strong note of amazement. "Why?"

"Might've been exploring. You might've been in the way. Might've been to get your attention."

The last seemed most likely, since the horse had sidled up closer to Val.

"May I pet her?" She nearly whispered, as if it might be rude to ask loud enough for Storm to hear. Also as if the thousand-pound animal were a foot-long poodle. To his surprise, he had to stifle a grin.

"Him, not her. Hold out the back of your hand. Let him sniff. Okay, now reach slowly toward his side and stroke his withers."

"Her — *his* where?"

"Withers. High up on the shoulder, there, where his neck comes in. Nice, steady rhythm."

"How do I know if he's okay with this? And why not his nose? You always see people in the movies stroking a horse's nose."

"Movies are a lousy research source. Get a lot wrong. As for why, think about it from Storm's viewpoint — literally, considering where his eyes are — the hand of a stranger would be coming right at his face then disappears."

She slowly nodded. "That makes sense. They might think they're being attacked." She looked up at the horse. "If he decided to defend himself, I don't think I'd come out of it very well."

"When it comes to fight or flight, most horses' first choice in most circumstances is flight. Run first, think later."

"You don't have to be insulting, does he, Storm?"

He snorted. "As for whether he likes it or not, he's not moving away, so there's your answer."

"Excellent," came Donna's voice from behind them.

They both turned, the movement letting their gazes catch. Damn. He better stick to looking at her from the corner of his eye.

Donna continued, "You did very well for your first encounter with a horse, Valerie. That gives me an idea."

Val smiled warmly, but she hadn't been around the older woman as much as he had. "What's your idea?"

He braced himself.

"The best way to see the ranch is on horseback, so Jack will teach you to ride. And since I'm here and can keep an eye on Addie and Brennan, there's no time like the present."

"I've got to check the grass in the Sask pasture and the alfalfa in that Broken Creek field."

"Perfect," Donna said. "That'll be a nice, easy first ride for Valerie."

Chapter Seven

Addie was fascinated that he was going to start teaching her mother to ride.

For the first five minutes.

With the prospect of also having to teach Addie once she mastered staying outside corral fences, Jack deliberately made those first minutes as boring and technical as possible. He went over equipment first, detailing the tack and what it did, using the patient mare Bo as the model.

He lost Addie during the discussion of halters, especially when Brennan piped up about how he used grain to get horses to lower their heads so he could put on the halter, making it clear to Addie that the boy knew a sight more about the topic than she did.

"Let's find Vegas," she announced.

Before Donna followed the kids out, she said with suspicious sweetness. "You'll teach Valerie how to mount from the ground, won't you?"

"I suppose—" Just in time, he caught the glint in the older woman's eyes. He coughed to fill the gap left by his change of direction. "Suppose we'll use the block the first few times."

"Oh, but she needs to know how to mount from the ground in case anything happens where there's no block. Ed always emphasized that when he was teaching me to ride when I first came to the Slash-C."

The glint grew stronger, and Jack suspected Ed and Donna had wrung every last bit of enjoyment from that process. Helping another rider into a saddle could be a pedestrian act … or not.

"She's got enough to learn," he said sternly.

Donna chuckled as she started away. "I'm confident Val will learn very quickly in some areas."

Valerie looked from Donna's departing back to him. "Is that something I should learn?"

"You will. Later." And with someone else teaching her if he had anything to say about it. "Right now more basics to cover."

She didn't argue. She paid close attention and picked it up quickly.

That left him a choice. Try to stretch this out enough to avoid putting Valerie in the saddle, then drive out alone to do his checking … and have Donna insist on a second lesson later. Or satisfy Donna at the same time he checked those areas, which would take about the same amount of time overall.

He stepped back from where Val had neatly adjusted Bo's cinch strap as he'd instructed.

"Ready?"

Her head snapped up. "To ride?"

"In the corral first. That goes okay, then on out."

Her eyes widened with what he recognized as a mix of excitement and uncertainty.

"Sure thing." She swallowed.

He ducked his head, hiding that he'd been ambushed by a grin, as he led Bo out. "You'll do fine."

"Right. Everything'll be okay."

"Yeah, it will."

He didn't give her time to think about it. Watched by Storm from the middle of the corral, he led Bo to the block and issued step-by-step instructions to Valerie. She wiped her hands down her jeans, then swung into the saddle as if she'd been doing it for years.

He handed her the reins.

She dipped her head, down and to the side a bit, and rocked forward.

"He isn't moving," she announced, as if it were news.

"She."

"B-E-A-U is a she?"

"B-O. Short for BoPeep, because Lisa Currick thought her mane sticking up like that looks like a bonnet that character wears."

"Oh, yeah. And this part—"

"Forelock."

"—turns under like the bangs. I see that. But I don't think using the wrong pronoun is the crux of this problem. Especially since I only called her him *after* she didn't move."

She said it all in a rush, not cranky at being corrected, but serious. Like he'd given her a viable theory to explore, she'd given it consideration then — reluctantly — found it lacking.

He felt an unexpected fullness in his diaphragm. He realized he'd held his breath a moment, and now let it slip out from between his lips.

She repeated that head-dipping, forward-rocking motion. It looked like one person indicating to another that the second one was welcome to pass through a doorway first. As if the horse could see it, when she had eyes in the front of her head and she was sitting behind. Not to mention not many horses were versed in polite society's body language.

"Gotta tell her what you want."

"Oh." She leaned forward, and said, "Let's go."

Bo's ears flicked, but that was about it.

A tickle hit Jack's throat, and he rubbed the back of his hand across his mouth.

"Gotta tell her in language she understands."

She looked at him, her lips already parting, and he hurriedly added, "No, not like Spanish or French or something. Not words at all. Thunk your heels into her sides."

"Really? I always thought that was a cliché from cowboy movies. Like white hats and black hats. And you said movies weren't reliable."

"No."

She did that head tip again. "No, what?"

"No, that's not a cliché. Movies might've gotten one right. And no, it won't hurt her," he tacked on because he saw that coming. "Try it."

"Okay, but ... if I don't get the same pressure on both sides will it make her turn?"

"Not likely. That's what the reins are for." He heard a stifled sound from the shadows at the entrance to the barn. Not Donna, because he saw her over by the foreman's house with the two kids.

"Oh. Okay, here goes."

She kicked her feet out wide like she was going to wale away with them, then brought them back soft and light. More like a breeze along the horse's side than any real contact.

Maybe Bo had gotten tired of standing still, because she stepped forward.

"She's moving!" Val called out. "Keep it up, baby. Good horse, good, good horse."

Bo's ears flickered at hearing more praise than she'd probably earned to that point in her life. Val brought the horse around the corral and back to him.

"What a great horse. You and me, Bo! You and me! Isn't she brilliant?"

Bo looked startled.

He laughed.

Val grinned at him, but he recognized another reaction, like a change in the air pressure, he felt surprise billowing from the shadows at the barn door.

He half-turned that way, was aware of movement, as if a figure withdrew deeper into the barn.

But Val was talking, and that drew his attention back to her. "Now that I have this moving thing down, let's *go* somewhere. You have to check somewhere, right? I can go with, can't I? I won't get in your way. If Donna will keep watching Addie—"

"No problem," Donna called from just around the corner of the far doors to the barn, proving the woman's hearing rivaled radar. But if she'd been the figure at this end of the barn, she'd been jet-propelled to get there that fast. "Go ahead and have a good time, you two."

"Can we, Jack? I never realized how much better the view is from up here. Even better than Matty's truck because nothing gets in the way. The view's so good, and I want to *see* things."

He never actually said yes. Didn't matter, since they were heading toward the Sask pasture.

Slower than he'd have taken it alone on Storm. But not too bad a pace.

And he could hardly complain.

Because he'd realized that the figure in the barn was Bryan. He'd had plenty of time to call to him out, order him to accompany Val on her first ride. Then he could have gone on alone. Could have done that, easy.

He hadn't.

****

They'd swung by the Sask pasture on the way to the Broken Creek field. The pasture was rebounding nicely from spring grazing. The alfalfa was a little behind. Needed rain.

Val was doing fine on Bo.

At first she'd concentrated so much she'd been quieter than usual. Then she got the rhythm and gained confidence. As they started back, she'd started talking. Should have irked him. He liked peace and quiet. But somehow her silence had made him uneasy.

He settled into the saddle more comfortably as she rambled from what they were seeing — with occasional brief answers from him to her direct questions — to taking some pictures of the landscape for her blog to how she'd learned about photography in one of her many jobs.

Bo had taken a slight lead, since they were headed back to the home ranch now. He watched Val rolling easily with the horse's motion. As short as she was, her legs looked long now. Long and sleek. They'd feel that way, too, out of those jeans. His hands stroking slow up the curve until—

He jerked the reins along with his thoughts. Storm sidestepped in justified indignation.

Both Bo and Val looked back to see what was up.

"Sorry," he said, letting Storm toss his head once as they pulled up even. "Thought there was a hole. You were saying."

"I was saying I'd never done that great taking care of myself. Okay but not great." She tilted her head and stared straight ahead. "*Mostly* okay. I mean, everybody has dips now and then, right?"

She looked at him.

He looked back.

She dropped her head and one shoulder, the way she had when she'd been trying to get Bo to move. An invitation.

"What?"

"Now you say, yes, everyone has dips now and then."

His mouth opened.

He snapped it closed again.

He'd almost said he'd sell his soul to have *dips*.

She kept looking at him expectantly. He faced the horizon as he said mechanically, "Yeah, everyone has dips now and then."

She nodded. "But since I've had Addie I've been so much better. Let's say I look both ways before I risk a dip."

She grinned. The muscles of his mouth eased. That was okay. He could even smile. Because he wasn't in danger of saying anything now. Not anymore.

"You know how they say it's cheaper to feed two than one? That's baloney. Absolute baloney, because you'll buy cheap for yourself — well, I'd buy cheap for myself. But not for Addie. So no way is it cheaper to feed her and me than it was just me. But in a way it's easier to think ahead for two.

"Especially being back in Gloucester near my cousin Eleanor. You and she would get along great. She's the planner. Had college funds set up for son kids before he was conceived. Heck she had a college fund set up for Addie practically before she was conceived. Well, okay, maybe not that early. But before she was born. She's even got me saving for retirement." She chuckled. "Sneaky about it, too. Gave me all this stuff to read about how the best gift you to give your kid is not worrying about supporting you in your old age. When it was just me, I always figured I'd get by, I'd find a way out if I got in a sticky situation. But that's not good enough for Addie. I have to ..."

He turned toward her when her words dried up. She was staring off, and she didn't look like whatever she was seeing made her happy.

He resettled in the saddle. She kept staring.

This wasn't right. Not for her.

"What is it, Val?"

She blinked. "Huh? Oh . . ." She glanced at him, then quickly away. That wasn't right, either. "I was going to say that I looked ahead, thought things through for Addie. But I didn't, did I? Not when I headed East and only got this far."

"Can't always plan when a baby's going to come."

She twisted her head and slanted a look up at him. "You of all people are going to let me off the hook for driving around in a snowstorm when I was that pregnant? If it hadn't been for you..." He saw the sheen in her eyes before she looked away.

"Turned out fine," he said gruffly.

"You have no idea how many times I've said that in my life. You could say it was my mantra." Clearly, she'd tried for her usual lightness. She hadn't made it. "In and out of jobs, towns, relationships, plunging ahead, taking risks. It all turned out fine."

She faced him again. Her mouth grim, her eyes sad — and that was so not right he almost reached out to her, with some strange thought that his touching her might return her to how she should look.

And that was about as strange a thought as there could be — that his touching her or anyone would lighten them.

"I endangered Addie's life and even my own with that stunt, and it was only because of your knowledge and kindness and the providence that brought you to us that everything was okay."

Their gazes met. He wanted to lean toward her. To— No. It wouldn't help her any and he wasn't sure how any more.

"And look at this." She spread her hands and made a face. "I did it again. Coming out here. Springing this on you. Not at the level of having my baby in the back of a car in a blizzard in Wyoming, but still springing the party on you that you didn't want, hanging around when you wanted us gone, now getting you dragged into teaching me—"

"You're a great mother."

"What?"

"You heard."

"Now you're being nice because I was having a pity party and—"

"Shut up, Valerie. You're a great mother and Addie's a good kid. But you're right. I was dragged into giving you a riding lesson and your next one will be with Bryan, is that understood?"

"Am I doing that bad?"

"No." Their eyes met again. Then the movement of the horses unsynced and the look broke, and he could only be grateful. "Now, shut up and ride."

"Okay," she said in a small voice so unlike herself that he wondered if that shared look had shaken her half as much as it had shaken him.

Chapter Eight

Donna called out good morning, rising from a rocking chair on the porch of the trim little house in the Slash-C compound and coming down the steps to where Val had extracted Addie from the child's seat in the back of the rental car.

"Matty said you might come by. She's not back from town yet. She took Brennan with her while she gets her hair cut."

"Cut?" Not Matty's long, thick sweep of hair, whether loose and flowing or partially tamed into a braid.

"Trimmed, I should say for Matty. Don't know what they're going to do about Brennan's." She made a wry face. "Bubblegum. All over his head."

"Oh, dear."

"Seems to be a rite of childhood. They should be back soon, if you'd like to wait."

"Thank you, we will. I want her okay on some photos of the ranch I want to post on the blog. I told her and Dave I'd run them past them both before I put them up, but Dave said—"

"Whatever Matty says is fine with him," Donna finished for her.

Since that was exactly what he'd said, Val smiled at how well his mother knew him. "Must be nice to have always been this smart."

"Oh, I wasn't always smart about the important things in life. If it hadn't been for Ed coming after me, I might have had an entirely different life. Possibly a good life. But not *this* life."

Her tone indicated this life was far, far better than good.

"How did you and Ed meet?"

"That's a long story. Why don't you come back and join me on the porch and we'll be comfortable while we wait for Matty. I have some coffee for you and—" She patted Addie's head. "—some juice for you."

The small house Donna and Ed had was set at a comfortable distance from the main house. Easy walking distance, but not close enough to trample on each other.

Once on the porch, Val saw the house's angle offered a view across fenced in areas to the mountains beyond. Only because the entry road looped around an old pump and trough was someone sitting on the porch able to see arrivals at the main house. And she'd seen from the main house that there were limited views of Donna and Ed's place. Some very careful planning had gone into the placement of this building. That said a lot about respect for privacy. She wondered if the Curricks could give lessons on the topic to some of her relatives in Gloucester.

Donna finished giving Addie a small glass of apple juice and supplied her with a well-worn picture book on horses. She poured coffee into a clean mug — "Ed took off in too big a hurry this morning to even have coffee with me." — and handed it to her. "How did your brownies turn out?"

She blinked at the older woman. "How did you know I made brownies?"

"You bought all the ingredients to make chocolate brownies in town before having lunch at the café with Addie, with a side order of conversation with the stool-sitters. Matty told you the oven in the Flying W foreman's house was unreliable, which might or might not be a figment of her imagination, and urged you to use the oven in the main house. There was also some discussion of Jack's birthday."

She felt her eyebrows rise.

"Welcome to Knighton, Wyoming," Donna said with a smile. There was also a faint hint of warning. She'd been wishing the Curricks could give a lesson on privacy to her relatives, but perhaps this was Donna's way of saying how little might be private in this small town?

She said, "Right on all counts. The brownies turned out great, if I do say so myself. Which I have to do, since we gave most of them to Jack for his birthday and haven't heard if he liked them. Next batch, which will be soon, since now I need to test that oven in the foreman's house, I'll bring you some."

"That would be delightful. Ed will be your greatest fan. So, you haven't heard anything from Jack about whether he liked his birthday brownies," she said. "Not surprising, considering how much he keeps himself to himself, especially with some goings on here at the ranch."

"Keeps himself to himself," she repeated. Then asked bluntly, "Is that all it is? Hugh Moski said Jack was like a zombie when he first came here."

Donna's eyes widened. "Did he? You know that's the danger of thinking you have people pegged. They go and surprise you. Who'd have thought he'd be that fanciful. Or that accurate."

Val blinked at the last sentence. "Jack *was* like a zombie?"

"Mmm."

True, he'd been extraordinarily matter-of-fact about the death of his parents and the "reliable" couple who had fostered him. And when she'd introduced the topic of doing better now that she was no longer on her own, he hadn't opened up any about what sounded like a history of his being on his own most of his life. But a zombie? No.

"Why?"

Donna looked at her directly. "You need to find that out from Jack."

"I'm sorry. Of course. I didn't mean to ask you to break a confidence, but you said you didn't know—"

"No. You misunderstood, Valerie. You need to find out from Jack why he was that way for his own good. He needs to tell you. He needs to tell someone."

Oh, yeah, she got it.

She'd been handed a mission. Possibly an impossible one ... if she chose to accept it.

No reason she should. She could happily spend these weeks exploring this part of the country until her house was hers again. Plus, she had absolutely no reason to think she'd get through to him if people like Donna Currick hadn't.

Though if she *could*, it would be for his own good.

Probably.

And she did owe him.

Certainly.

True, she had pushed El. Of course, so had Cahill. Look at her now. Married with a son and running her own business and happy, happy, happy.

If pushing did that for El, what might it do for Jack Ralston?

Donna's voice brought her back to the present. "Maybe he needed to go through days like a zombie to heal at the beginning, but it went too long. We let it go to long. It's a habit now. A safe, comfortable habit. It's going to take something sharp and strong to get him out of that habit."

Implicit was the question: Are you up for that?

Addie's voice cut across her thoughts. "There's Jack," she announced.

Val looked around, a sudden hitch in her breathing. "Where?"

"Way, way over there."

She followed the direction of Addie's pointing figure. He was visible in a large enclosure at some distance. Enough distance that there were three other enclosures plus the driveway between them.

"What's Jack doing?" Addie asked.

He appeared to be sitting on a chair in the center of the fence-enclosed space. It was hard to see details from this distance, but he appeared to be reading a book. "I don't know. You can ask him later."

"We go ask him now."

Donna put her palm on the crown of Addie's head, forestalling her from starting off immediately. "Not right now, dear. He's working with that horse."

Valerie broadened her focus and realized that there was, indeed, a horse in the same enclosure.

Without dislodging Donna's hand, Addie tilted her head up and sideways then slanted her eyes even more. "He's just sitting."

Donna nodded solemnly, though the corners of her mouth lifted. "Sometimes that's the hardest work of all. Come sit here by me, and I'll tell you about it."

When Donna had ushered them onto the porch, she'd gestured Val toward the chair she'd been sitting in and took the other. She'd noticed, because most people return to where they'd been sitting, but hadn't though much of it. Now she realized this seat gave a clearer view of Jack as he sat, reading calmly.

The horse trotted first one way, then the other, looking at the still man.

"Sometimes horses aren't cared for as well as they should be," Donna said to Addie. "Jack's very good with those horses. And people around here have gotten to know that. So if they know about a horse that needs extra help — the kind of help that Jack's so good at — they'll tell him about the horse or sometimes they just bring them here. That's what happened very early this morning with this mare. That's why Ed left in such a hurry this morning. He's helping fill in for Jack."

"So it's not just Jack who's helping this horse," Vail said.

Donna smiled. "No. Ed doesn't count, because he's delighted at these occasional bursts of getting back into running the ranch. But it means more work for Dave and the other hands, too. Nobody minds. Not with the miracles Jack can perform."

"Miracles? He's sitting," Addie said.

"That's what the horse needs right now. For Jack to sit there and not do anything to her that might make her more frightened or nervous than she is now. The first thing he has to teach this horse is that she can trust him. Trust Jack," she added, her gaze flicking to Val, then returning to Addie. "That might take a while to learn."

Addie nodded. But then, as if that understanding had stretched her beyond her not-yet-four-year-old tolerance, she hopped up from the corner of the chair she'd been sharing with Donna, said, "Ant!" in an enthralled voice and scooted to the far corner of the porch.

"How long will he sit with the horse?" It was better to ask the question than to risk Donna expanding on that "Trust Jack" theme.

"As long as it takes."

"Takes for what? The horse to go to him? Or be touched? Or—?"

"Long way from any of that," Donna interrupted smoothly. "First step with these rescues is for the horse to calm. Helping the animal figure out that it can soothe itself even with a human in the vicinity. That can take quite a while. That's why Jack always asks Dave first when someone calls about one of these poor creatures. Even though Dave always says yes. This first day can be particularly long."

She shaded her eyes with her hand. Val followed the direction of her look. Saw the horse do the same trot one direction, pivot and trot the other way routine. But now the horse was giving the man longer, almost questioning looks, at each turn.

"Ah, the mare's already starting to wonder. That's good. This should be easier than with Storm."

"Storm? He was a rescue? But he's gorgeous."

"Not when he came to Jack. This mare's scared, jittery. But that's easier in a lot of ways. Storm … well, Jack gave him that name because he said that horse had surely come through the worst of storms. He was nearly starved to death by some worthless idiot. The horse had given up. On humans — with good cause — and on living. Jack sat out in that paddock with him all one day, through the night, and into the next morning. Never left, never let anyone come in, hardly moved. And neither did Storm. Stood there listless, his head hanging. Not moving at all. First light, we were out here, and I was all for insisting Jack give up. Get off that chair, come in, have something to eat, get some sleep before he was in as bad shape as the horse. Then Ed spotted it — Storm had started swishing his tail."

"Swishing his tail?"

Donna nodded. "When I say he wasn't moving at all, I meant at all. He wasn't even using that automatic response to disrupt the flies. He'd let them land and bite. Never twitched, never swished his tail. Not until the next morning. And here sat Ed and me, with tears trickling down our cheeks because the sorriest looking piece of horseflesh you'd ever seen was swishing his tail at flies."

Val felt her own eyes prick.

"Took Jack more than a week of long, long days before Storm got enough life in him to be curious enough to go near him. There were times when everyone else was as ready to give up on Storm, as he had on life."

Donna's words repeated in Val's head. She knew what the older woman was trying to draw from her, yet she couldn't stop herself from saying, "But not Jack."

"No, not Jack."

Chapter Nine

Addie's attention had progressed from the ant to a spider web under construction to a large forked stick leaning against the wall. Donna had noted all that with the expert divided attention of a long-time mother and grandmother.

She'd seen the brewing discontent in the child and wasn't surprised when she plopped herself back on the corner of her mother's chair and demanded, "Wanna go see Jack."

And because she suspected Valerie wanted to do the same thing, she spoke quickly and firmly. "Not now, Addie. He's still working with the horse. He wouldn't want to be interrupted because the horse needs all his attention right now."

The child's mouth pursed. "Jack likes me."

"I'm sure he does," she said before Val even pulled in a breath to scold. "That doesn't alter that you should not interrupt him."

The mulishness creeping into the girl's expression disappeared. "Alter? Brennan says alter goes on a horse."

"That's halter with an h," Val said. She drew the shape of the letter on the thigh of her jeans with her finger. "What Mrs. C said is alter. That means change."

Addie lost all interest in vocabulary, letters and Jack at the sound of truck tires approaching. "Brennan!"

"Stay on the porch," Val commanded, as Addie ran to cut the distance to the approaching truck. "Those two are thicker than—What?"

Donna shook her head, blinking back quick tears and smiling

reassuringly. "I had a flashback to Dave and Matty when they were young."

Val laughed. "Oh, c'mon. You're saying Addie and Brennan have made a lifelong match? That doesn't happen."

"Oh, I don't know. These Currick men have a powerful draw. Someday I'll tell you that promised story about when I met Ed. Turned my life upside down … or maybe right-side up."

They were both smiling as they went to meet Matty, Brennan, and little Finn. But Donna saw the look Valerie sent toward the distant corral, where Jack Ralston still sat, still and silent, waiting for a horse.

****

Matty was unhooking Brennan from one of the two children's seats in the back of her new truck.

"You were right, Donna. They couldn't get it out. Bubblegum," she added over her shoulder to Val. "Worst was at the crown of his head, right in close to his scalp. How I missed it last night…"

"You probably didn't. Probably got in there overnight and then he slept on it," Donna said. "That was one of his father's favorite tricks. Have you checked the pillow yet?"

"No. Oh, Lord. If it's the S-p-i-d-e-r-m-a-n pillowcase and it can't be saved, we're all in deep trouble."

Addie examined her friend as he scrambled out of the truck to stand beside her, his close-cropped head giving Val the strongest urge to run her palm over it. "I want my hair cut," she declared.

"We can give you a trim—"

"Cut. Like Brennan."

Val gasped, shocked that her daughter's words felt like a blow to her chest. Her baby girl's gorgeous curls sacrificed to a buzz cut? Not only would it break her heart, her family would break her neck.

Matty came to her aid. "Oh, honey, you don't want to lose all your beautiful curls."

"Like Brennan," Addie said stubbornly.

"That's a cut for a boy, sweetie, because they're not as good at looking after their hair as we are."

"A boy cut," Addie confirmed, undeterred by the rest. "Like Brennan." She started, "Addie-"

"And Jack," her daughter interrupted.

"Jack?" But his hair wasn't this short. Long enough on top to think about running fingers through it, then tapered closer down the back and sides that showed when he wore his hat. "No—"

"Yes. Like Brennan and Jack," Addie repeated.

Before Val could respond again, Donna said, "Brennan, why don't you and Addie go play a bit. Didn't you have a new truck you were going to show her, Brennan?"

"Yeah. New truck like Mom's. Come see," he invited, and haircuts were forgotten as they headed away.

"Not by the pump, Brennan," Matty called out. She added in explanation, "The guys still use that pump and trough all the time, but they're so old, they leak and it's a quagmire."

Donna sighed. "Right there where anyone who drives in sees it. Been that way since before I came here. I kept asking Ed…"

"And I keep asking Dave." Matty nodded. "But repairing those leaks is so far down the to-do list we'll have Twenty-Third Century Curricks doing the job if we're lucky. In the meantime, it's a magnet for the kids and an eyesore for visitors. I remember you trying to plant things there year after year, Donna, and I've tried a few more. Everything dies. A flat of marigolds have already bitten the dust — or should I say they've gone under for the third time. Under the muck and mud."

"The only spot on the place where flowers die by drowning," her mother-in-law commiserated.

"I swear, this year I'm going to get something to survive here. But I don't suppose you came by to discuss my black thumb, did you, Val."

She chuckled. "No, I came by to get your okay on some photos. We can look at them on here—" She held up her phone. "—or attach it to a bigger screen if you want to see them better."

"The phone sounds great. We can sit on the porch and watch the kids at the same time. We'll have something to drink and look at the photos. Donna, you want to join us?"

She did.

While Addie and Brennan busily created roads and at least two avalanches in a pile of sand with Brennan's truck, Matty quickly approved the photos Val had selected. "I particularly like this one with Jack's shadow."

Damn. If Jack was identifiable from his shadow she wouldn't be able to use it. How had Matty known? The slice of his hat that showed? Something about the shadow? "How'd you know it was Jack?"

"Because the horse is Storm, so it must be Jack."

Ah, then she could use the photo. The only people who'd know it was Jack's shadow by recognizing Storm were those who already knew him, so he couldn't complain.

"In fact," Matty went on, "I'd love a blown up print of that to put in the new office. Let me know the cost and—"

"Absolutely not. With all you've done for Addie and me, it would be my pleasure to get that for you. Please," she added as Matty started to protest. "I want to do this, and I'd be honored to have one of my pictures hanging in the Slash-C office. Besides, I have another favor to ask you."

"Shoot."

"I'd like to read up on this area, especially the history. Would you — both of you — recommend some books for me? I thought I'd try the Knighton Library first, then order some."

"You can start right here. We've got some great books. And we finally gathered them all together — well, most of them," Matty added with a gesture to the window that revealed a stack of books on the kitchen counter. "—in the library in the new office. Tell us what you're interested in and we can recommend some titles. Then you can go and collect them while I give our pint-sized construction crew a snack."

****

Val pulled open the screen door to the new ranch office building, then stepped back abruptly. Jack Ralston stood just inside the door. He'd apparently been about to walk out of it when she'd opened it, but now stood rock still.

She looked up. His hair was definitely long enough to run her fingers through.

No.

"Oh. Sorry. Matty told me to come over here and take a look at the office library for some reading material. I didn't know you were here." But she wondered if Matty had. She was beginning to suspect Matty Brennan Currick hid ulterior motives behind her wide eyes.

Jack stepped back, gesturing up. "There it is."

Most of the small building had ceilings that went to the roof. In the back quarter, a second-story loft topped a small bathroom under construction

88

and storage closets. The loft was deep enough for bookshelves from its floor to the roof and a balcony in front of the shelves that held a couple plastic-wrapped easy chairs. Plastic hanging in front of the shelves smudged the colors of the spines into an Impressionist rendering of a library. A metal spiral staircase on the far right accessed the loft.

"Be careful on the staircase. It'll hold you, but it's not up there permanent yet. Has to come down for some other work to be finish. Retape the plastic when you're done. More construction to do, so more dust." He started toward the exterior door again, but so wide of her that he almost tangled with a plastic-wrapped couch on one wall.

"Thanks. That was fascinating to watch."

She saw his reluctance to stop. That stung. But not as much as it would have if he'd kept going. "What was?" he asked.

"What you did with that horse."

He gave her a disbelieving look. "Nothing fascinating about sitting."

"There is about why you do it. Restoring a horse's faith in humans. No, don't tell me that's not what you're doing. I know it is. And it's got to be difficult. To spend so long being ... *patient.*"

"Not so bad."

"Jack, don't give me that. You were out there for hours and I heard you sat without moving all day and all night with Storm. Weren't you tired? Hungry? Thirsty?"

He grunted.

"I suppose no mere human needs dared to get in your way."

When he flicked her a look, a corner of his month hitched. "Could've used a brownie or two long about three a.m."

She swatted his arm, but grinned. "Okay, so you sit with the horse the first time for as long as it takes for it to have that one moment of relaxation. What's next?"

"Get her on a routine. Food the same time. Me showing up and sitting with her the same time. Looking for relaxing quicker, longer."

"How long does that take? No, don't tell me. As long as it takes. So you're going to sit out there each day until she relaxes?"

"Pretty much. Shouldn't take too many days. Then we get on a regular routine. And I add in other stuff."

"Like?"

"Depends on how she reacts."

"You're not going to tell me."

He shrugged. "It depends on the animal and my best guess each day, so there's no telling. Besides, it's boring."

"How can it be boring when the end result is a beautiful animal like Storm?"

"Because it is boring to look at."

"But not to do?"

He sidestepped that. "You want to know about the deworming, too? Killing all the parasites? Can't do it too fast or the horse gets impacted from the mass of dead critters being expelled from its system at one time."

She narrowed her eyes at him. "You think you can gross me out with that? You've clearly never been a mother with a kid expelling the entire spectrum of disgusting stuff from every orifice simultaneously."

"Nope, never have been a mother. But you've succeeded in grossing me out, so I'm going to work, where all I have to worry about are stepping in cowpies."

But he was grinning as he turned away and walked out.

As she climbed the spiral stairs, she realized she was grinning, too.

****

Two days later she came by the Slash-C to drop off some groceries she'd picked up for Matty while she'd been in town.

Matty was on the back porch, looking through binoculars.

They restricted the kids to the porch while they sorted out perishables and frozen food. Matty persuaded her to stash her things in the fridge and freezer for now and to stay for a cup of coffee on the porch, letting the kids play a bit longer.

She agreed, then added, "But not for long. Someone needs a nap. Still adjusting to time change."

"Oh, that sounds wonderful," Matty said, making Val chuckle. Outside, Matty handed her the binoculars. "See that far corral? Take a look."

"Where Jack's working with the rescue horse?"

"Oh, that's right. I forgot you were here the first day Phantom arrived. Jack's getting quite the reputation. A neighbor of the guy who was mishandling her started calling around and heard about Jack. Went and had a discussion with the neighbor, loaded her up, and trailered her right here. First thing we knew was when he drove in with the horse trailer."

As she listened, she focused on the man sitting in a chair in the middle of the open area once again. This time he held something in his lap and his mouth was moving. His motions, while methodical, were easier, not as constrained as that first session.

"It looks like he's talking. But he's not looking at the horse."

"Reading out loud. Some folks talk, but I guess Jack'd have to worry about running out of words." Matty chuckled, not appearing to notice that she didn't. "He's been doing that off and on. Also walking around — never at her, but getting her used to the idea that a human moving around isn't necessarily bad news."

"How long is he spending out there?"

"An hour or so the past couple days. He's got her on a schedule now. Horses like consistency. Plus, he's introduced her to a couple of our other horses. Even had her out with Storm for a while yesterday. Today he's got an alpha gelding waiting in the wings. He'll leave them in neighboring corrals when he's done. Being herd animals, horses can get anxious of they're isolated but you also want to make sure they sort out the herd pecking order without any blood. So far, so good. There's Buster, over to the left. See? He's listening to Jack, too. Farther to the left."

She reluctantly slid the binoculars to the left to see a broad-backed gray horse who did, indeed, seem to be listening to Jack.

As she swung back toward Jack, the lenses caught the mare, and stopped. "She's listening to him."

"She's not looking at him." Matty sounded a bit skeptical.

"I know, but she's definitely listening. Her ears are like … like fine-tuning antennae. Oh, and she looks so much better. I can't believe it."

"Amazing what good food, decent water, and some attention can do, isn't it?" Matty's dry tone indicated that she didn't have much tolerance for the previous owners' failure to provide those necessities.

"Matty." She eased away the eyepieces just enough to flash a look at the other woman. "She's moving toward him."

Matty moved to the railing, cupping her hands to form a visor over her eyes. "She is."

"But she's behind him. Will he know..?"

"He knows."

"She's backing up now."

"That's okay. Forward and retreat, forward and retreat. That's the pattern. Just like some people." She was aware Matty had turned toward her, but she didn't return the look. "She's getting closer with each pass. Is she looking at him?"

"I can see both of them now. And — yes, she did look at him. Not long, but she did. Backing up again."

"Horses don't have the best vision, and lousy depth perception. She's getting a handle on him bit by bit, sort of like using a magnifying glass and moving it closer and farther away until you find the right spot."

"Oh. She touched him on the top of his shoulder. With her nose." And she'd seen him grin, even as he kept talking.

"That's a breakthrough."

"What are you two staring at?" Ed Currick asked from the office door behind them.

"That mare Jack's working with," Matty said.

If she'd been honest, Val's answer would have been: *Jack. I'm staring at Jack Ralston.*

"She's approached him already has she? God bless the innate curiosity of horses. That'll move her rehabilitation along well."

"What will he do next?" she asked, reluctantly lowering the binoculars and offering them to Matty. She shifted a mug of coffee to her other hand and held them up.

"Keep talking to her. Maybe approach her. Each step bit by bit. Then comes the big hurdle. Getting her to let him touch her. To be okay with it. Eventually, to like it. Teach her a man's touch is a good thing when it hasn't been in the past."

"Jack's great at that," Matty said.

Horses. They were talking about horses. Not Jack Ralston touching her. Nope, not talking about that at all. No reason to feel heat rising up from her chest to her throat … and dropping down to pool considerably lower than that.

"I've been meaning to ask you. I, uh, heard something about if a cowboy sold his saddle it meant he was giving up cowboying completely."

"Yep. That's how it was in the early days," Ed said. "If they kept the saddle they might be heading a long way away, but they weren't done yet. Selling the saddle was the end of that kind of life."

Matty offered the binoculars to her father-in-law with a gesture, and he took them with a nod of thanks.

"If you're interested in reading about it, there are some wonderful books on the early era of cowboying. They're all in the office library now," Matty said.

"I am. Thank you."

"Jack's the one who's read all those books. He'd be a good one to ask about which to start with," Ed said without lowering the binoculars. Before she had to respond to that, he added, "Those hoofs of hers need attending. Was that jackass trying to lame her?"

She met Matty's eyes and they both smiled slightly. Ed Currick's indignation on behalf of the horse was endearing.

"That's down the road a bit," Matty explained. "Need to build up the trust before you go picking up an abused horse's feet."

Her smile faded as she caught the significance in Matty's look.

"Got to build up a lot of trust. And that takes time. Time and patience." Unaware the topic had shifted, Ed still managed to hit the bull's-eye with his words.

Chapter Ten

"Mo-om," Addie whined as Val unhooked her from the child seat in the back of the rental car outside the Slash-C home ranch.

They'd had lunch at the Knighton Café with Matty and Donna Currick, Taylor, Ruth Moski, and a couple other women from town, discussing plans for the Fourth of July. Brennan, Addie, Cassie, and her little brother Rob, had their own lunch at their own table under the care of the waitress Rainie.

Donna had asked for a ride back to the ranch, saying she wanted to hear about Val's progress after two more riding lessons — these given by Bryan.

Val had a feeling the older woman wanted to talk about something else, but if so, she hadn't had the chance to talk at all. Addie's determination to get a haircut like Brennan's had resurfaced more strongly than ever.

"No more, Addison Rose."

Donna Currick coughed, poorly covering a would-be chuckle, as she exited from the front passenger seat.

Matty and Brennan had arrived first and came around the front of Matty's truck to join them, clearly having heard the exchange.

She felt Matty's knowing gaze on her. "Tough drive?"

Before she could answer, Donna said, "Matty, would you mind looking after Addie for a moment? I'd like to have a word with Valerie."

"Sure thing. Why don't you two go on in the house. There's some iced tea in the fridge. And in the meantime," she added, looking from Addie to Brennan, "I heard a rumor that Rapunzel the barn cat had kittens recently. Who'd like to see little baby kittens?"

That not only received a resounding response, but both kids headed full-speed toward the barn.

"Hold up, you two. Wait for me." Matty started after them.

She and Donna were crossing the porch toward the back door when a call of "Hey, Val" came from behind them.

They turned to see Bryan coming from the barn toward them, crossing paths with Matty and the two kids.

After hellos, he said, "I want to get your email address so I can send you some pictures I took. I've had 'em on my phone ever since and I totally forgot until I was downloading some the other day."

"Sure, but pictures of what?"

"Of the three of you—"

"The three of who?"

"You, Addie, and Jack."

"That's— You can't think—" She produced a laugh. "You make it sound like we're a unit."

"Sure," he said casually.

"No. No we're not."

He looked surprised. "But *you* think of the three of you as a unit."

"What? Why on earth would you think that?"

"Because you said it." He grinned at her.

"*I* did? No way."

"Yes, ma'a— sir, you did. You said it the day you had Addie, when you kept referring to Jack and you and her as *us*."

"Under the duress of childbirth. No woman can be held accountable for what—"

"And you said it the morning after the party when you came here with Addie, looking for Matty. You said 'You were the first one to come help *us*.' That had to include Jack, because he was already helping you," he said in triumph.

"That's a general us. You can't read anything into—"

"Language can be so telling, can't it?" Donna said. "Without our even being aware of it."

"Yes, ma'am." Bryan grinned.

Val glared at him.

His grin dimmed. "Uh, I better get back to work now. Gotta, uh, organize the tack room."

"That would be an excellent thing to do, Bryan." Donna smiled as he departed, though she was looking at Val. "Let's get that iced tea now."

"Why he would think …" she protested.

"Iced tea," Donna said firmly.

In the main house kitchen, Donna poured two glasses of iced tea and ushered her to the table off the kitchen, saying as they sat, "What you're doing matters, Valerie."

"I don't know what—"

"Jack," Donna said unflinchingly.

"It you mean that nonsense Bryan was spouting—"

"I don't. Not directly, anyway. It is interesting that even Bryan's picked up on the connections among you, Jack, and Addie. And don't waste your breath arguing with me about it," Donna said briskly. "I wanted you to know that it's a good thing you're doing. It takes courage to reach out, especially to a man as bent on discouraging real contact as Jack Ralston is."

"I'm not doing anything. Just being a—" She stumbled a bit there. Hoped the other woman didn't notice. "—friend."

Donna gave her a look that said that particular hope had not been fulfilled. "A couple days back when you and Addie came by and first saw Jack working with Phantom, I overheard a bit of you talking with him in the office." Blandly, she added, "Voices can carry so easily when that door's open. You said something to Jack about what he was doing was fascinating."

"And he denied it."

Donna nodded. "He did. But you didn't accept that. You said it was fascinating because of why he was doing it. To restore an animal's faith in humans. You also mentioned how hard you thought it must be to be patient." Her eyes warmed with a smile that never quite surfaced. "Remember?"

"Yeah, I guess."

"That's what you're doing, Val. What you're doing for Jack. You and Addie." She looked at her steadily. "But mostly you. You're restoring his faith in humans."

"What? No."

"Yes."

"But he *has* faith in people — in all of you, and in the people in this community. You know he does. You've said how much he's done for people around here."

"Yet won't ever let them get close. Not truly close. He pulls back, always pulls back."

The truth of that stopped Val's protests.

"Something happened," Donna said. "Something that wounded him deeply. He's too good a man, too generous a man not to help others. But he doesn't trust them. He is like some of these horses he rescues. Wary, staying at a safe distance, isolating himself. Hurting himself even as he tries to protect himself."

"But … not me. I drive him nuts."

"Yes. That's a definite advantage."

Val looked up to the woman's smile, knowing, teasing, and wise, then looked away, feeling heat rising up her throat and into her cheeks.

Donna continued in a neutral tone. "That, along with your connection from Addie's birth, are what've let you get in the corral with him."

"Jack is nothing like a nervous horse. He's calm, in charge—"

"He'd given up. Just like Storm."

Again Val looked into the other woman's face. This time there was no smile, no teasing. She meant exactly what she'd said.

"That morning after Jack had been out all night with Storm, I didn't cry just for the horse beginning to switch his tail. I cried for Jack Ralston, too. He was as dead inside as Storm, maybe more. What started to draw him out of it was helping that horse. The first step on a long, long road. After he helped you give birth to Addie … But you left — oh, I'm not saying you shouldn't have. You had to go home to your family and take care of your baby. Of course you did. And it became a moment, an incident that Jack set about putting behind him. Until you came back."

She felt her breath coming faster, her lungs burning as if she'd been running. "I… He doesn't—"

"He doesn't know if he does or not, Val. But he's curious now. You have no idea how big a step that is."

She was shaking her head. "I'm not… My history with men. This isn't…" She rallied. "I wouldn't want my daughter to get attached to him."

Donna gave her a steady look.

"Any more attached," she added. Then she mitigated that confession, quickly adding, "Or any man. I mean not any man who's likely to go out of her life. The people in her life now are ones who'll stay. Family, friends I've had all my life, neighbors. People who aren't going to disappear from her life the second they have a chance."

Donna patted her wrist. "That's understandable. No mother likes to let her child feel pain. Although sometimes it's necessary so they learn — sometimes to learn to avoid what caused the pain, like a hot stove. But sometimes to learn how to deal with the pain that happens in all our lives. How can any of us go through life without experiencing the pain of people going out of our lives? Some drift away, some leave, some die. That's the nature of things. No matter how a mother might want to shelter her child from that, she can't. At some point, if nature follows its course, it will be the mother's own dying."

Val looked at her quickly.

Donna smiled. "No, no, I'm perfectly well. This is hypothetical only."

"That's the problem, though. It *isn't* hypothetical for Addie. She likes all of you, but she's really latched on to Jack. Maybe it's seeing Brennan and Finn with Dave and Cassie and Rob with Cal, but whatever it is, she's going to be devastated when he walks away without a backward glance."

"You think that's what Jack will do?"

"More like he won't be part of her life in the first place."

"Then there's nothing to worry about, is there? Ah, here comes Jack now." She nodded toward the window that looked out toward the barn. Val glanced up to see Jack closing in on the porch. Beside her, Donna's hand on her arm took on a warning pressure. "Probably headed for the office. I do believe the house-side door to the office is open and voices do carry easily."

As did the sound of boot heels on wood floor, Val realized. Jack was definitely in the room next door.

"I should scoop up Addie and get back—" She sat up when she heard Addie's voice in the next room, apparently having followed Jack in to the office.

She started to rise to remove her daughter — though which of them she was protecting from the other was hard to tell.

Donna rested a hand on her arm. "Wait," she said in a soft but commanding voice.

****

"Scissors," Addie demanded.

He considered the small face looking up at him, fully expecting his immediate obedience. He'd dealt enough with her and her mother by now to proceed with caution.

"What do you want scissors for?"

"Cutting."

"Cutting what?"

"Hair."

He narrowed his eyes. Her brown eyes looked back with limpid innocence. Only he wasn't so sure they were telling the whole truth. "Whose hair are you thinking of cutting, Addie?"

"Mine."

"No."

"Yes. Like your hair. Like Brennan's hair."

"You will not cut your hair, Addison Rose Trimarco. And neither will anyone else, not if I have anything to say about it."

Her eyes widened. He thought it was at the use of her full name. He, on the other hand, felt burning from an abrupt, molten ball in the pit of his stomach that had nothing to do with using her full name.

Not if I have anything to say about it.

Where the *hell* had that come from? He had no say about anything to do with her — no ifs, ands, or buts about it. Nothing.

The pint-sized version of Val stared up at him, those brown eyes wide and soft, but so damned *seeing*.

"Why?"

It took him a second to come back to what they'd been talking about. "First, because I'm scared of what your mother would do to me if I helped you cut your hair."

Addie's giggle floated between them. "You're bigger'n her."

"Small can be dangerous. Don't ever count your mother out, Addison Rose. And the other reason I won't give you scissors is I like your hair the way it is."

Addie tipped her head, absorbing his words. Then she nodded with the decisiveness of her mother and said, "Okay," and was gone.

His breath came out in a whoosh of relief and something else.

****

Val heard Bryan's voice called Jack from the direction of the barn, and the slapping of the door closing behind him announced he'd followed Addie back outside.

Not if I have anything to say about it.

But he didn't.

Did she want him to?

No need to worry about that, because he didn't want to. … Did he?

Val was saved from her own thoughts by Donna's voice.

"You said you were worried about Jack walking out of Addie's life, Val. But you'll be the ones leaving. Going back to Gloucester. You and Addie will walk out of his life. Not the other way around."

Chapter Eleven

Unaware that her mother-in-law had landed a blow, Matty breezed in with a big smile, a glint in her eyes, and one hand behind her back.

"Oh, good, you're still here. Jack's waiting to take you for your next riding lesson."

"Jack? But Bryan—"

"Bryan saddled up Buster for you. You can't ride only Bo. Need to try other horses, too. And with an unfamiliar horse, it's better that Jack takes you."

Donna made a sound that might have been a cough. Or not.

"Now?" Val asked Matty.

"Yup. Right now."

"But—"

"We'll watch Addie, won't we, Donna?"

"With pleasure."

Val raised one sandal-shod foot. "But—"

"Got that covered, too. Ta-da." She swung her arm around from behind her back to reveal she was holding a pair of well-worn boots. "As long as Donna doesn't mind you wearing these old ropers of hers. You two must be near the same size."

"Of course I didn't mind."

Val tried a third time. "But—"

"I know Jack said riding boots," Matty interrupted again. "But we all ride in ropers most of the time and Bryan said you were doing great, so

I think he's overly cautious. Here are some socks, too," she dug a pair out of her vest pocket. "I said I'd leave it up to Donna — and you, of course, Val, if you're worried about wearing ropers, though you should at least try them on. What do you think?" she concluded, looking at her mother-in-law, and making it clear whose opinion mattered most.

"Absolutely try them on," Donna instructed.

Val obeyed while they entered into a discussion of the distinctions of heel and toe shape that distinguished a roper from a riding boot from a dress boot to a cowboy boot. She almost commented that she thought they were *all* cowboy boots, but was glad she didn't as the conversation became more detailed about shaft and toe height.

She stood, testing the fit of the boots.

"How do they feel?" Donna asked.

"Good."

Matty pressed down on the toe, then squeezed across the instep. "Feels like a perfect fit. Great, you're good to go."

"If Val wants to ride now," Donna amended gently. "No matter what, you should take those boots with you. I don't use them anymore, and there's no sense you buying new ones if you're not staying here."

Val's head came up at that and caught a flicker of a look between mother-in-law and daughter-in-law.

"Thank you very much, Donna. I would really appreciate having the use of these boots while I'm here — until I go home to Gloucester," she said firmly.

"And you'll start using them by going riding now," Matty said.

****

"You okay with this?" Jack asked.

"Sure. Why wouldn't I be?"

He made a sound. "Because you didn't have a lot of choice."

"No more than you had, huh?"

This sound had some amusement in it. "Matty can be a bulldozer. Suppose I should check up on Buster anyway."

"On Buster? Was he a rescue horse, too?"

"Not abuse. Neglect. Like any of them, they face bad situations, and they start reacting in certain ways. They fall back on that way of reacting. Nothing easy about breaking bad habits. So you've got to do things that stop them from heading down that familiar path. Make them stop and think. Jolt them out of doing the same thing they've been doing."

"If you jolt them too much, could that be bad?"

He eyed her. "Yeah. I suppose."

Addie, Brennan, Matty, and Donna lined the porch railing, waving as two of them headed out.

She waved back, but quickly focused back on Buster. He was so much bigger than Bo that everything felt new.

"Bye, Mom!" shouted Addie. "See you later—"

"Addie-gator," she called back, and heard her daughter's wonderful giggle.

He chuckled, and she turned toward him. It was a nice sound. One that came from him too seldom.

He looked back over his shoulder toward the house. A move that happened to block her view of his face, too. Just a coincidence, of course.

"She looks a lot like you," he said abruptly.

"Yeah. She'll outgrow that."

"Not if she's lucky."

Feeling her cheeks warm, she cut him a look. He was looking straight ahead now, his expression giving no indication he knew he'd paid her a compliment.

"What I mean," he added evenly, "is there doesn't seem to be much from her father's side."

"No." It was her turn to look straight ahead, though she was aware of his glance toward her.

"Addie's father...."

"Isn't in—"

He completed her sentence. "In the picture. You said that before."

On the day she'd given birth to Addie, she remembered. "He's not a bad guy. Intelligent, educated, employed, sense of humor, nice looking, kind to animals. Just not interested in having kids. Good genes."

"Good genes," he repeated thoughtfully.

She laughed. "Yeah, you and El. She half accused me of using him as sperm donor." She grew serious. "Maybe I was, at some level. Unconscious — I swear. But still... When I told him I was pregnant and he wanted nothing to do with it, I felt this huge rush of something. Only later did I realize it was relief."

"He might change his mind, come back into your lives."

She shook her head. "He signed away his rights. El found a great lawyer, and it's all tied up, nice and legal. But I don't think he would anyway. One of our first dates, I saw him with some kids at this company picnic we were at, and it was like he'd encountered an alien species, not one he was interested in getting to know. He lived in one of those buildings that's adults only. You practically have to get a papal dispensation to bring anyone under twenty-one to visit. I swear they carded the pizza delivery guy."

"He's never…? Addie?"

"You mean asked about her?"

"Or wanted to see her."

"Nope. Didn't want to know anything about anything having to do with the b-word."

He said a word that started with a different letter and drew an amused huff from her.

But he wasn't amused. What an idiot. To leave Val, to never see or know Addie, the life he'd helped create. At least the punishment of never being allowed into their lives suited the crime.

"So, no she doesn't look like him or — as far as I know — his family." Val laughed. "Heaven help us, she looks like my Great-Aunt Susan."

He didn't want to ask. Wasn't going to ask. Rarely even had the urge to ask with most people.

Valerie Trimarco wasn't most people. It's what caught him every damned time.

"Why heaven help you?" he asked.

"Great-Aunt Susan was my grandmother's sister — El's grandmother's sister, too. So El isn't really my cousin. Not a first cousin. Didn't mean to mislead you about that back when I told you about her."

"You had other things on your mind."

She grinned. "I did. So did you. Didn't want to distract you from delivering Addie with the intricacies of our family genealogy."

He was momentarily distracted by her grin. "Uh, but now you're ready to hit me with the intricacies of your family genealogy?"

"You bet. So there were three sisters, El's grandmother made a 'good' marriage and settled down to raise solid citizens — solid on the outside anyway. My grandmother, Eliza, was the rebel and married a Trimarco. Scandalized the whole family. Not only did he have an Italian last name, but he also had—"

"Portuguese and Irish and ..."

"Finnish. Everybody always forgets the Finnish. Ta-dum-dum. Get it?"

He felt amusement brewing, and tamped it down.

They were passing Phantom's corral. She'd been visiting three other horses in the next closer corral to the home ranch, but now trotted near to where they were, her ears pricked forward, watching intently.

"I think she's jealous — of Storm, I mean. That you're riding Storm," Val said. "That's wheat over there, right? And this road goes to the southwestern part of the ranch?"

"Uh-huh." She was trying to bury her comment about Phantom being jealous with a flurry of words in case he thought she'd mean the mare was jealous of her. It surprised him a little to realize that amused him, too.

"Oh, is that the path that leads to that big rock field between here and the Flying W?"

"The Narrows, yeah." He could encourage her to ask about scenery, talk about ranching, cattle, crops. It would be easy. He asked, "And Great-Aunt Susan?"

She shot him a you-really-want-to-talk-about-this? look. He nodded.

"She married Great-Uncle John, had seven children and was quite the businesswoman."

"Successful and happy marriage?

"You'd think so, wouldn't you?" She relaxed into telling the story. "But here's the thing about Great-Aunt Susan and Great-Uncle John. They only lived together the first three years of the marriage. Then he built a second house down the next beach. That's where he lived, while she kept the family home."

His brows rose. "Three years of living together, seven kids?"

"And no multiple births. Math doesn't work, does it? You should have seen El and me trying to figure it out after we first learned about babies. At first we thought you had to be married to have kids." She grimaced slightly. "After we learned more about the mechanics, we couldn't figure out how she had five kids after he moved out. And, yes, by that point we were aware enough to think about other men. But one time Mom was scolding me about being wild and I said I had a long way to go to beat Great-Aunt Susan who'd had five kids after her husband moved out, so she must've been fooling around. And Mom started laughing and laughing, saying nobody who'd seen them doubted they were Great-Uncle John's offspring."

She seemed prepared to leave it there. The woman who could talk a blue streak went silent now?

"Okay, tell," he demanded.

"Sunday dinners."

"Sunday dinners?" he repeated.

She nodded. "For twenty years, Great-Uncle John had Sunday dinner with his family. And after Sunday dinner, John and Susan retired to her bedroom to 'discuss business' and were not to be disturbed. I told you she was a good businesswoman."

He turned a chuckle into a snort. "*Eliza* was the scandal?"

"Absolutely. She did something that couldn't be ignored. Besides, I wasn't kidding about Great-Aunt Susan's business acumen. She made great investments. She was doing micro-loans before they'd been invented. Was sharp, sharp, sharp right up to the day she died. She left her money to her kids, but she left the two beach houses — hers and Great-Uncle John's — to El and me as joint owners. She said if she'd been born when we were, she would've been a career woman like we were. Course El had a real career, working as an accountant. I'd hopped around from cook to radio to chef to restaurant manager to marketing and more. But to Great-Aunt Susan that was enough. It had to help that El and I were both single at the time. Great-Aunt Susan wrote in her will that the houses were to remind us if we ever contemplated matrimony that the only way to avoid misery in marriage was through distance."

"How'd her kids feel?"

"About us getting the beach houses? Fine. She left them plenty. Or do you mean her thoughts on marriage? That came as no surprise to them. Great-Uncle John had named the house he built to live in alone The Fishwife, telling anyone who'd listen that it was in reference to Great-Aunt Susan. El and I started a restaurant there and that's what we called it — The Fishwife. That's how she got to know Cahill — her husband. It was all my doing." She smirked. "I knew they should be together from the start. They didn't have a chance. Same thing with my older brother Anthony. I introduced him to my piano teacher's daughter because I knew they'd be perfect together."

But apparently she hadn't found herself that perfect match. He didn't point that out. None of his business.

"Anyway, Great-Aunt Susan would be delighted with the success El's made of The Fishwife and now the Inn, even if that is with Cahill as a full partner."

"What about you? You helped start the restaurant."

"Yeah. Mostly I pushed El into taking the chance. And I cooked there. Stuff like that. But she's the real business brain."

"No restaurant without a cook. No restaurant without your half of the inheritance."

She shrugged. "Suppose." Then she grinned. "Great-Aunt Susan would love the blog and podcasts. Not the subject necessarily, but the idea of women helping women."

"You admire her."

"I do. Doesn't mean I want Addie to be quite that strong-willed and outspoken."

"You mean like her mother?"

"Hey, I'm the soul of tact compared to my Great-Aunt Susan."

"Setting the bar low?"

"You bet. Now it's your turn."

"For what?"

"Telling me about your background. You mentioned a foster family. No, you said no siblings, so only foster parents?"

"Yeah. The Bazerocks."

"You went to them after your folks' died?"

"Went to their farm a year later. I don't remember much before." Crying. That's what he remembered. Loneliness. He said quickly, "Older couple."

"So that's how you learned about animals? Living on a farm?"

"Yeah."

"But they never adopted you."

"No. Don't go assuming they just wanted a kid to do chores. They wouldn't have taken a five-year-old if they had. They couldn't afford to adopt. They needed that foster care stipend to keep afloat. They were decent people. Solid. Reliable. Honest."

He clamped his mouth closed, abruptly aware he was repeating a long-ago argument, not responding to Val.

She didn't seem to notice. "You were fortunate to find people who helped you deal with the loss of your parents, to talk that out and heal— What was that grimace for?"

He hadn't realized he'd grimaced. "All that stuff."

"Talking and healing and dealing with loss? All that stuff?" she asked wryly.

"Yeah. The Bazerocks were a good match for me. They believed in hard work, being reliable, and if you had a problem, you worked it out yourself. They left me alone."

She reached down and patted Buster. When she straightened she said, "Maybe that made them not such a good fit for you."

"They took me in and gave me a home, food, education."

"I'm sure they were wonderful people. But maybe you would have benefited from someone who drew you out more. Someone who encouraged you to participate in the world—"

"No." The word came out harsh because his throat was suddenly raw.

"—to be part of a community," she finished, her eyes studying him.

"I help out when somebody needs help."

"To have interaction with other people, to enjoy being around other people," she picked up as if he hadn't spoken. "To believe relationships don't have to be based solely on working hard. To accept their friendship and caring."

I tried that and it didn't work…

The words almost came out of his mouth. He held them back just in time.

Someone who drew you out more. Someone who encouraged you to participate in the world … friendship and caring.

Val's words, spoken in Val's voice, with her crisp delivery.

Yet somewhere in those words, he'd heard another voice. Not saying the same words, but expressing the same sentiment. Doing more than talk, too. Tugging him into the circle of her friends and family. Urging him to believe. And he had.

Until…

Never again.

"This part of the ranch was added on by Ed's parents. The home ranch was the original section. Each generation has added on." Better to talk history than to relive it.

****

The rest of the ride focused on the history and running of the Slash-C, when it wasn't silent.

For once, she preferred the silences. Her eyes enjoyed the scenery while she sorted through what he'd said.

He'd lost his parents when he was not much older than Addie. And he hadn't had the grandparents, aunts, uncles, cousins, and more swoop in with waves of love, as well as providing a continuity for a child whose world had been turned upside down.

And then he'd been fostered by people who might have had the best of intentions, but had set him more firmly on the path of withdrawal.

Maybe you would have benefited from someone who drew you out more. El would be proud of her for being so tactful. For not saying his foster parents had been utterly and completely wrong for letting — encouraging! — a little boy who'd suffered a tragedy indulge his recluse tendencies. That allowing a child to apply the do-it-myself model to his emotional wounds qualified as child neglect in her book

And yet, that wasn't when he'd shut down. That didn't happen until she talked about accepting friendship and caring.

He'd started to say something — to keep arguing. Then his face stiffened and his eyes went cold.

Maybe he needed to go through days like a zombie to heal at the beginning, but it went too long. We let it go to long. It's a habit now. A safe, comfortable habit. It's going to take something sharp and strong to get him out of that habit.

A safe, comfortable habit — that's what Donna had said.

Nothing easy about breaking bad habits. So you've got to do things that stop them from heading down that familiar path. Make them stop and think. Jolt them out of doing the same thing they've been doing.

Interesting that was Jack's prescription for his wounded horses' bad habits.

****

Val sat on the porch of the foreman's cottage, editing her next blog, while Addie played with a stuffed frog and a teddy bear, reenacting her version of Jack working with the mistreated mare.

She couldn't wait to tell Jack that he was the frog.

A truck came into sight from the direction of the main house.

109

Her heartbeat picked up.

Not Jack's.

Her heartbeat should have known better. He'd proven himself quite adept at avoiding her.

As she looked closer, she realized it wasn't any of the trucks she'd become familiar with from the Flying W and Slash-C. Then she recognized the trio in the front seat.

She took Addie's hand and went to meet the new arrivals — Taylor and Cal Ruskoff, with their four-year-old daughter Cassie and just over one-year-old son Rob. But the first out of the truck was an adult collie. The dog trotted toward them, sniffing and tail wagging.

"That's Sin," Taylor said. "He's friendly. In fact, he might walk right in because he thinks that's still our house."

Addie was entranced by the dog, and the feeling appeared to be mutual. He circled around Cassie and Addie, as if inviting them to play together by urging them closer together.

After hellos, Taylor said, "Cal's meeting Dave here for some horse-trading."

"Actually tool trading," Cal said with a smile as he held his sturdy son. "I picked some things up at an auction I knew he was looking for, and he has some extras I can use."

"Cassie, Rob, and I came along for the ride and in hopes of seeing you and Addie."

"I'm playing horse rescue," Addie said to Cassie. "Wanna play."

"Sure."

"You're the teddy bear. I'm the frog," she informed the other girl, leading the way back to the porch, with the dog Sin right behind.

"She's the frog?" Taylor repeated in a low voice.

"Teddy's a mare who needs rescuing and the frog is the rescuer."

"Ahhh. We heard about Jack working with another abused horse."

"Does a damned good job, too," Cal added. "Even if he isn't green and not a great hopper."

By the time the second truck pulled in, they were sitting on the porch steps, drinking iced tea, while the kids played behind them.

Dave and his mother joined them, with pleased hellos all around.

"Would you all like to stay to lunch after your tool trading?" She could pull together sandwiches and an interesting salad from what was in the kitchen.

"Sorry, I've got to get back to see a client," Taylor said. While she maintained her law office in town, she also saw clients at home for their convenience and hers. "Can only stay another forty-five minutes or so.

"And I'm the designated driver," Cal said with a grin at his wife that proclaimed that wherever she was going, he wanted to go, too.

"I'm afraid I'm promised for a lunch meeting at the church," Donna said.

"And I've got a meeting with a client in town. Going over the proposed settlement drawn up by some shyster lawyer named Larsen," Dave said.

"Hey," Cal protested, drawing such an immediate grin from Dave that it was clear that had been his goal all along.

"So, what are your plans since we're all deserting you, Valerie?" Donna asked.

"Finish editing my blog so I can upload it tonight, feed Addie lunch, then— As long as you're all here, I can ask the experts. I want to pick up a few things. Photography supplies," she said, purposely vague. "Only, I was hoping if there's a somewhat bigger town…"

Dave exaggerated a double take. "What? The metropolis of Knighton isn't fulfilling all your shopping dreams?"

She grinned. "I'm not much of a shopper, but it's not strong on photography supplies."

"There's a shop in Jefferson that does framing and sells cameras. Would that do?" Taylor asked.

"Perfect. I also wanted to pick up something for Matty as a thank you for all she did with the party. If you have any ideas…?"

"Help her find a couple plants that'll survive by that old water pump near the drive, and she'll be ecstatic," he said.

"With good cause," his mother said to him. She widened her next words to include Cal and Taylor. "We were telling Valerie about the problems growing anything there. The plants get drenched every time the pump gets used, and water's always sloshing over from the trough. I tried all the usual suspects and they'd die in weeks. Now Matty's having the same bad luck. You'd need to talk to someone who really knows flowers."

Cal Ruskoff looked up at that. "Dave, don't you know a place by the courthouse?"

The men exchanged a look. As it ended, both gave a small, strange smile.

"What are you two—?" Taylor started.

But Cal put his arm around her and squeezed as Dave talked over her. "Yeah. As a matter of fact, I do. There's this little shop. I'll write down all the information for you, Val." He did that as he kept talking. "It has the usual cut flowers, but ask the woman behind the desk for some help, and I'll bet she'll know what to get. And you can ride in this afternoon with Jack, because I was about to call him to let him know I need him to go into Jefferson on an errand this afternoon. So, I'll go do that right now. One o'clock suit you?"

"Sure, but I can drive myself—"

"No, no, it can be confusing in Jefferson. So you ride with Jack. C'mon, Cal. Let's see what you've got."

"Sure thing," Cal said.

The two men headed off, Cal clapping a hand to Dave's back as if congratulating him.

Val turned and looked at Taylor, who was watching their departing backs with a hint of a frown. "Was I imagining it, or was there something weird going on?"

"Definitely something weird," Taylor said. "For one thing, since when is Jefferson confusing? All straight roads and you can see the courthouse from just about anywhere in town, so to get to a shop near it all you have to do is open your eyes."

Donna nodded at the piece of paper Val held. "What's the name of this shop my son recommends?"

"Flower Power," Val read.

They looked at one another, trying to imagine Dave or Cal shopping at a place called Flower Power.

"Wait a minute," Taylor said slowly. "I think — I'm almost sure that's where Dave got Matty's bridal bouquet."

"Ah. The Indian Paintbrush," Donna said. "So appropriate."

"Wyoming's state flower," Taylor said in response to Val's questioning look. "Bright and tough and stubborn. Suits Matty to a T. And it was amazing that Dave got it for the bridal bouquet. Yes, I said Dave got it. Though it was a close-run thing whether she was going to whap him over the head with it or appreciate it. C'mon, let's have some more of that iced tea, and I'll tell you all about it."

How Matty and Dave came to marry first and court afterward was such an entertaining story that Val forgot all about the strangeness from Dave and Cal until she was in the truck being driven by Jack that afternoon.

Chapter Twelve

"Can you imagine Lewis and Clark coming all the way out here in the early 1800s and seeing this for the first time?" Val asked Jack.

In the car seat in the back seat, Addie was catching a nap as she often did in moving vehicles. Val had alternated staring out the windshield or passenger window, craning her neck to see everything at once.

The Slash-C and Flying W were tucked up closer to the mountains. It took some distance, as they were getting on this drive to Jefferson, to get the full impact of the Big Horn range.

"They didn't see this. Weren't around here."

She grimaced at Jack, then looked back out her window, where a long V-shaped valley cut into the line of mountains. Wheat was growing in much of it, rippling under the wind like water.

"I was speaking metaphorically," she said with great dignity. "The way people speak of the ocean and the mountains being similar."

He said something under his breath, but all she caught was *stream*. "What?"

"Guess you know about the ocean," he said.

It was a diversion. That was okay. At least he was talking.

"Some. Not as much as the folks who make their living from it. It's like they *feel* it in their bones. We've lost that. Some generations back, our family members went to sea. A number of them didn't come back. Their widows were adamant that the following generations would not be fishermen, so the various family lines gradually moved away from it.

"In a way, Gloucester has, too. Except it's still there, at the core. Something more than history. Or tradition. I worked with a chef once who used to call it Fish Fry Town. I wanted to pop him every time. I finally did." She turned and grinned at him. "Actually, I dumped a big bowl of batter on his head after he took credit for that particular recipe for frying fish, which I'd brought to the kitchen from my Great Aunt Susan."

Her grin faded as she looked out the window again.

"I grew up there, and then I wanted so much to leave, to see other places, to do other things ..."

"Not when you were having a baby. You talked about that a lot. You wanted to be in Gloucester."

"I wanted my baby born there. Right by the sea." She quirked an eyebrow at him. "As you know better than anyone else, we didn't quite make it. But it's turned out okay, she's still getting the feel for Gloucester and the sea right down into her bones. Gloucester's sort of like us — or we're like it. A mix of things. Italian and Irish, with Portuguese and Finnish thrown in. And then a dash of Puritan New England. All mixed up together. And that's what Gloucester's like. The fleet, sure, and all the businesses that support the fishing, but also the art colonies, the summer people. Coast and harbor, rocky heights and marsh. Freshwater and saltwater, and spots where they mix. I want Addie to grow up with all that. To grow up with the connection to the ocean. So you don't go by a day without thinking about it, what it does, what it can do. It keeps you connected to reality. You know?"

"Yes."

One word. After all those words she'd spilled. Yet that word might have said more than all of hers.

Turning to keep tracking the valley as it slipped behind them, she blinked slowly, as if to shift her focus from visions of the craggy coast of her hometown to what was right in front of her.

Then she turned to him and saw that he wished he could take back that single word. She wouldn't let him.

"I believe you do know, Jack. As they say, there is something of the ocean in the mountains, too. Or vice versa. Maybe it's the perspective they're always talking about — that their grandness make us feel small, our problems not worth worrying about, but I don't think so."

"No," he said, agreeing with her.

She nodded. "The ever-changing-ness, if that's a word. No day's like another. You can't ignore them."

Now he nodded, though perhaps a bit reluctantly. "You have to respect them."

"Yes. Yes, you do. I wonder if a blog musing on mountains and the ocean would entertain my readers. I— Why do you do that?"

He looked at her, then quickly back to the road. "What?"

"Make that face when I talk about my blog. In fact, why do you always make that face when anyone mentions my blog?"

"I don't."

"There. That face. Exactly that face. Like someone who caught a bad smell just before he was turned into a statue."

"No idea what you're talking about."

He had his facial muscles under strict control, but the lines at the corners of his eyes became more visible, like the rays Addie drew around her yellow blob pictures of the sun. Somewhere inside he was smiling, at least a little. She was sure of it.

And that warmed her in ways she didn't want to think about right now.

She shifted around in the seat and eyed him. "So, if you're saying I'm imagining you making a face whenever anyone mentions my blog, does that mean you're in favor of my blog? Approve of it? Think it's a great thing for humanity, mothers worldwide, and peace on earth, goodwill to men?"

He was going to sidestep it. She saw that in his eyes.

His mouth opened, and out came, "No."

He'd thought he was going to sidestep it, too. He was as surprised as she was that he hadn't.

"So you're in favor of my blog? You approve of it?" she persisted.

"No."

No doubt, no wiggle room on that answer. She propped her hand on her hip. "Okay, explain. What's your problem with it?"

"It's public."

"Of course it is. I don't mind that."

"You make yourself vulnerable."

She shrugged. "I don't mind that, either. I know a lot of people do, but it's like starting a new job or trying something you've never done before. It's scary and exhilarating at the same time." She sat up straighter. "You know, that might be what I love the most about motherhood — after Addison Rose, of course. It's always something new. Even if it's not new for me, it is for Addie, so it's like seeing and doing things new through her. That could be a great podcast topic. I should write that down."

As she dug for her notebook to write it down, her gaze skimmed across Jack's face again, and she was instantly reminded he did not share her enthusiasm for blog topics.

"Hey, I'm not Pollyanna," she said to that grim profile. "I know people can be mean on the Internet. I've had the nasty commenters, people who get their jollies from being hateful and crude. Showing their worst sides because it's not face to face."

He dismissed that with: "Words."

"Oh, no. You're not going to give me the sticks and stones lecture, are you? Words *do* hurt. And they can do a lot of harm. I'm not going to let the few nasty people's words stop me from doing what I want to do. Especially not with all the good and kind people. Their words count, too, you know. Folks can focus so much on the cyber-bullying and the diatribes in comments on news sites and the other cruelties that they forget the kindnesses that are done, the support given, the friendships formed. So being vulnerable— Oh, you don't mean emotionally, do you? You're thinking of those jerks who broke into my house? I told you, I learned my lesson there. I'm not announcing when the house will be empty anymore. Plus, family and friends are keeping a close eye on it when I have a public appearance, so there's no need to worry about my house."

"Not your house. *You*. You and Addie. You open yourself up to a lot worse than a break-in. Whatever's on there. It's there forever. You open yourself up to … "

Apparently he wasn't going to complete that, so she did. "To the crazies. But there are lots more good people than crazies."

"The crazies can hurt you. Some aren't satisfied staying on the other end of the computer writing nasty notes."

"I take precautions. I'm not public with my information." Well, not any more, anyway.

He hitched one shoulder dismissively. "Anyone who wants to find out can. They can track you down easy."

"Oh, come on. Isn't that paranoid? Why would anyone want to find out who I am, much less where I am. I can't imagine anyone wasting their time on tracking me down."

"You have no idea who's on the other end of that computer screen. Watching you."

She opened her mouth to respond, but stopped. There was something in the way he'd said it that set off her antennae. Only she couldn't sort out what they were picking up. Only thing she was sure of was that what he'd said was significant.

"Do you have experience with—?"

"No. Don't know a thing about it. And it's none of my business. Shouldn't have said anything."

"That's okay, I don't mind discussing…"

She let it die, because from the firm line of his mouth and the rigidity of his jaw, he clearly wasn't going to add another word.

For a second, she'd thought …

But maybe she had it all wrong. Maybe it was simply his apparent allergy to even the concept of opening up. If that was the case, she was tilting at windmills. And even with Donna as her windmill-tilting coach, the windmill was going to win this bout.

****

Shortly after they passed the county courthouse, Val said, "There it is," pointing to a sign painted across a shop window that proclaimed Flower Power.

Jack grunted.

That's about all he'd done since their conversation about her blog.

No, she took that back. He'd also issued an order — in as few words as possible — to stay in the car when they'd stopped at the Ranch Supply store.

She'd ignored him, freeing Addie, newly awakened and restless, from the child seat in the back of the truck. Then held onto her daughter's hand for dear life and stuck to the main aisle to find a bathroom.

That didn't stop Addie from straining to go look at the shiny metal of what appears to be machetes on a display straight ahead. Or to examine a bright red *Poison* label. Or to play with those with what looked like a pre-made noose. The place should have been renamed a thousand and one ways to maim a nosy three-and-a-half-year-old.

After the successful trip to the restroom, she'd distracted her daughter with a lollipop from a jar on the counter. As much of it transferred to her hands as got in her mouth.

So he'd been at least partially right about telling her to stay in the truck. That didn't improve Jack's mood as far as she could tell.

The child seat and the truck had laid the foundation for his bad mood well before the blog and internet discussion. Needing a child seat for Addie had been the center of a long, convoluted discussion, which ended up with Jack driving Matty's new truck, which had child seats already installed.

Jack clearly hadn't been happy about the instructions Matty had given him to keep her new vehicle pristine. Val had definitely heard him mutter about *kid gloves.*

But she suspected his bad mood had started even earlier, when Dave instructed him to drive into town with her as a passenger. Despite the lollipop, he didn't seem to mind Addie nearly as much. Which was a good thing, considering what had happened at their second stop.

It was at the store that sold cameras, printed and enlarged photos, and did framing.

She and the clerk had sorted out the enlargement of the photo and which frame she wanted, but they were still discussing mats. The clerk was friendly and — with no one else in the shop — generous with his time and suggestions.

Jack had been uninterested in the entire process. Probably a good thing, because if he'd seen the photo was of his shadow, he'd probably have put the kibosh on the whole project, when, really, it was for Matty and Dave, not him.

So his wandering off toward a rack of magazines near the front of the shop suited her fine.

As she switched back to a second pairing of mats she'd considered, Val caught a glimpse of Addie's red shirt, and realized her daughter had headed after Jack.

Unfortunately, Addie had been distracted on the way by a display of photography books artfully arranged on the rungs of a ladder. From the corner of her eye, Val saw her daughter look up at a photo hanging on the wall near the ladder's top. A photo of a blue truck remarkably similar to Matty's and, likely of more importance to Addie, remarkably similar to Brennan's new toy.

"Addie, no—"

But her daughter was already climbing the ladder, edging around the stacks of books, and stretching her short legs to their maximum from rung to rung.

She started forward.

"No! Stop, Addie."

Of all the stupid things to say. Her daughter had no off button. To her stop was an invitation to go faster.

Addie reached toward the truck photo, her lean breaking the laws of physics and gravity, but only for a breath before she started to fall.

Valerie lunged toward her, horrified to know she was going to be a quarter of a heartbeat too late.

"Oh, God—"

Addie launched herself toward the photograph. Val's heart clogged her throat, strangling her cry.

Jack caught Addie in mid-air.

Without hesitation, without seeming to hurry in the least, without even blinking. Which, for some reason, made Val feel even guiltier about taking her eyes off her daughter for that slice of a second that would have been disastrous if he hadn't been there.

She wanted to shout at Addie. She wanted to fall on his neck and thank him. She wanted to scold her daughter up one side and down the other. She wanted to cry.

She did none of those things. She pulled in air in grateful, would-be calming gulps. She remained standing under the knife-thrusts of guilt.

Jack gave her a quick, assessing look.

"She's okay," he said, as if she'd done all the things she wanted to do at once. As if she were overreacting. "I'll take her up front so you can finish. Soon."

She accepted her deep human frailty for experiencing unreasonable and unfair delight as they walked away from her at the moment when Addie plunged her lollipop-sticky hands into his hair.

Then she wrapped up the details on the photo for the Slash-C office so they could go on to their last stop, Flower Power.

****

A woman behind the counter t-shirt proclaimed "True Flower Power" smiled broadly at them as they entered.

"What a charming family," she said.

Val looked behind her. Nope, no charming family trailing them. "Us? No. Not a family. No."

"Ah. My mistake. In any event, welcome to Flower Power. What can I find for you?"

"Thank you. I need to look around a bit first."

"I meant perhaps you'd like an iced tea? Sparkling water? Lemonade? Would you like that, young lady?" she said to Addie, adding in an aside to Val, "Your daughter?"

"Yes."

"Yes, please," Addie said in a suddenly shy whisper.

"And you, sir?" the woman asked Jack.

"The ranch hand chauffeur," he grumbled.

The woman blinked.

Val caught the insides of her cheeks with her teeth to keep from grinning as she started down a tight-packed aisle.

The shop carried almost anything associated with flowers. Books, magazines, window boxes, pots, soil, plant food, bagged mulch, hoses, paintings, and — massed together or occupying a sliver of space — plants, plants, plants.

"Here you are dear." The woman handed Addie a paper cup with snapdragons painted all around it. Then she added, "*Mimulus guttatus.*"

"Excuse me?"

"*Mimulus guttatus.*" Apparently recognizing that repetition wasn't going to do the trick, she added, "That's the plant you're looking at. Also called yellow monkyflower or common monkeyflower."

"Monkey," repeated Addie.

The woman beamed at her. "That's right. Such a smart little girl. Can you see how the face of the flower looks like a monkey's face?"

"Uh-huh." Addie's agreement sounded skeptical. Then she brightened. "I see. Eyes. Mouth. Ears."

"Exactly." The woman nodded.

Val read the tag filled with information, most of which went over her head. "The photo of the bloom resembles a snapdragon."

The woman now turned the beam on her. "Yes, it does."

"Would it bloom this summer?"

"Oh, yes. They're about to bloom now. Then they'll rebloom some throughout the season."

"Will it come back next year or do you have to replant it each year."

"As long as it's in a situation that's right for it, it returns here in Wyoming every year. And spreads when it's happy, so you have masses of blooms."

"So it would be good for—?"

Before she could specify the conditions Matty was battling, the woman enthusiastically took over. "Oh, yes, it's good for a great many ailments with many intriguing properties. It has been frequently used as a poultice because one of its main properties is to cause flesh to contract. That makes it particularly beneficial for wounds. The Shoshoni would crush its leaves to apply to rope burns. Other tribes favored it to treat soreness in the chest."

Jack humphed in disgust, which prompted Val to give the woman her rapt attention. Served him right if she drew this out as long as possible. "Really?"

"Yes, indeed. Scientists have confirmed its astringent qualities. In fact, while many in science scoff at the healing properties of flowers and other elements of nature, they are quite interested in *mimulus guttatus*. It has so many varieties and they have adapted to such diverse circumstances that it is valued for studies in ecology and evolution. Geneticists, in particular, find it fascinating. Also," she added cheerfully, "you can use the leaves in a salad. Though most find the taste a touch bitter. Some boil it, but I don't care for that texture."

"I was thinking more along the lines of whether it could be planted in a garden. Not that I'm interested in all the rest, too," she added hurriedly, "but I was hoping to get someone a gift that would return each year—"

"A perennial."

"—and wasn't just the usual flowers for sale everywhere."

"Oh, yes, this would be an excellent choice."

"We pull those out of ditches." Jack's expression match his gruff words.

"They fall in ditches?" she asked with false sweetness.

"They grow around ditches. They're invasive."

"They *are* water lovers," the woman confirmed. "That's where another of its names come from — seep monkeyflowers. They can grow, ah, enthusiastically in some situations."

"Invasive water-lovers. Did they come from back east? Maybe by the ocean?" Jack grumbled under his breath.

But not deep enough under his breath to keep from being heard. The woman looked from him to her.

Val put her hands on her hips as she said, "It sounds like the perfect plant for that area by the water pump and trough that Matty's planting, which is what Dave suggested I look for. She and Donna said they had a real hard time getting anything to grow there because they keep getting drowned when you and the other men use the pump. Invasive water-lover might be exactly what's needed."

The woman said, "There is another property of yellow monkeyflower I forgot to mention. It can turn someone who suffers from heightened caution into someone who lives with cheerful enthusiasm."

Val looked directly at Jack as she said, "You'd have to corner the entire market to pull off that trick."

He glared at her. She frowned back.

"Mad Jack," Addie said, then giggled, breaking the standoff.

Also, Val realized later, as she bought enough plants for Matty to give them a fair trial in her problem spot, though nowhere near enough to transform Jack Ralston, Addie's comment or her giggle or both had broken Jack's glare.

Maybe she didn't have enough Common Monkeyflower to get Jack living with cheerful enthusiasm, but she might have discovered another secret weapon. Addison Rose Trimarco.

If Addie being herself got to him, who was she to interfere? Especially since it was for the man's own good.

Chapter Thirteen

"Good heavens, Jack. Looks like you've turned the back of my truck into a garden." Matty called out from the porch of the Slash-C's main house. She'd come outside as they pulled up, with Brennan on her heels.

Jack swung out of the driver's door as Val extricated Addie. "No dents or damage, so you shouldn't have any complaints."

"I'm not complaining. I'm delighted. Sure looks better than bags of feed or a load of tools. But what's the occasion? Did you get these for Val?"

"What? No," she said quickly. "They're for you, Matty. We — Addie and I — brought you some flowers as a small thank you for all you've been doing for us, all the dinners, and letting stay here, and that party." Better not to pursue that topic. "I hope you like them."

"There's absolutely no need for that, Val. You're great to have around and you and Addie entertaining Brennan has been priceless. But I sure appreciate you thinking of this." Matty peered over the side of the truck bed. "What are they? Look sort of like snapdragons, but the bloom's so much bigger."

"Monkeyflower," Jack said. "She bought an acre's worth of monkeyflower."

"No," Matty said in disbelief.

"Yup," Jack confirmed with dour pleasure. "Just what you'd want along a fast-moving stream that was cutting away at mountain that was there first, minding its own business."

With that he turned on his heel and headed toward the new office.

"What was that about?" Matty asked.

"I have no idea. The woman in the shop didn't say anything about fast-moving streams or mountains. She did say they're called common yellow monkeyflower. *Mimulus guttatus.*"

"Huh." Matty stared at the plants, hands on hips. "Monkeyflower can be a pest in the ditches and such if we have a real wet stretch. But they are kind of cheerful."

She grabbed onto that. "They are. The woman in the shop said they can spread across the top of the soil to make new plants, but she swore they wouldn't be invasive unless conditions were ideal."

Matty snorted. "Fat chance of that."

"I thought I'd plant them for you by the trough where you've had such trouble getting anything to grow."

"Oh." Matty turned her head to look at that offending patch of muck, then back to Val. "You know, that might be a really good idea. Well, let's see how they do."

****

Matty stood, brushing off her hands, head tipped as she surveyed their work. "I like it," she declared.

"You should have let me do all the planting." Val nested the now-empty pots together.

"No way. Especially after being kind enough to get me these flowers. You all were a great help," she added, extending her smile to their pint-sized not-so-helpful helpers. Then she spotted a familiar figure cutting across from the office toward the horse barn. "Hey, Jack, come see what we've accomplished. Thanks to all of us, we'll now have pretty yellow monkeyflowers to enjoy every time we use the pump, instead of a bed of mud."

Val watched Jack stop, then change the angle of his path to come toward them. Slowly. With reluctance. Geeze, why didn't the man just shout that he'd rather not join a group that included her?

"We planted all the monkeyflowers you brought back from Jefferson, so thanks to you, too, for helping Val get them. Doesn't it look great?" Matty asked Jack.

"Very nice."

"Monkey," Addie said. "Because it looks like a monkey face."

"Monkey face," echoed Brennan Currick.

"That's right," Matty said. "Monkeyflower. Don't forget the flower part."

"Monkey's better," Brennan declared.

"Flower's better," disputed Addie.

"And they're off," muttered Val. She and Matty grinned at each other as their offspring debated the relative values of flowers and monkeys with the highly developed logic of "is not" and "is so" until Val interrupted with, "Aren't we lucky that this has *both*. Monkey *and* flower."

Addie stared at her mother a moment, then turned to Brennan and pronounced, "Storm."

"Storm," Brennan confirmed.

Unified, they headed for the closest corral fence, where Storm stood.

"You stay outside the fence," Matty reminded them. She turned back to the bed they'd just planted. "You know, there's an area at the Flying W could use some flowers, too. Would you pick up more, Jack?"

He nodded. "Now I'd better go. Not sure that fence will protect Storm."

Val pivoted. He daughter had one foot on the bottom rail. At least she hadn't tried to go between, the way she had last time. "Addie!"

"It's okay," Jack said, striding away. "I got them."

That figured. Most single men ran the other way from a woman with kids. This man would rather herd a couple of rambunctious kids than stay where she was.

"He's so good with kids," Matty said, putting a much more positive spin on the situation. The woman should work for D.C. politicians.

Though, he *was* good with kids.

****

After they'd collected the kids, cleaned them up, then themselves, Matty insisted Val and Addie stay for dinner. A low-key affair of burgers and hotdogs on the grill, she said. Donna arrived from a trip to town to visit with friends, and added her voice to the invitation. "Do stay. I want to hear how you and Addie are liking Wyoming."

Matty nodded. "Sure. This'll be a good chance to catch up. We're saving the fancy stuff for when Lisa and Shane get here. You know we're having a party for them, don't you? And of course you and Addie have to come. Oh, and come to the dinner we'll have a couple nights before, too. Lisa's dying to meet you in person. She's so impressed with your blog."

"We better get busy so the men have something to grill." Donna's easy tone broke the silence.

"What can I do to help?" Val volunteered.

"Go get Jack," Matty said.

Before she could do more than open her mouth to propose an alternative, Matty added, "That's not as easy as it sounds because you have to walk over to the corral where he's working with the mare. Jack doesn't allow anybody to drive around the rescues at first. And you need to approach slow and calm and quiet — in other words, he doesn't let me around the rescues at first, either."

Val couldn't help joining Donna in laughter, and soon she found herself walking toward the far corral, slow and quiet and calm on the outside.

If that wasn't good enough for the horse and Jack Ralston, too bad.

****

Val didn't make noise as she came closer and he couldn't say she disturbed the mare, who watched her with apparent interest.

Which didn't mean he had to do the same. He kept his gaze on the horse.

Val reached the corral fence a dozen feet from his position inside it and stopped.

The mare looked right at her and made a sound.

"Oh." Apparently feeling obliged to explain her delight, Val added, "Matty said when a horse makes that sound they're saying hello."

"Pretty much."

The mare's ears flickered at Val's voice. Alert but relaxed.

"And when they make that other sound, like a whinny, that's like asking if there are any other horses around, because they're such herd animals they naturally try to find their band. And other horses respond with this same sound to say, yes, here we are. But this sound—"

"Nicker."

"Nicker," she repeated, "is definitely hello. Only there aren't any other horses around."

"They use it to greet humans, too."

He saw her recognize that they were only two humans around, and since he'd been here all along there was no need for the animal to vocalize a greeting to him.

"Me? She's greeting me?" Without waiting for an answer, she turned toward the horse. "Oh, you big, beautiful sweetie you."

The mare moved toward the fence, hesitated a moment, then put her head over it.

"I know. Let her sniff my hand," Val followed the words with the actions. "Stroke her on the withers. Steady strokes. Right, Sweetie Pie?"

He snorted. "Her name's Phantom. There," he added as the mare lowered her head slightly and turned it more toward Val, "that's saying she's okay with what you're doing. But that's enough now."

Val patted her twice more, then stepped back from the fence. The mare almost seemed to nod, then ambled toward the far side of the corral.

Still watching the horse, Val said, "I've been sent to tell you it's time for dinner."

"I don't eat with the family."

She looked at him then. "Ever? Because I kind of doubt Matty sent me out here to tell you it was time for dinner if she didn't expect you to join us."

He wouldn't put it entirely past Matty Brennan Currick. But Val had a strong point that it was far more likely that this was Matty's way of informing him this was a command performance.

If he'd known socializing was going to be part of his job when he'd signed on …

"Give me a minute," he said, keeping his voice even — for the mare's sake. He repeated his end-of-session routine.

But the mare didn't do any more than that as he exited the gate and walked to where Val still stood. So no harm done. And it had vented a bit of his irritation.

Val turned and headed toward the house as he came along beside her, walking in silence.

They'd covered three-quarters of the distance to the house when she broke it. "Going to put a saddle on her soon?"

"Good bit to do before that."

"But she has to be able to be saddled, right? I mean for her to be useful around the ranch."

He doubted any of the Curricks would push him if he said this horse was more likely to be a pleasure horse, maybe even more of a pet than a working horse. Interesting the way she'd reacted to Val. Maybe she'd had good experiences with women. She sure hadn't with men. But no need to discuss all that with Valerie Trimarco. "Look at it from the horse's point of view."

"You mean who wants leather strapped around your belly, then people climbing on your back?"

He felt the tug of a smile but kept his tone serious. "More than that. Out in nature, they're prey animals. If something lands on their back, their instinct say it's more likely to be a mountain lion intent on dinner than a hunk of leather that's just going to lie there."

"So you work with the animal to get her to accept that it's the hunk of leather, not the mountain lion, just like you did to accept that the human sitting in the corral isn't going to do something awful to her."

"Something like that."

"It's too bad you don't know what happened to her before she came here."

He shrugged.

"Wouldn't it help to know how she got to that state?"

"You can't always know what happened to them before. Maybe you don't want to. No matter what, you move forward slowly, steadily. Cautious. Just like with people. Because you can't know who you're dealing with. Not really. Not ever."

"Oh, sure you can. Just listen to your instincts."

"I've read your blog."

****

I've read your blog.

Where on earth had *that* come from?

She'd thought they were circling around whatever it was that had happened to him that had put him so off of humanity. Hinting that she'd be better off if she knew. Possibly edging toward his telling her why he made *cautious* look like a party animal.

And then he said *I've read your blog*, as if he'd confessed a sin.

"Have you? What did you think?"

"That's not the point."

"It is to me. If I draw in male viewers, I double my audience. Maybe

129

do segments on dads and—" She stopped herself, looking at him. There was something more here. "Did you hate it?" she asked, more to give herself time to think than because she thought he'd tell her if he had.

"No."

She believed him. But there was definitely something else behind his words and she had no idea what.

"Jack, you're going to have to give me more to go on if you want me to know what you're getting at."

He gave a kind of growl. "It's what I said before. You don't know who's on the receiving side. You look into the lens, all open and honest and vulnerable, as if everyone who's watching you is just the same, and you have no idea who's out there. What they're thinking. How they could take what you give and hurt you."

Whoa. She didn't think he'd said that many words to her all in one breath before.

But she was finally waking up and putting pieces together.

"You wouldn't, Jack. You wouldn't take what I give and hurt me. Yet you were one of the watchers." He didn't look away. He seemed to want to, but he didn't. "What were you thinking when you were watching, Jack?"

"That I wanted you in my bed."

He'd meant to shock her. Possibly to scare her. And he'd done it just as they approached the group on the patio, no doubt trying to maximize both her flusteredness and her inability to respond.

She had the eminent satisfaction of shocking and silencing him when she smiled broadly and said loud enough for everyone to hear — but with only him knowing the significance — "Oh, good."

****

Yes, she'd shocked and silenced him, but she was the one who didn't sleep that night.

Dinner had been no problem.

There'd been plenty of distraction from the gathered Curricks and Ruskoffs, who were happily planning for the arrival in a few weeks of Lisa and Shane and their five-month-old baby Alexa.

They drew Val into the conversation with easy expectation that she would join in all the activities.

"So, we'll give them a couple days to relax while we have Alexa all to ourselves, then have dinner here with the gathering of the clans on that Thursday," Matty said, consulting a July calendar. Donna and Ed had gone to New York to help Lisa and Shane when their baby was born. The rest of them were looking forward to meeting the newest member of the family. "Then Friday is party prep and Saturday we have all of Lewis and Clark counties for the party."

There'd also been the distraction of the dark looks Jack darted toward her when he thought she wouldn't notice.

At one point, Taylor had given her a brows-raised look, silently asking if everything was okay. She'd smiled brightly to say everything was fine.

And it had been.

Until she got home — to the foreman's cottage, she corrected herself — put Addie to sleep and slid into bed.

Then came Jack's voice into her head.

That I wanted you in my bed.

Did he want that?

She thought so. Part of him, anyway.

Did she? Oh, hell, yes.

But should she?

What about the part of him that wanted nothing to do with her? The part that tried so hard to avoid her. That pulled back time and again even when he didn't — or couldn't — avoid her.

Yes, there were moments …

But it was the other moments she needed to think about.

Especially with Addie the most important factor to consider.

Between those thoughts and much steamier ones that slipped in whenever she started to drift toward sleep, she spent most of the night awake.

Addie was fractious all morning.

After lunch, she insisted her daughter lie down for a short rest. Addie resisted with words, pouts, and stomps.

For a full minute, she laid resolutely stiff on her bed, her face turned to the wall. Then she released a long breath and was asleep.

Val considered a nap herself, but she was too restless… And then there were those thoughts she could hold off while she was awake, but that slipped free if she tried to sleep.

She looked at her laptop, reminding herself she should work on her blog.

Instead, she pulled out her phone and dialed a familiar number, not bothering to say hello.

"Have you ever heard of monkeyflower?"

"What?"

Her cousin Eleanor Thatcher Cahill wasn't much of a gardener. Val didn't know why she'd asked. Didn't know why she'd been hopping around the Internet looking at information about the plant, either. Nothing she'd found was going to say whether or not it would survive in Matty's garden, and that's what mattered. All that mattered. "Never mind."

El ignored that order. As usual. "What about monkeyflower?"

"It's a wildflower out here. Blooms all summer, I'm told. Bright yellow with touches of red. According to what I've been reading, Merriweather Lewis of Lewis and Clark found it on July 4, 1806."

"That so?" El said dryly.

"It's also supposed to help heal wounds, especially rope burns. Relieve tightness in the shoulders. Ease somebody who's suffering from anxiety because of a specific cause. Impart faith and optimism and inner peace."

"That's a lot for a flower." El sounded like someone feeling their way across ice they suspected might crack any second.

"Uh-huh. Also can use it in salads. That's why I'm interested. All that other stuff? A bunch of hooey."

"What does it taste like in a salad?"

"Bitter."

"Okay. Well. That sounds like a winner."

Val held onto her own bitter mood for another beat, then heard the echo of their conversation in her head like it had been on a delay.

She laughed. She laughed hard. After a while, El joined in.

When they stopped, El said, "Blog seems to be going okay."

"I guess. Got behind for a while, but I'm caught up now."

"So it's not the blog that's bothering you. And you'd have spilled right away if it was Addie. So what is bothering you?"

"Why does something have to be bothering me to call you?"

El chuckled briefly. "I don't know why. I just know you." There was a pause and then she said in a different tone. "It's the guy, isn't it? Jack. The reason you went out there."

"He's not the reason I came out here, not the way you make it sound."

She heard her own defensiveness.

So did El. "Valerie, it's me. I know you are deeply grateful to him and always will be. I also know that on another level completely, you've wondered about him ever since the day Addie was born. And now I know you're worried. What's going on? Does he pose a danger to—"

"No. Never. Not to anybody else. It's himself he's beating up on." She sucked in a long breath then let it out slowly. "El, he's in pain. He's really, really in pain."

****

"What are you doing?"

At the sound of Val's voice, he turned, slowly, reluctantly. When he saw her eyes, wide with something that reminded him of those hours in the back of her station wagon, he knew an urge to soothe. Then he noticed the dark smudges under those wide eyes and the urge strengthened. He pushed it back.

He set the saddle down in the back of the trailer. "Packing up."

Her eyes on that saddle were the way he'd expect her to look at a snake. "Jack—"

"I wouldn't be packing up the Curricks' horse trailer if I were leaving for good." Dammit, he *had* soothed, even if the tone hadn't been the least bit soothing. Hell. He should have let her think… But at least her expression had eased. "Got to check cattle up in the mountains. Move them to new grazing. Be up there a few days."

"You're taking that?" She nodded toward what was in his hand.

He had to look down to remember what he held. A flask of whiskey,

Her brows were tucked. "I mean, if you're drinking — anybody's drinking — it's more likely something could happen to you — an accident — and nobody would know …"

"First, I'm not going to be alone. Hands from a couple other ranches will be there. Second, who have you been talking to?"

She stared back at him. "I don't reveal my sources."

"Oh? You Woodward or Bernstein?" He saw a laugh fighting with the concern in her eyes.

He spoke to the concern. "Listen, I drank too much when I got here — before I got here, mostly, but that was a long time ago."

Damn, damn, damn. Why was he soothing?

"Before you got here?"

"Yeah."

He saw her questions piling up like clouds behind the Big Horns' peaks.

He braced himself. But all that came out was, "How'd you end up here, Jack? Had you worked at cattle ranches before?"

"Some."

"You grew up on your foster family's farm. Is that what got you interested in cattle?"

He shook his head. "Learned the basics, but not much about cattle." Maybe it was because he'd expected worse, but he added, "I was … in some town in Nebraska. A little motel with those old metal chairs out front under a tree. The legs are all one piece, so they sort of rock. One day I was sleeping there and a guy stopped with a cattle truck. A fastener had broken on a divider gate. He had an arm in a cast and couldn't get it. I rigged it temporarily. But he was going to need help unloading and I had nowhere to be. Drove behind him to what turned out to be a cattle sale. Somebody else there needed help. Then somebody else. Along the line somebody needed a hand at their ranch, so I went there. The next spring, Ed Currick and I crossed paths. Hired me on."

She looked at him for a long moment.

He braced again.

She surprised him again. "What about Phantom while you're gone?"

"Some of the others are going to work with her a bit. Get her to trust a few more folks."

She nodded. "Well, have a good time in the mountains. Being up there should make it easier."

"Make what easier?"

Devilment glinted in her eyes. "Avoiding me." She turned and started away with an exaggerated flounce. After four steps, she looked back over her shoulder at him and grinned, making light of her words and her motions. In her normal voice, she said, "Bye!" and waved as she disappeared around the front end of the horse trailer.

Out of sight. Not out of mind.

Chapter Fourteen

Jack being gone did not leave her life empty or boring. Not at all. She hardly noticed his absence.

For starters, she had two riding lessons from Bryan. True, every other sentence from him started with "Jack says," so she couldn't completely forget about the man. But she wasn't mooning about him. Not one bit.

And there were regular gatherings with Matty, Dave, and their kids, or Taylor, Cal, and their kids, or all of them. There were lots of play dates, alternating location and the designated Mother in Charge, which gave one or more of the other parents' time for work projects. Many of these days ended up with all of them sitting on the porch at wherever the play date had been, eating some simple supper, talking, and watching their kids into the long, lingering evenings.

On the second of such evenings — the day after Jack left — Val was heading into the foreman's cottage to clean up and make pasta salad to go with the burgers to be grilled when Dave and Cal arrived. She'd been helping Matty plant yellow monkeyflowers by a pump near the Flying W barn.

"Jack went into town day before yesterday special for these, and if I don't get them in the ground, they'll all die," Matty had said when she arrived.

Taylor, dressed for her law office, became designated child-watcher on the porch, while Matty and Val planted.

"Looks good, doesn't it?" Val said to Taylor as she headed up the front steps. The kids were on one side of the porch, Cassie telling a story to the two youngest, while Addie and Brennan apparently saved the world through the efforts of a teddy bear and a stuffed frog. "Matty's worried they're a little wilted, but I think they'll bounce back with some water."

Taylor didn't answer. She was staring at the water pump, or maybe the trough, like it had raised a real important legal issue.

Val almost kept going, prepared to shrug off the woman's absorption. She wasn't sure what made her stop and ask, "Something wrong, Taylor?"

"What? Wrong? No. No, nothing's wrong. Not wrong. No." Except the usually unflappable lawyer was spitting out words erratically.

"Okay. Well, if there's anything you need while I'm in the kitchen, holler and—"

"Wait, Val. Uh, come sit with me for a minute. I, uh ..." Her voice trailed off as she returned to staring.

Val followed the direction of her stare, which had shifted to the right, and saw only a rough ranch road that disappeared into a hilly section of the Flying W.

Taylor blinked several times. "Sorry. Sorry." She smiled. "This might sound crazy, but I'm going to say it anyway. You've heard the story of how Donna and Ed met, right? And when he went after her, he brought her a bouquet of snowberry?"

Val nodded. It was one of many family stories the Curricks had shared with her.

"And I know you know about Matty and Dave and the Indian Paintbrush, because I told you about that."

Val nodded again.

"Well, there's another flower that grows around here called fireweed, and it . . ." Taylor's eyes reflected remembered pain, quickly covered by joy. "It has a lot of meaning for Cal and me, from when we went through rough times, and then better times. Much better times."

Val shifted on the chair. Where was this going?

Taylor's voice took on a brisker tone. "And then there's a flower called bur marigold. Lisa has a broach that looks like it, made by a jeweler who took her under his wing in New York. You, uh, know that jeweler got in trouble with the law?"

"Yes, and Shane came here, following up on the case."

Taylor smiled. "I think the case was his excuse to follow up on Lisa.

He already knew about the bur marigold broach Alex had made her, and while Shane was here, he tracked down some of the flower and gave it to her. And now it's yellow monkeyflower." Taylor looked at her expectantly.

Val looked back blankly. "What's yellow monkeyflower?"

Taylor nodded at where Matty was finishing up the planting. "That is."

"Yeah," Val agreed. "It is."

"That's what you got for Matty to plant at the Slash-C when Dave sent you to that shop in Jefferson, isn't it?"

"Yeah."

"And then Jack brought these for you."

"No — not me. He got them because Matty asked him to pick up more plants."

"Uh-huh. And he just happened to pick yellow monkeyflower, which meant he had to drive back to Jefferson and go to that store again. To buy what you'd bought when the two of you were together. A flower that has healing properties. Those were your very words when you were telling me and Matty about the plant before you two started digging. You might even say properties for healing what anyone can see has been ailing Jack Ralston since he came here. And you know what? Each of those other flowers I mentioned has special properties that applied to the situation — snowberry for Donna and Ed, Indian paintbrush for Dave and Matty, fireweed for Cal and me, and bur marigold for Lisa and Shane."

Taylor stood, put a hand on her shoulder, and smiled broadly. "*That* is what I meant when I said 'And now it's yellow monkeyflower.' "

Val shook her head. "He got them for Matty. She asked for them. Because they'd survive here. There's no significance for him and—" She bit off the *me* that could have made it sound like she and Jack were a couple. "It's not like all you others. There's nothing…"

She let it go because Taylor was walking down the steps to greet Matty, chuckling and saying, "Right, right."

Taylor didn't bring it up again, but she must have said something to Matty, because there were a couple of pointed remarks about yellow monkeyflowers and how perfect it was that Val could see them from the foreman's house and maybe she should plant some by the Flying W's main house to surprise Jack when he came back.

"Sounds good," Dave said to his wife, but he wasn't looking at her. Instead, Val saw him exchange a look with Cal.

She opened her mouth, but how did you argue with a look?

Better to let time — especially this time with Jack away — make it clear they were wrong. All of them. In whatever they were thinking.

Yes, she was concerned about Jack.

Yes, she was attracted to him.

But as for some connection between them that had to do with yellow monkeyflower … it was absurd. As she clearly displayed by not acting one bit different with him gone than she'd been with him around.

She would admit to feeling an absence, but that was Donna and Ed being away over the long Fourth of July weekend.

On July Fourth itself she might have let herself be a little blue — not because a man chose to stay in the mountains while all the other hands working with him came down to Knighton to celebrate. No, it was because she was a little homesick, missing Gloucester and her family.

Not that she didn't have fun in Knighton. There was an afternoon parade in town with horses decked out in more red, white, and blue, the high school band, 4-H members, and any kids who wanted to join. Then there was a leisurely potluck picnic, with grills and picnic tables set up on the library lawn. As the sun started to set, watermelons were sliced and impromptu seed spitting contests took place.

Then blankets were spread and the fireworks began. Addie jumped up to "oooh" and "aaaah" with nearly every explosion.

The instant the applause for the finale ended, Addie curled up on the blanket and fell sound asleep.

Trying to keep a sleeping Addie hoisted on her hip, Val was considering how to also get their stuff to the car, when a familiar, male voice came from over her shoulder.

"Here, let me help you," Bryan said, picking up her three jammed totes and the blanket.

She wasn't disappointed it was Bryan. She wasn't. She'd recognized his voice immediately. There had not been a flash of … whatever. Not even a flicker.

At the car, Bryan said, "Hey, before I forget again, give me your email address and I'll send you those pictures I took."

They were there in her inbox when she opened it after getting Addie to bed, unloading the totes, and washing what needed it.

The first one gave her a shock of surprise. They weren't from these past weeks. They were from the day Addie was born.

A series of her and Addie being loaded into the ambulance. She held the red-swathed bundle she knew was Addie in one arm while her other hand clasped Jack's for dear life. She'd forgotten that he'd wrapped the newly born baby in a section of her cape that he'd cut with a knife. She hadn't even minded.

She smiled now, looking at the pictures.

One finger touching the red-wrapped bundle. Then traveling over to Jack's calm, sure face. And then to where their hands joined.

****

He strode into the Flying W foreman's house fueled by the cleansing fire of anger.

He didn't let the back door slam, but other than that he made no attempt to hide his presence.

Val's hands were on the keyboard, but weren't moving. Her head had come up with a frown between her brows. Her hair was as wild as it got in a Wyoming wind.

"Jack? You're back." Her smile faltered as he kept coming. She raised up as he reached the opposite side of the small table she was using as a desk. "What are you—?"

He leaned down under the table and yanked her computer's plug out of the wall.

"Hey!"

"I told you — nothing about me on the Internet."

"I didn't." She dropped her voice. "And if you wake up Addie from this nap, I'll shoot you."

She'd been the one to raise her voice, but he didn't point that out, which was pretty damned big of him, considering. "Hugh Moski said my picture's on your blog. You saying he's a liar?"

"You were in town—? Your picture—? Oh."

In the instant of that last syllable, he thought she'd admit her guilt. Thought he'd found the lever to pry her out of here. Thought she'd be packing up and heading out with Addison Rose sooner rather than later. Thought he'd gotten what he needed. Wanted. Because he *did* want it. And need it. Her and Addie far, far away.

He also thought the band around his heart had just been tightened into a tourniquet.

Then she said, in an entirely different tone, "Oh, for heaven's sake."

She uncoiled from the chair, glared at him, bent over so she was partway under the table, and jammed the plug back into the socket.

"I told you—"

"And I told you, Jack Ralston, that I wouldn't write about you or name you or put your photo out on the Internet. So now I'm going to show you. Could have done it right away if I hadn't run out of battery power. Or—" she added with heavy emphasis as she sat again, this time with her legs tucked under her so she practically was kneeling, "—if you'd asked instead of jumping off the deep end. So now, just be quiet and wait for my computer's system to recover from your assault on it."

He waited. He didn't say anything. But he'd be a liar if he said his mind was quiet.

The problem was the waiting left a vacuum for his attention, and that vacuum soon sucked in all the details of her presence in the Flying W's foreman's house.

He'd been in it a few times when Cal lived here, and the basics hadn't changed.

He'd come in through the small mudporch off the back door. That opened into a compact kitchen and eating area. The living room where she was working had gotten the majority share of the space. A fireplace and bookcases occupied most of one wall, with a sofa and coffee table facing it. Bookshelves extended from the north side of the fireplace, turned the corner and stopped only at the double doors that led to the bedroom and bathroom. The doors were closed, presumably with Addie behind them, napping.

But the evidence of the two females was everywhere. Two small, soft knitted blankets pooled on the sofa cushions and dripped over the edges, as if mother and daughter had been curled up there. There was iced tea brewing in the sunlight from the kitchen window. The fireplace mantel held glass jar vases with exuberant mixes of wildflowers trying to burst from them.

And the place smelled like them. Not that it stank when Cal lived here. But then the underlying scent had been man and horse and leather. Now it was female and lollipop and … whatever the hell that was she smelled like.

Valerie had set up her laptop on a table in front of the front window.

Sitting with her side to the window the way she was, she could see the view if she turned her head, but wouldn't be distracted by it each time she looked up.

Not that he knew — or cared — about her working habits or productivity. In fact, the less productive she was the better.

And it looked like she hadn't been as productive as she would have liked. Not only was there a pad with scribbled drawings of mountains and flowers at her side, but her hair was even wilder than usual. As if she'd been driving her hands through it.

It would look the same if he put his hands in it to hold her head to kiss her deep and thorough. It would feel just the way it looked, like a cloud designed to surround a man in welcoming softness. And in that subtle scent that teased him every time he was near her. Clean and fresh. Tart, but not harsh —

No. He was not going to pull in a deep lungful, just to try to store it in his cells. At least not again. He'd heard himself do it once, unaware. But now he was aware and there was no excuse—.

"Oh, quit sighing. The computer's loading now."

"About damned time."

"How can you be so patient with Phantom and such a grouch the rest of the time?"

He wouldn't have answered, but he was spared her recognizing that fact — and no doubt commenting on it — by the computer screen coming to life at that moment. Her fingers flew over the keys.

"There. Look." She gestured in triumph to the screen.

Too late he realized that to look at the screen, he'd have to come around to behind her chair. Since her chair was already about as far as it could go into the corner of the room, that meant being close and leaning even closer.

He couldn't retreat, tell her never mind, he'd look some other time. Not without her wondering more than she already was.

He stepped in, peering toward the screen. Standing right over her.

With her hair practically under his nose because now she'd straightened up so she was basically kneeling on the chair. The softness right there. The scent all around him. The nearness—

"Do you see?" she demanded impatiently.

He brought his focus to the end of her extended finger, which nearly touched the screen.

"*There* is this photo of you that you're all bent out of shape about."

Her finger pointed to a sliver of shadow on the dusty ground beside Storm in a photo that took up the entire screen. You could make out it was probably a man's form and you could see the outline of a cowboy hat. That was about it.

"The only people who'd know — who'd *suspect* it was your shadow, because nobody could know for sure — are the people who already know you well enough to know you ride Storm and to recognize *him*. So the only one who has a right to complain is the horse."

He stepped back to a safe distance, but he didn't give any ground. "You will not put anything about me on the Internet. Not pictures. Not words—"

"I told you I wouldn't."

"Not hints. Not shadows. Nothing. Do you understand?"

She propped her hands on her hips and looked up at him. "What? Are you wanted by the police or something? An escaped murderer? Or — *Whoa*. What was that?"

"Good-bye, Valerie."

"No way, Ralston. The way you just reacted? You can't walk away—"

"Can and am."

****

The door had closed behind him before she got herself even half untangled from the chair.

A black hole, right there in the man's eyes. Not just darkness, but a light-sucking, matter-destroying black hole.

She hadn't imagined that. She hadn't.

The question was whether *wanted by the police* or *escaped murderer* had triggered it.

Not a great choice.

She ran.

****

He'd made the same mistake as when he'd left Addie's envelope. He'd automatically used the back door, like most folks did, leaving her to take the shortcut of coming out the front door. It was like he didn't have a brain cell left in his head.

He'd gone to town to push back the moment of seeing her again.

Because he'd wanted to see her too damned much. Way too damned much. Then Hugh and the other stool sitters had started razzing him about being an Internet star and how the next thing would be a reality TV show of his own, and he'd felt the pure, safe fire of anger building.

No worries about seeing her again after that. No worries at all.

She caught him as he came around the side of the building.

"Tell me," she demanded, planting herself in front of him.

"Go away, Val."

"Can't, because I can't take the wondering. Was it *wanted by the police* or *escaped murderer?*"

"Are you crazy?"

"No. Tell me."

"No. And you are crazy. You come out here — alone — to ask a man if he's wanted by the police or an escaped murderer? What sort of idiotic reckless behavior is that? You do not take risks like that, do you understand?" His hands were around her upper arms, resisting the urge to shake her. "You do not take risks. You have a baby. You have a family. You have — You do not take risks like that."

He dropped his hands from her, breathing hard, his heart hammering at where his words almost took him.

No. No, no, no, no.

Only after a long moment did he realize she'd remained motionless, all her energy condensed into the bright, fierce light of her eyes as they studied him.

"Tell me."

He turned his back on her. "Go away, Valerie." He sounded — he felt — a couple centuries old. "Go."

He heard a sound behind him, but didn't turn. That didn't stop her. She was back in front of him. Not relenting. Not going anywhere.

"You said something to me that day, Jack. The day you delivered Addie. The day that divides my life from black and white to Technicolor. You said it was you and me. And that everything was going to be okay. Now I'm saying that to you, Jack Ralston. It's you and me. And everything will be okay. Tell me. So you're not carrying it alone anymore."

He didn't know when he'd started shaking his head, but the motion was steady by the end of her words.

"Why?"

"I carry it alone."

"Jack—"

"No." He'd said it loud enough to make her blink. "Take Addie and go away. Go back to Gloucester. Get out of here. Just go away, Val."

He saw the tears in her eyes. "I—"

He couldn't take it. Not tears, not anymore words. "Then I'll go."

CHAPTER FIFTEEN

The first day, alternating swells of determination and troughs of uncertainty had battered at her the way a riled ocean could. A hundred times Val considered packing up and leaving so he wouldn't.

Because he could have meant that. She didn't *think* so. She thought — hoped, prayed — he'd meant for her to go all the way back East until she hit the Atlantic Ocean, but that his "then I'll go" was only as far as the Slash-C.

So, a hundred and one times she decided to stay. She wouldn't push him right now by crossing his path if she could help it, but she wouldn't leave, either.

Still, she called the Slash-C once on the flimsiest of excuses — to tell Matty she was going to be busy a few days after falling behind on her blog — only to hear Bryan cheerfully fill her in on how Jack had been working with Phantom that day... when she'd carefully *not* asked about the man.

She'd also heard that Lisa Currick and her husband Shane Garrison were arriving from New York that evening. Some of Shane's family had already arrived for the week. And one of Taylor's brothers and his family were visiting with them at their ranch.

The second day, she practically jumped Ed and Dave when they briefly stopped by the Flying W. Her would-be casual questions about if anything was new had them giving each other puzzled looks. Since she was as sure as she could be that even with Lisa and Shane newly arrived, the news that their valued foreman was up and leaving would have been considered worth mentioning, she decided she'd been right: Jack Ralston was waiting for her to leave.

Thank God he wasn't turning his back on this place.

Damn him for trying to push her out.

The third day, she cursed his stubbornness and secretiveness with inventive phrases in several languages — none of them spoken aloud because Addie would be sure to repeat one or all of them at the most inopportune time. Especially since her daughter was a little testy about not getting to see her buddy Brennan for three days in a row.

The fourth day, the heavens opened and rained like the ocean had somehow gotten above them and was emptying itself onto Wyoming. Since that perfectly suited her mood she didn't even mind when it continued into the fifth day.

Not until she realized that the bogs and ponds that had appeared on the road from the foreman's cottage to the highway meant she was trapped alone in the tiny house with the cranky bundle of energy and Brennan-less dismay who vaguely resembled her daughter. Again.

There were tears. There was pouting. There was ill-humor. And Addie didn't have a good day, either.

On the sixth day, Matty called and asked if she wanted to take an outing in her all-wheel-drive truck.

"Even after the storm my truck will get us around so you can see more of the ranches this afternoon before you come to dinner tonight to meet Lisa and Shane and Alexa — what a doll."

"That's great news." Her enthusiasm might have been a bit forced.

"It is. They're with the Garrisons now. I'll leave Finn with Donna, but I'll bring Brennan and we can have a snack outside with the kids. I don't know about you, but I'm nearly as ready for him to be outside as I am. We'll be back in plenty of time to get ready for dinner. So, are you up for it?"

"How soon can you get here?"

****

Val watched the horizon rise and fall and sway from the front passenger seat of Matty's new truck. She listened with only half her attention to Matty's explanations of how they used the fields. First year in wheat for this one, letting the next one rest a year, testing alfalfa seeds in another, those two were grazed in spring.

Both kids had thoroughly enjoyed shouting over the storm-raised voice of a small waterfall, and eating their snack while sitting on a relatively dry boulder at a safe distance from it. Now they were heading back by a new route and new commentary by Matty.

"...so the seeds worked out great and— Oh, look. It's Jack's truck." Matty's extended arm nearly took off Val's nose. "Gee, I wonder what he's doing here?"

Instead of looking in the direction of the pointing finger, she turned to the driver. "That was the least believable *Gee, I wonder what he's doing here?* I have ever heard. Taylor warned me about you."

"Like she has any reason to complain," Matty shot back.

She tipped her head. Acknowledging the point, but not conceding it. Taylor and Cal were clearly happy with each other and their lives. But they were entirely different people from her and Jack.

"So, shall we go see what Jack's doing or not?" Matty asked.

"I don't—"

Val was drowned out by voices from the back seat.

"Go see Jack!" demanded Addie.

"See what he's doing," corroborated Brennan.

"The back seat has spoken. Try to say no now." Matty grinned at her as she turned the steering wheel to follow tire tracks leading down toward the water.

She pulled up about fifty feet to the side of Jack's truck, waving out the driver's window. Jack, standing down closer to what looked like a creek of its banks, raised a hand, then turned back toward the water. No, not toward the water, which rushed along, but to an area this side of the water.

"Uh-oh. Critter's got himself bogged in," Matty said. "These bog holes can appear after the kind of storm we've had. The water sweeps through but gets trapped in an area. The older animals usually know enough to tread carefully, and the young ones are usually strong enough to get themselves out. But we always have to check after a storm to clear any. Good thing it's a steer with horns."

Only then did Val see the dark head of an animal.

"Why?"

"Jack can throw a catch rope around the horns. Much easier on the animal than around the neck. Boy, he's stuck."

The downward slope of the land turned the car into stadium seating, with the kids able to view what was happening through the front windshield as well as she and Matty could from the front seat.

"Jack caught it! Jack caught it!" Addie shouted.

"That's nothin'. My Daddy coulda done it better," Brennan said.

Val bit the inside of her cheeks to keep from laughing.

But Matty seemed intent on the scene in front of them.

Even from this distance they saw the effort Jack was putting into pulling on the opposite end of the rope. The steer's shoulders appeared above the muck, then his progress halted.

A frown pulled Matty's brows down. Abruptly she leaned over, popped open the glove compartment, and pulled out a pair of gloves that she dropped on Val's thigh. "These should work."

"Work for what?"

Pulling on a battered pair of gloves she'd retrieved from the console between the front seats, Matty said, "He's going to need a hand. C'mon."

"But—"

"C'mon," Matty repeated the order impatiently as she got out, closing her truck door behind her. "You kids stay put." With both of them still buckled in, they weren't likely to go anywhere.

Matty headed straight toward Jack.

"Mommy?"

Val looked back at her daughter. "I'll be right back."

"They're gonna he'p Jack," Brennan said, patting Addie's arm.

Val followed Matty down the slope.

"You going in, Jack?" Matty called. "We can hold the rope."

Jack turned toward his boss's wife first, then his gaze came up to her, trailing behind, and he seemed to pause for a moment before saying to Matty, "Gotta get his back legs up."

"Think you'll need the truck?"

"Going to try it without first."

Matty said something else to him that Val didn't hear, since she'd used a lower tone as they neared each other.

"...come out spittin' mad," Jack said as she came up to then. She saw he wore rubber boots. "She should get back in the truck."

"Don't worry, We'll leave you the honor of pulling him free."

"Matty—"

"Go on."

Jack's gaze flicked from Matty, now holding out a gloved hand for the rope, to her. "Put on the gloves," he ordered.

She drew the gloves on as she watched him walk around the edge of the bog until he was at right angles to the steer's length, then began to wade in slowly.

Matty explained, "You can haul them out with the truck, but it can be real hard on them. Sometimes there's no choice because they're so deep or so exhausted. But this guy's still got some fight."

The animal rolled its eyes toward Jack is if wondering what had possessed the crazy human. Val shared that thought.

"This looks like a young one," Matty added in an even tone. "Think he was swept in?"

"Could've been. Had another one caught upstream by the Three Rocks fence." Jack's voice went beyond even, to calming, almost crooning.

Yet the animal kept rolling his eyes toward the man now nearing his flank.

"Jack'll get around and raise up his rear. Legs can sort of fold up under. When he's ready, we'll pull on the rope and Jack'll lift. He's got to be careful he doesn't get kicked. And we don't want to pull so hard that we totally free the steer. Just want to get him up so he's not so deep."

Val listened closely to Matty's explanation while she watched Jack, now near the animal, reaching into the muck. He came out of it with the tail.

"Ready," Jack said.

"Okay. Val, grab the rope behind me. When I say three, pull. One. Two. Three."

Val pulled with all her might but Matty was doing most of the work. Jack, she saw, was pulling the tail. The steer seemed to rise. He certainly shifted position, but he didn't come loose.

"That's enough," Jack said, still in that calming voice.

They released the tension on the rope. "He's not all the way out yet," she protested to Matty.

"Nope. Jack's too smart to let him all the way out."

With his belly now clear of the mud, but his legs still mired, the steer tried to heave himself up again, while swinging his head around to watch

Jack retreat out of the mud.

"Hold on," Matty ordered her. "We don't want to lose the rope after all this."

The animal subsided as Jack, stomping off mud with his first several steps on solid land, came toward them.

"Why not pull him all the way out? Isn't he going to wear himself out?" she asked.

"Learned my lesson," Jack muttered.

"Fine line," Matty said. "Want to wear him out enough to discourage him from chasing us, but not so much that he has trouble recovering. Somehow the critters never appreciate the service we've done them."

Jack took the rope. "You two get back now."

Matty gestured her toward Jack's truck.

"The kids," she protested, looking toward Matty's truck.

"They're fine inside the truck. But we won't have enough time to get there if he charges. Jack's is closer. Hurry up, he's nearly free."

She looked over her shoulder and saw Jack hauling back on the rope, exerting steady pressure. The animal's front legs came out as it struggled to gain purchase.

Matty grabbed her arm and tugged her to the open truck door. "If he starts coming this way, hop in," she ordered. "No hesitating, because I'll be right behind you and Jack after me."

The animals' back legs extended, and for an instant it appeared he'd go head first into the bog, but Jack pulled even harder, and after a breath-held moment, the steer came clear.

Jack reached in with a quick motion, apparently loosing the rope, because he started reeling it in as he backed away from the steer and toward his truck.

The animal, looking decided cranky, swung his big head toward Jack and lunged. Jack turned and ran toward the truck.

Val's muscles tensed in instinctive preparation for jumping in the truck.

The steer stopped, apparently slowed by the mud still clinging to him as well as tired from his struggles to extricate himself.

Matty called out, "He stopped." She laid a hand on Val's arm and added more softly, "It's okay. Jack's fine."

As Jack neared, Matty said in a normal tone, "Nice throw. Nice save."

He grunted. Nice to know that response wasn't one he reserved only for her.

"Thanks for the help," he added, looking at Matty.

"No problem. Guess we'll be getting along. Walk us to my truck, will you, Jack? Just in case he decides to get frisky."

He shot Matty a look, but didn't say anything as he pulled off the rubber boots and put his working boots back on.

Val, looking at the steer plodding slowly in the opposite direction, didn't think he was much of a threat.

"You should be wrapping up work now to get cleaned up, Jack. Because you *are* coming to the dinner for Lisa and Shane." Her emphasis made it something between an order and a threat. "And I need to get you back, Val, so you can get ready, too. But that's going to make things tight for me."

Jack tossed the muddy rubber boots in the back of his truck. His jeans showed generous swipes of mud above where they'd been. He could have used all-weather bib overalls like the fishermen wore in Gloucester.

"I'm sorry, Matty," she said. "I didn't think about that. We shouldn't have come out—"

"Of course we should have. We had no way of knowing we were going to be needed to rescue a steer. Oh, wait. I have an idea," Matty said with unconvincing innocence. "Jack, why don't you take Val back to the Flying W to change for dinner, then bring her to the Slash-C. I'll take the kids back, get some supper into them so they aren't raving hungry when we're all trying to eat."

"I could take—"

"That's not nece—"

Matty waved off both protests with one hand. "No, you can't take the kids, Jack, because the car seats are in my truck. No way on this earth are we transferring the car seats after the trouble we had getting those things in right. But there's also no way I'm letting you drive my baby after you waded into that muck hole. And, Val, yes it is necessary, because I don't want to be rude, but you appear to have stepped in something. I might let you get in my truck if you took your shoe off and wrapped it in an old blanket and left it in the bed, but I really don't want to sit through dinner with you like that. And your foot would get cold."

She'd been backing toward the driver's side of the truck as she talked, and now she called in reinforcements.

"What do you think, Addie, you want to come have some supper with Brennan? Then your mom will come over later, okay?"

"Yeah," the kids chorused.

"Good. So let's check that you two are still buckled up right. You want to get Addie settled before you go, Val?"

"Matty—"

Jack grumbled, "Give it up. I'll wait for you in the truck." He turned and headed away.

For a couple breaths, Val stayed where she was, then headed to the passenger side of Matty's truck.

"Matty," she started as she checked Addie's belt. "Pushing him is not going to work. I don't want—"

"Oh, go on. It's just a ride. He won't bite," Matty said.

He might. She fought down a shiver.

"Jack won't bite," Addie proclaimed.

"No," agreed Brennan. "Jack won't bite Addie's mom."

The two women's gazes met across the back seat, sharing the instant of dismayed amusement that their children had followed the conversation that well.

"Bed bugs bite," Addie solemnly informed her friend. "Have to tell them *No!* before you go to sleep."

Jack looked at her as she climbed into the truck with a faint lifting of his brows.

She explained her grin by relaying Addie's advice to Brennan, leaving out any hint of what led up to the discussion of biting.

****

During the rest of the drive back to the Flying W home ranch, she asked a couple questions about where they were and what she saw.

He answered in a minimum number of words.

Between every word either of them spoke were the ones she was certain they were both still hearing.

You said it was you and me. And that everything was going to be okay. Now I'm saying that to you, Jack Ralston. It's you and me. And everything will be okay. Tell me. So you're not carrying it alone anymore.

I carry it alone.

As they crested a ridge, the buildings of the home ranch came into sight, with the foreman's cottage not far from a cluster of barns and other outbuildings, with the main house beyond them, facing the highway.

They also saw the worn ranch truck coming toward them. Bryan waved out the driver's window and both vehicles slowed, coming abreast and stopping at the edge of the big corral behind the barn.

"Where you headed?" Jack asked.

"Out to repair that fence in the Gray Wolf pasture while there's light."

Jack nodded. "Check the Three Rocks section, too, if you have time. Couple of steers in the mud the other side. Make sure they're not getting through there."

"Will do. And with those things done …"

"Yeah, if those are done, you can leave early Friday."

Bryan grinned. Looking past Jack, he said to her, "Group of friends from school are getting together for the weekend over in Cody."

She smiled back. "If I don't see you, have a great time."

"Oh, I will." Jack's truck started easing forward. "Wait. Almost forgot. A friend of yours is here, Val. At the foreman's house."

"A friend of mine?"

"Yup. Left 'em on the porch."

As he Jack his truck roll on, he asked without looking at her, "You expecting somebody?"

"No." Catching the narrowing of his eyes, she downplayed her surprise to add, "Isn't it delightful that a friend has come to give me a great surprise?"

He didn't even bother to grunt.

Chapter Sixteen

In a moment, he pulled up near the front of the foreman's house. She caught movement in the shadow under the porch roof, but had no hope of recognizing anyone.

El. It had to be. Nobody but her cousin would fret enough about her to trek out here, and she had told El … well, enough to make her fret. But only because Eleanor Thatcher McRae had a very low fret threshold. Still, this was the busiest time of year for the Inn. She wouldn't have left Cahill on his own with Sam, would she?

Unless — Oh, God, it couldn't be her mother. Surely, Bryan would have said her mother was here to see her, not a friend. And would Lucy Trimarco has been pulled away from Gloucester with her other kids and grandchildren at hand? Val never would have thought so. More than once in her life, she'd counted on that to keep her mother from descending on her.

All that went through her mind as she rounded the front of the truck, aware of Jack's eyes on her through the front windshield.

A plump woman rose from the rocking chair on the front porch. Val tried to keep her face neutral, her pace steady.

The driver's door of the truck swung open, and Jack got out.

Apparently, her face and pace hadn't been neutral or steady enough.

She tried to get ahead of him, but he was right there beside her as she reached the steps.

"Hello," she said, hoping her smile masked her confusion.

The woman clasped one hand over the other atop her heart. "Oh my, I can't believe it. I just can't believe I'm actually standing here with you. Valerie Prudence Trimarco."

"Yeah. Uh, pretty surprising."

Jack came up another step toward the woman, and Val didn't think it was an accident that his head was now slightly above the woman's. "You're a friend of Valerie's?" He shaved the edge of hostile while landing dead-center in suspicious.

"Jack—"

"Oh, dear, I know it was presumptuous of me to say so to that young man — *so* good-looking, and a real cowboy — but I do feel like I know you, and you have been such a good friend to me. I've watched you almost from the beginning—"

"On the Internet," Jack said in deep disapproval. Val felt rather than saw that he had sent her a dark, significant look. She kept her eyes on the stranger — no. That was Jack's view. That anyone he didn't already know was a stranger — a suspicious stranger. This was a woman. A viewer. A *potential* friend.

"On 'Mommy: The Truth Zone,' " the woman said almost reverently. "I can tell you, there were days and days and days when only 'Mommy: The Truth Zone' kept me sane. I can't thank you enough."

As the woman wiped at tears, Val advanced up to the step Jack stood on, though that still left him looming over her, so she had to look up when she shot him a look of *See. My* blog does good.

Val took one of the woman's damp hands and pressed it. "Thank you for saying that. It's so wonderful to hear. We all need some help staying sane sometimes."

Jack muttered something. Val didn't need to hear the words to get the gist.

"I never dreamed in a million years that I'd ever get to meet you. Not with you living way back East in Massachusetts. But when you came out here, I knew I had to come see you."

"But I never said anything more than Wyoming."

"Oh, you didn't need to. I saw the mountains in the background and that got me close. Then one picture had the truck in the background, really small, but eventually I made out the name of a ranch, and the people there told me where to find you."

Each detail the woman gave felt like a hammer blow on Val's head, pounding her deeper and deeper into a hole. Jack's stare followed her down.

But the woman's happiness never dimmed. "And of course you—" She beamed at Jack. "—must be the reason."

"What? No. No, he's not the reason. I mean, not really. Just—" *Just wanted to thank him for delivering my daughter.* She couldn't say that. She'd promised him. Not only that, but a finger of uneasiness poked at her at that moment, because she suddenly felt grateful that her daughter wasn't here. That this woman — okay, damn it, this *stranger* — wouldn't see Addie.

"What makes you think that?" Jack demanded of the woman.

She didn't seem to take his interrogation tone amiss. "I recognized you."

"You recogni—"

"You *couldn't* have," Val protested, appalled. "He's never been on the blog. I never mentioned him or had a picture—"

"Oh, yes, the picture with the shadow." She beamed up at Jack. "Your shadow."

Jack went still an instant, then shifted his eyes to Val. He had her pinned with his gaze, with its accusation, with its shout of I-told-you-so.

"I recognized the hat as soon as you got out of the truck because it's just like the shadow. *Oh!*"

The woman's exclamation, followed by a giggle finally let Val break Jack's look. "What's wrong?"

"Nothing. Nothing at all. It's… I'm so silly." Her eyes filled with tears. "The good-looking young cowboy who greeted me and had me sit here to wait for you was wearing the same kind of hat. So, I suppose it could have been him?"

Relief and triumph flowed through Val, welled around her, lifting her right out of that hole. She shot Jack a look to be sure he'd heard. He had.

"It certainly could have been," she said to the woman. "Hard to tell one cowboy hat from another."

"Especially from just a shadow like that," the woman said, apparently back on the edge of giggling. The woman's moods certainly came and went quickly.

"Exactly." Val beamed at her new best friend.

The other woman blinked at her, then gave a kind of hiccupping sigh. "This is so wonderful. Amazing. Being here chatting with you like this. Meeting you— Oh!"

She jumped at the woman's exclamation. "What?"

"I've never told you my name. Where is my head, not to mention my manners? I'm Angi, Angi Pilson." She extended her hand.

Val shook. "It's good to meet you, Angi."

"Oh, it's so good to meet *you*. So good and such an honor. A true honor. It makes it all worthwhile."

"All what worthwhile?" Jack demanded.

"The drive and all."

"I know. You have to drive far to get almost anywhere in Wyoming, don't you," Val said. If she kept talking, Jack couldn't ask his demanding questions. Clearly, she was simply a devoted fan. One with perhaps a little too much time on her hands, which had allowed her to put together the few teeny-tiny hints Val had let drop. "The distances out here amaze me. Where'd you drive from?"

"Baxter."

"Sorry, I don't know that town. Just Knighton and Jefferson."

"It's near Brainerd. It's a real nice town. And the people are good people. But you know how it is when you're new in town and most everyone else has lived there forever, and they have all their friends from the time they were in diapers, not to mention their families, so their lives are so full that it's natural they don't have time for newcomers."

Val was so struck by the woman's words that she waited a beat too long. Her "That must be so hard" was run over by Jack's "Where's Brainerd?"

"About the very middle of Minnesota."

"Minnesota?" Val repeated. "Baxter's not in Wyoming?"

But Jack's "*Minnesota?*" had a lot more impact. Especially when he followed up with, "You drove here from Minnesota? How many hours?"

Angi Pilson pulled in her bottom lip. "About fourteen, but that was with a few stops."

"Fourteen. That's, uh, that's a long drive." Val couldn't stop herself from looking at Jack again. Not in triumph this time. He was intent on the woman.

"Long drive," he said, "even with sharing the driving."

"Oh, I drove alone. Regina gets car sick, so I it would have been cruel to bring her, and it wouldn't have been fair to bring Petra and not bring Regina."

"You left your kids at home?" There was a slight rawness in Jack's voice.

"Yes. Got up before dawn so everyone was still sleeping. Then I wrote the note to Tim, and told him he'd finally have to take a couple of the vacation days he's been piling up like a miser and look after the kids himself. I left him lists of the girls' schedules and what they should wear each day and when to wash their hair. And the baby will be fine. I pumped enough to leave a week's supply of milk in the freezer. And that was no easy task because that boy's a good feeder, that one. Brought the pumps, sterile bags, cold packs, and a cooler with me, of course."

Jack's usually stoic face held the usual male expression of dazed disbelief when the topic turned to breastfeeding.

Val nearly sagged with relief. Jack Ralston was contagious, and she'd momentarily caught a dose of his worst-case scenario bug. But a woman who made sure to have a week's worth of breast milk before leaving on a trip was definitely looking out for her child. She straightened abruptly. A *week?*

"A week's a long time to be away from your husband—" That drew no response. "—and kids."

A fresh spurt of tears appeared. "I might not make it the whole week. But that's what I told Tim. So he didn't think he could just let things slide a day or two and I'd be back to clean up."

Jack appeared to have recovered from the discussion of breastfeeding, because he was slipping his phone from his pocket while still listening closely.

"So your husband, uh, Tim knew you wanted to come here?"

"Him? No way. He'd have to listen to me to know that. I wrote in the note that I needed to do something for myself. Then, like I said, I gave him the schedules and instructions and such,"

"The note?"

"Uh-huh. The note I left when I dropped the baby off at his work before I started driving yesterday."

"Don't you think you should call him? Let him know where you are— Okay, maybe not that." Val shifted approach as Angi vehemently shook her head. "But let him know you're okay. And be sure the kids are okay."

"Maybe."

"And you'll need to find a place to stay, to get some rest before you start the long trip back."

"Oh, that's so kind of you to invite me to stay—"

"I didn't mean—"

"*No.*"

This time Val didn't mind having her words overridden by Jack's strong voice.

"No room," he added in a tone that didn't invite discussion. "Nearest motel's an hour away. I'll call now. Make sure there's a room. And get you headed out before it's dark." He retreated down the stairs, but didn't stop watching the woman and her.

"Oh, I can't spend money on a motel. I brought just enough for gas. And that's money I've saved from using the coupons Tim's always making fun of. Talks about how important it is we save, but then he laughs when I do. So I don't tell him. I just put it aside. He's not interested, so he doesn't need to know."

"What about food? You have to have some money for food, right?" Val asked. Mostly from curiosity, but it did also cover that Jack's call — supposedly to the motel — only consisted of three numbers.

"No, no, I packed the cooler. As I eat the food, there's more room for the breastmilk. I planned it so it'll all balance out." Angi began detailing what she'd packed and how she'd estimated how much room she would need for each stage of her trip.

During this, Jack was talking to someone in a low voice, though she'd caught the phrase "we've got this woman at the Flying W" and something about driving from Minnesota.

His head came up now, and he looked intently down the road toward the highway. She turned her head that way, too, and saw dust clouds rising as vehicles turned off the highway and headed toward them.

"They're here," Jack said into the phone. "Yeah."

He hung up, turned, and gave her a long, steady look.

Message received. This could be the dicey part.

She'd recognized that the trucks were from the sheriff's department. To get here so fast someone must have called earlier. Angi had said she stopped at the Slash-C. Someone there?

Angi Pilson didn't seem to notice, focused on wrapping up her inventory. "… and of course mustard for the bologna. But that doesn't take up much space. And keeping it fuller keeps everything cooler."

"I've heard that," Val said with a nod. But at least three-quarters of her attention was on the trucks pulling up in front of the porch.

"Oh, dear. You're not in trouble with the law, are you?"

Angi sounded so disapproving that Val bit the inside of her cheeks to keep from laughing.

"Are *we*—?" Jack started. After the barest glimpse of the affront clear in his posture, she looked away or she'd risk losing it completely.

"No, no," Val assured Angi hurriedly. "Jack and I have a social engagement this evening and we didn't want to leave you without providing some assistance for getting settled tonight. You know there's so little crime out here, the sheriff's department helps with situations like this all the time."

The bulky sheriff had emerged from the lead truck by then. Jack walked down the steps to meet him. They talked in low voices.

Angi frowned. Val searched for a way to distract her and found it when a young woman emerged from the front passenger door of the other truck. She hesitated long enough to glare back inside at the driver before slamming the door and starting for them.

"Looks like she isn't too happy with her driver. Deputy Jessup can be awfully full of himself," Val said.

Before more could be said, the young woman approached with a big smile. "Hi. I'm Zoe Parisi, Ruth and Hugh Moski's granddaughter. I thought I'd come out and see if I could give a hand. You must be Val. It's a pleasure to meet you."

Val returned every bit of the smile as they shook hands. The woman was taller than her — but who wasn't? — and very attractive in a no-time-for-makeup kind of way.

She also was tactful and smart. Tactful because Val had heard enough from Matty, Donna, and Taylor to know that Zoe was a newly minted doctor who was working with the long-time local doctor with a goal of taking over his practice when he retired. Yet she hadn't said a word about being a medical person, which likely would have put Angi on the defensive. So, clearly, she was also smart.

"We have a report—" Started the thin deputy in a formal, officious tone.

The sheriff cut across it without ceremony as he clapped Jack on the shoulder and headed toward the porch. "Well now, welcome to Wyoming, Ma'am. We're sure glad you came to visit. I'm Sheriff Kuerton of Clark County, at your service, happy to help."

"Thank you, Sheriff. But I don't need any help."

"I can see that, Ma'am. You clearly have things under control. The thing is, your husband Tom—"

"Tim."

"Tim. That's right. That's me all over. Can't remember my own name most days. Well, Tim called us and he's real worried."

She snorted. "About all the work he has to do. Surely not about me."

"Well, now, that's the thing. He is worried about you." His eyes twinkled as he looked only at Angi Pilson. "Mind you, if he's anything like most of us men what he's most worried about is that you won't come back soon, and he'll be stumbling this way and that like a moon calf the rest of his days."

Angi snorted again. This one held more satisfaction. "He *would* be stumbling all around. But he'd never admit it."

The sheriff nudged the angle of his hat back with two fingers to its brim. "Oh, I think he'd admit it now, Ma'am. From what I heard on the phone, that baby hasn't stopped crying since you left. That seemed to be upsetting one of the little girls past bearing—"

"Petra. She has a very soft heart."

"And that set the other one to shouting at her to quit blubbering and for her Dad to do something instead of standing around."

"Oh, dear." But Angi didn't sound upset, and her mouth kept trying to find a grin while her brain kept telling it to stay serious. "Perhaps I should cut my visit short."

The sheriff nodded in admiration of such good sense. "That's a fine idea, Ma'am. It's clear they can't get by without you."

"You're not going to send this woman home to her family without a chance to rest up," said Zoe with light indignation. "That's a long drive back to Minnesota, and the first thing is to get her someplace for a good meal and a rest."

Angi looked at Val. "But I can't leave you and think only of myself."

"Yes, you can, and you should. You know how we say on the 'Mommy: The Truth Zone' that the Mommy needs to put her own oxygen mask on first, or she won't be around to help anyone else. That applies here, too."

"If you're sure… And if you really have an engagement tonight and weren't saying that to make me feel better."

Zoe moved in closer, giving Val a quick nod toward the front door.

Val retreated a step, letting Zoe take her place beside Angi. "We truly do. In fact, I need to excuse myself to take a shower and get changed. It's been a pleasure, Angi—" Before she finished, Val found herself surrounded in a plump, slightly damp hug. As she returned it, she realized some of the dampness came from Angi crying again.

"I will remember this all my life. Thank you, Valerie. You're a great woman."

"Thank you. I'll never forget it, either."

Val thought Jack's mutter was "You better not," but she didn't ask for a repeat to make sure.

The sheriff was ushering Angi Pilson down the porch steps as Val slipped inside. She waited by the front door, listening to the sheriff and Zoe adroitly arrange it so the two women would be "relaxing" in the back of his vehicle, while the officious deputy left alone.

Served him right for annoying that nice, competent young woman, Val thought. She felt absolutely satisfied that Dr. Parisi would not let Angi go anywhere unless she was up to it.

Perhaps she just needed a little time away. A little time to herself, even if it was devoted mostly to driving. And a little time for that husband of hers to get a clue.

Val caught sight of the clock, uttered a curse, clapped her hand over her mouth, then remembered her parrot with the sonar ears wasn't on hand to hear, and dashed toward the shower.

****

It occurred to her as she toweled off to wonder if she'd misread Jack's reaction to Angi Pilson asking if they had trouble with the law. Had it been affront? Or had it been something deeper. Like his expression when she'd asked him if he was wanted by the police or an escaped murderer. An expression of someone confronting a truth he'd ignored for a good, long time.

She was still considering how she might introduce the topic to get more information when she came out to the porch, wearing the jeans that always made her feel good and a white blouse with seaming that conformed perfectly to her figure … and totally forgot the issue.

Jack was still there, sitting sideways on the porch, his back against the pole, his bent legs down the steps. Everyone else was gone.

He turned his head, looking up at her.

The instant held, stretched, expanded. Possibilities hanging above them like puffy white clouds that only made the blue sky bluer.

Then he looked away.

Her heart thudded heavy against her ribs.

Stupid, stupid, stupid.

Any clouds in the sky above them were storm clouds. It wasn't like he felt anything toward her. Or was attracted. Or interested.

And yet …

He stood. "Let's go. I need to shower and change before I drive you over. You'll have to wait for me at the main house."

She blinked. She hadn't stopped to wonder why he'd stuck around. "I'll drive myself."

"I'm driving you."

She shook her head. "I'll need my car for the car seat for the trip back tonight after dinner."

"I already talked to the folks at the Slash-C. It's been decided. Addie's staying there tonight and so are you."

"It's been decided?" She propped her hands on her hips. "Do you think you're giving me orders?"

"No. I think Donna Currick is. But I *know* I'm saying that you and Addie are not coming back to stay alone in this place tonight when we don't know where that woman or her husband are."

"Her husband?" Damn. He'd distracted her with her own curiosity.

The glint in his eyes said he knew it, too. "What if he's coming after her? What if he's not happy with the person who lured his wife away?"

She snorted.

He kept going. "Until we know they're both wrapped up tight, you and Addie are not going to be here alone. Now, c'mon. We're already late. You don't need to worry about getting dirty from the truck. I cleaned it out and put a towel over the seat and floor."

As if that had been her objection to having him drive her to the Slash-C, to having him — and Donna, apparently — decide what was best for her and her daughter, to having him arrange it so she'd have to sit downstairs in the Flying W main house trying her best not to think about him taking a shower somewhere above her.

Chapter Seventeen

Val slowly breathed out her relief to get out of the Flying W main house and back in the truck. Slowly, just to show her breath who was in charge here.

The following intake of breath informed her she might have jumped from the proverbial frying pan into what felt like a fire crackling away inside her.

Her inhalation had drawn in the scent of clean, damp, warm male. And another scent that was all male because it was *Jack*. Completely Jack.

She desperately wanted to lean close and place her nose against his neck and sniff it in so deeply that she would carry it with her forever.

Conscious of exerting control, she leaned away from him, wedging herself against the passenger door. A move that bought her about an inch and a half. She'd become accustomed to Matty's bigger truck. This compact older truck had oddly intimate confines.

It wouldn't take much to stop hugging the passenger door, slide a bit to her left, maybe reach out to touch him...

No. How could she think about touching him when what mattered was his pain?

I carry it alone.

Was she using an attraction to him as a distraction from what truly mattered? Was she—

"How do you know Duane Jessup is full of himself?"

His abrupt words didn't make sense at first. "What?"

"Deputy Jessup." How'd you know he's full of himself."

She laughed. A short, surprised spurt of self-directed amusement. Her heart had been hammering over a look from him, and he'd been thinking about Deputy Jessup.

"What's funny?"

"Nothing. Really, truly, nothing. Not funny at all." She almost had her voice back under control. "Matty and I ran into him in town. Later on, she told me some about him."

Jack "huh'ed" acknowledgement of her answer, then cleared his throat. "Sheriff Kuerton says there's no reason to worry."

"I'm not worried." Not about Angi.

"That's the damned point, Valerie. You *should* have been."

She huffed. "There is no satisfying you."

He partially turned toward her, their eyes met. She saw in his the thought that she could satisfy him, and how.

She also saw that he wanted to look away. So did she. Against their combined better judgment, the look held. Stretched.

… get you in my bed.

Oh, good.

If the attraction was distraction, it wasn't one-sided.

Was it as unsettling to him as it was to her that it mixed in with that other element between them?

You said it was you and me. And that everything was going to be okay. Now I'm saying that to you, Jack Ralston. It's you and me. And everything will be okay. Tell me. So you're not carrying it alone anymore.

I carry it alone.

But what was *it?* Was it because he withdrew from people? Or did he withdraw because of whatever it was? It didn't seem to do with his parents' death or his upbringing, though they certainly must have laid a groundwork for his solitariness.

"What you need is yellow common monkeyflower," she blurted out.

"What?"

She couldn't fault him for his confusion. But at least it had broken the look. His eyes were back on the road.

"In fact, lots and lots of yellow common monkeyflower. That woman said it makes someone who had too much caution live with cheerful enthusiasm. That's what you need."

"What can you give someone who has too much enthusiasm? Something that'll serve up a damned good dose of caution?"

"I didn't need caution with Angi. She's a nice woman. She just needed a break. She's stressed and lonely. You have no idea what it's like."

"She's crazy."

"She's harmless."

"She knew your name — including middle name — your hometown and your occupation. And she tracked you down here. What if she wasn't — or isn't — who you think she is? Or even, what if you're right about her, but someone else puts the same pieces together?"

"You can play what if forever. What if that cow over there started flying and hit the windshield? What if a meteor struck in front of us? What if a tsunami hit us?"

"In Wyoming?"

"See, the fact that you picked that one out means some part of you thinks the others are possible." She reached across the space between them, placing her hand on the hard, warm strength of his arm below the turned-back cuff of his shirt. "You can't keep living like that, Jack. It takes too much out of you, bracing for every possible bad thing you have to be prepared for, trusting nobody, being on guard all the time."

She swore she felt the warmth ebb from his skin as if he withdrew without moving.

So she wasn't surprised at his tone when he said, "I'm fine."

Not surprised at all, really, yet she blinked fast several times to beat back a sudden burn in her eyes.

In silence, they pulled into the drive to the Slash-C home ranch, passing the thriving patch of yellow monkeyflower by the pump and trough, then following the curve of the drive around to the back.

There were several unfamiliar vehicles, a couple sporting Wisconsin license plates that belonged to Shane Garrison's family, she knew from Matty and Taylor.

Jack slowed the truck. "Going to drop you off here, then park by the office."

"By the office? But everybody's gathered and it'll be time to eat soon."

"Might have to get a bit of work in after supper."

She turned and looked at him. He was already laying the groundwork for leaving early, for getting off by himself while everyone else had a good time.

She had a choice.

Jump on the man now for anti-sociability that would make a hermit look like a party guy. Or maybe, just maybe, lighten his mood a bit so he'd have some chance of sharing the evening's enjoyment.

"If you think you're going to hide away in the office this evening, you don't know your boss' wife very well. Or her mother-in-law." He grimaced, then tried to hide it. That sign of vulnerability lifted her spirits. "Besides, I know the truth about what's really bothering you."

He faced her, and she saw another reaction — surprise. Better and better.

She climbed out of the truck, looking back in to say, "You're just cranky because Angi kept referring to Bryan as the young, good-looking cowboy. So, what does that make you?"

"The sane one," he called out after her as she turned and walked away.

She waved dismissively without looking back, then grinned when she heard his chuckle as he drove off.

****

Jack didn't want to know where Val was every second. He made no effort to know. He made every effort not to know. It happened anyway.

He'd ducked into the office, intending to start checking the supplies list he and Dave needed to go over.

That lasted about five minutes before Ed texted to get over there for dinner. Pronto.

As he shook hands with Shane and received a quick hug from Lisa, it was clear they'd already accepted Valerie and Addie as part of the group.

That only became more clear as Dave serve up perfectly grilled steaks to add to the roasted corn, fresh green beans, fruit salad, pasta salad, and biscuits that Matty had spread down the center of two long dining tables.

At one point, Lisa said, "It's so nice to have this chance to get together with just us—" She waved around the group that included her family, in-laws, long-time friends in Taylor and Cal, Val and Addie … and him. "—before the party Saturday. It will be wonderful to see everyone then, but this is special."

Later, Jack saw Lisa and Valerie with their heads together, talking earnestly.

He'd also seen her talking with every other person in the gathering, getting hugs from Taylor and even Cal, drawing smiles from various members of the Garrisons, helping Matty and Donna with the food, exchanging comments with Ed and Dave, tending to Addie, Brennan, and the two Ruskoff kids with efficient calm.

Every second. Every interaction. Every gesture.

Might've been that damned white blouse that seemed to glow like a beacon wherever she went.

It covered her from above her wrists, where the cuffs turned back, to her throat, framed by an open collar that should have had ever damned button buttoned, to below her waist, so it disappeared into the waistband of those jeans that would not, under any circumstances, make him think in terms of flowing over her like a lover's hands.

Would. Not. Think. That.

He was having enough trouble with that damned shirt.

If the jeans were gone, how far down did the shirt cover? Did it fall to the tops of her thighs? Or higher?

He swallowed.

His mistake had been sitting on the porch steps at the foreman's house.

He'd known that the second she'd come out the door. He was used to looking down at her. Knowing she was smaller, weaker, in need of protection. Looking up like that had somehow shifted how gravity worked for them.

In that moment, he'd seen the strength of the woman raising a great kid on her own, a woman who'd made a success of her blog against the odds, a woman helping fellow mothers. The woman Angi Pilson so admired.

And he'd realized he hadn't looked at her blog once since Val had arrived. Not even when Hugh Moski's comment — "Good to see you've come around to letting Val put you on her blog." — had set him.

Did he not want to remember her strengths?

He'd pushed aside the question as they'd left the foreman's house, but it kept resurfacing, poking at him as he got ready, during the drive, and throughout his efforts now to not watch her.

A touch on his arm jolted Jack around, so Val was only in the corner of his eye.

That was better. Had to be better.

Except the touch had come from Donna Currick. And she was looking at him now like his skull was made of glass and every thought inside it was bright and clear for her to read.

"Haven't had a chance to talk with you tonight, Jack." She smiled. "In fact, I've hardly set eyes on you for weeks."

"Storm," he muttered.

"I'm sure that's kept you busy today, but it must be ..." She tipped her head, as if in an effort of memory. "Why, I haven't seen you to talk since you started giving Val riding lessons."

"Bryan's been teaching her."

"Filling in a couple times for you." She waved that away as inconsequential. She smiled brightly. "I was so glad to see you helping Valerie that way, especially that first time."

"Would have been happy to let you take over." At least partly happy. He didn't say that last part, but with his luck, she'd heard it in his silence. He'd had the feeling over the years that Donna Currick heard more than he said.

"Maybe at the very beginning you would have been," she said.

He cut a look at her and found her smiling up at him. Then the smile slid away and something else came into her eyes. "But not after you started laughing. I don't believe I'd ever heard you laugh before, Jack. Not once since you came here."

First, he was aware that silence had fallen around them, because everyone else on the patio was listening and watching. And then he realized what had come into Donna's eyes were tears.

A sound came from Val, off to his side. Before he could turn, she was thrusting Addie into Ed's arms and saying, "Look after Addie a minute, will you?"

"Sure." Ed gathered in the girl.

Val had already pivoted away. Now she took off at a full-speed walk into the shadows toward the barn.

He'd heard — they'd all heard — the shake in her voice. But nobody moved. None of them went after her.

"Shouldn't somebody...?" He looked around at the others.

Ed gave an arms-full-of-nearly-asleep-kid shrug.

"I'll take Addie," Jack offered, reaching.

Ed tightened his hold. "Val left her with me." And that was that. He wasn't giving up the girl and he wasn't going after Val to find out what was wrong.

He looked at Dave next. His boss didn't meet the look, instead stacking plates and gathering utensils from the table. "KP duty," he muttered.

"Matty? She's your friend," Jack tried.

She looked him straight in the eye and lied, "I hear one of the kids fussing. I need to stay here."

Taylor and Lisa stood in unison. "You're right," Taylor said. "We better go check."

Donna nodded with what looked to be approval. The tears were gone from her eyes as she looked at him now. "Go, Jack."

He looked over his shoulder in the direction Val had gone. She stepped from one of the circles of lights strung along the near corral fence, hidden by the shadows for an instant until she emerged into the next circle. Her hands were fists by her side, her head was down, her shoulders up. And moving. Like she was —.

He swore.

"Go now, Jack," Donna said from behind him, her small hands pushing at his back.

He was already going.

Val was moving at a good clip, but his longer stride ate up the difference as she turned the corner of the corral fence, heading into the barn.

"Val."

"Go away."

He could have caught up with her in the middle of the barn, but decided to wait until they were through the barn and out the other set of wide doors. The two horses in stalls were moving restlessly, probably picking up Val's emotion. Had nothing to do with being out of sight of the people on the patio.

The fact that he stopped her in a rare gap in the lighting was happenstance.

"Val, I don't know what's wrong, but don't cry."

He caught her shoulders and turned her around.

"I am not crying." But she was. Even in these shadows, he saw she had her eyes closed tight while tears slid out the sides.

"Don't be sad." What a damned fool thing to say. This was why he kept his mouth shut. This was part of why —

"And I'm not sad. I'm *mad*." She thunked a fist against his chest and he got the point.

Those thin arms and small hands carried more of a wallop than he would have expected. Yes, he got the point. "Mad?"

"Mad," she confirmed. "Angry. Irked. Irate. Furious. And if you can't tell the difference between sad and mad, it's the final proof that you have spent far too much time with cows, mister. Because let me tell you, I am not hard to read. This —" She made a whirlwind circling motion with her hand near her face. "—is not hard to read. It says what I'm feeling. Every Italian, Irish, Portuguese emotion right here. All right here."

"Finnish," he unwisely added.

"The Finnish and Puritan New England blood can go stand in the corner and be quiet, because I'm *mad*."

"At what?"

"At you, you idiot."

"What did I do?'"

"You laughed." And then she sobbed.

He froze. "You're mad? Because I laughed?" he ventured.

"Not *because* you laughed. But because your laughing was a damned *event* because you *don't* laugh. How many years? How many? Donna's known you all this time and she'd never heard you laugh before? How can that be? How can you do that?"

He'd laughed that last night. At the party. He was sure he had. Before their fight. Before she was gone.

"You have to laugh, Jack Ralston. Do you hear me?" Her hands were on either side of his face, making him look at her. No, he wanted to look at her. He needed to. "You have to laugh. A lot. All the time. And live. You have to live. And—"

He took her mouth.

Not a gentle kiss.

A taking. Possessing her mouth to ease all that wanting and needing in him.

She answered. Giving as strongly as he was taking. Reaching up to him, while he wrapped her tight against him to hold them both up.

Their mouths separated. They gasped in the damned oxygen their bodies demanded, overriding other demands of their bodies.

Then she came back to him. Arms around his neck drawing him

down, her breasts and abdomen pressing against him like she'd climb him if she had to. She didn't, because he wrapped her tighter, drew her higher, and then her tongue was in his mouth, taking now, too. He'd give her all she wanted, all he had. He'd —

He jerked away, breathing hard.

"Oh, Jack."

"No. Sorry—"

She reached toward him. He stepped back, then kept going. Into the dark.

Chapter Eighteen

Val rolled over, staring at the clock.

When she'd returned to the patio for Addie, the Curricks and their guests discretely pretended she'd done a better job of wiping her face than she had. They'd insisted she and Addie stay overnight, as Jack had said they would. Addie had been delighted to share Brennan and Finn's room. Matty and Donna had made up the convertible couch here in the new ranch office for her, making sure she had all the amenities.

Including the clock that told her that if she went to sleep right now, she'd get four and half, maybe five hours of sleep. If Addie slept in.

Addie wasn't going to sleep in.

And she wasn't going to sleep right now.

Jack wasn't going to let her.

He'd kissed her. He'd finally, finally kissed her. Oh, boy, had he kissed her.

And the disparity in their heights had this totally unexpected benefit. You'd think it might be awkward because they couldn't just lean forward and meet, mouth to mouth. He had to bend down, she had to reach up. To keep their balance as they kissed and kissed, they had to hold onto each other, and lean into each other, with the glorious friction of body to body. Yeah, there'd been the problem with his belt buckle, but that could be dealt with next time.

If there was a next time.

It wasn't the kissing that made her wonder if there'd be a next time.

Far from it.

It was his expression just before he said, "No— Sorry." And strode away into the dark.

He'd gone somewhere. Somewhere bad.

It made her stomach clench.

Breathe, Valerie Prudence Trimarco. Breathe.

It was like the time when she'd been fifteen and got caught in a riptide off Good Harbor Beach. As well as she knew that beach and the ways of the water, the panic almost took her under at first. She kept telling herself to fight the panic, not the water. Don't try to swim against the tide, don't try to yank yourself free of it. Swim parallel. Stay afloat.

Stay afloat...

That what the lesson to remember now. Don't try to go straight at it. Not now. Just stay afloat.

And try to keep him afloat.

To not let the riptide of what she'd seen in his face take him away. Far, far out where she couldn't reach him. Where no one could reach him.

****

Matty Brennan Currick was ruthless and direct.

"I'd sure appreciate your help today preparing for the party, Val," Matty said over breakfast. Her fellow family members exchanged meaningful looks. "I hear you make great brownies. Please say you'll stay today and help."

So, yes, Matty was ruthless, and, yes, Val stayed and helped, along with Lisa and Taylor. Donna and Shane's mother watched the collected kids.

In the morning, they baked Trimarco brownies, cookies, and sheet cakes while Pamela Dobson cleaned the rest of the house. After lunch, Pamela took on the kitchen and they moved on to patio. They swept, strung colored lights, and spruced up planters, while Bryan and another ranch hand set up a line of grills, then hauled in folded tables and chairs to be set up the next day.

When a battered truck pulled in and parked, Matty pushed back hair loosened from her braid and said, "Oh, good, Zoe's here. A great excuse to take a break. I'll get iced tea and lemonade."

The babies were napping, but the older kids swooped in for their share of refreshments, then were tasked with taking drinks to the two ranch hands.

175

"I thought you might want an update," Zoe Parisi said when everyone was settled.

"Thank you, yes. How's Angi?" Val asked.

"She was doing fine when I left her up in Billings. We thought some distance would be a good idea."

Donna tipped her head. "We? You consulted Doc Johnson?"

"Well, no. I made the decision after talking to the folks up there. It separates her from here — from Valerie — and now she's already accomplished some of the journey home. That helps starting to shift her thinking. They're talking to her and observing. If everything goes according to plan, I expect she'll be released tomorrow morning. Her husband's flying in to drive back with her. The folks up there will talk to him first, of course. Both on how to support Angi and to make sure she gets continued help when they get home. And the drive should give them time alone as a couple, which apparently they haven't had since their first child was born."

"Poor woman. I *said* she wasn't dangerous." Val became aware no one joined her in scoffing at the idea. "C'mon, she's not. She's a nice woman with way too much on her plate, a husband who's not helping and possibly her hormones out of whack from pregnancy and breastfeeding."

"Don't underestimate out-of-whack hormones," Donna said quietly.

"No kidding," Matty agreed fervently.

Zoe nodded. "She is a nice woman, but she's also under stress, feeling overwhelmed and isolated. Throw in hormones, and it's not a good combination."

Val snorted. "Most women deal with that combination all the time."

"Right. They deal with it. They don't run away from home," Donna said. "And fixate on someone they've never met."

"Fixate? That's an exaggeration—"

Donna interrupted. "Zoe?"

The young doctor responded with a noncommittal shrug. But then she said, "She'd planned this meticulously. Preparing food for her family, writing long, detailed instructions for her husband — a complete manual. Apparently that scared the man more than anything else. That he might be expected to live up to all those should-dos."

The group chuckled, but turned serious again as the young doctor continued, "She also put in an incredible effort to find you, Valerie. It wasn't like she'd just happened to recognize where you were. Apparently she spent hours and hours and hours over quite a few days methodically searching photos on the Internet for mountains that matched what you'd put on your blog.

"Once she identified the mountains and figured a rough area that would have that view, she bought expensive software to zoom in and focus in order to make out the ranch name from that fuzzy view of the side of the truck."

"That sounds like obsession," Lisa said with a frown.

"Good grief," Matty muttered.

Val chuckled, though she was a bit taken aback by the lengths Angi had gone to. "Don't tell Jack. I'll never hear the end of the told-you-sos."

No one else cracked a smile.

"Jack's concerned about you and Addie," Matty said with a hint of reproach. "I was glad he had the good sense not to let you two go back to the foreman's house last night."

Not let — ? Val fought the urge to bristle at that. "So now that we know Angi's all set, if I can catch a ride with someone to the Flying W—"

"Oh, no, you're staying here," Matty protested. "Tonight and tomorrow night for sure."

"There's no reason—"

"The party will go late tomorrow, Addie will already be asleep. You don't want to yank her up and—"

"She'll sleep through—.

"You're forgetting," Donna said. "Addie's already been told she's staying here tonight and tomorrow night."

Checkmate.

Donna smiled sweetly. "I'll drive you over to pick up anything the two of you need for the next few days, Val."

****

Ed straightened from checking Buster's left front hoof.

Jack had checked all of them himself yesterday. "Bryan did a good job," he said now.

"He did." The older man patted the horse and the two men walked in silence back toward the barn.

Jack said, "Ed, this party for Lisa and Shane tomorrow ..."

If Ed had been off with Donna on one of their protracted trips, Jack wouldn't have hesitated going to Dave. Even though Dave could be more unpredictable. Not with ranch business, but … other matters. Matty's influence was the X factor that sometimes made Dave's responses harder to figure.

But he'd had versions of this conversation often enough with Ed that they took on a familiar rhythm. Next Ed said …

"What about the party, Jack? Sure hope you're coming. Donna made sure to invite you special."

"Yes, sir, she did. The thing is, there's a lot of work to be done. We'll be doctoring the cattle in the Morton Creek field, if we go as long as light holds out we can finish up."

"Light holds out real long this time of year. You're going to keep all the hands there?"

"No. They'll want to go to the party."

"Ah, so you'll let the others go at noon like you did last year. And keep working yourself like you did last year. You know, there'll be just as much work to do the next day even if you do get to every head."

That was a bit of a deviation from the usual script. Ed didn't usually raise more than a token objection. "Yes, sir."

"We'd really like to have you join us, Jack. I can understand you not caring for the surprise of that party last month. The surprise and being put in the spotlight like that."

The older man gave him a sharp look from under his eyebrows.

Jack felt the concern behind it, but also its cut. He'd told Ed Currick — and only Ed — the bare outlines of his story when he'd been offered the job. He hadn't when he was drifting from job to job, but Ed had made it clear he was offering something steadier. So he deserved to know. And the man was plenty shrewd enough to piece together more.

"But this won't be like that. No surprise, no spotlight," Ed went on. "This is just a gathering of folks who enjoy each other's company."

That was a stretch. It was a gathering of the extended Currick clan and their wide circle of good friends, which included much of Lewis and Clark counties and a swath beyond..

"Nick Hustine and Nancy are coming," Ed added, naming a former part-time hand at the Slash-C and his wife. "And of course that nice gal, Valerie Trimarco will be here. Cute as can be. Her and the little girl, Addison Rose. And nobody's connected as close to them as you are."

Jack remained silent.

Ed sighed deeply as they entered the barn. It was a concession. There'd been a detour, but now the conversation was back on track. "No one's going to tell you what to do. I certainly won't say you should or shouldn't—"

"Well, I will." At Donna's calm voice both he and Ed turned and stared as she came toward them down the barn's wide center aisle.

She gave her husband a look that seemed to Jack to carry a lot of messages.

"You are a wonderful man, Ed Currick," she said with a warmth in her voice that tugged hard at something deep in Jack. It didn't feel comfortable, but somehow he wasn't ready to shut it out, this tugging. "If someone asks you for help, you give it. I've seen you do it time past counting in our years together. Even if someone doesn't ask you. But then there are people who don't want help. People who are determined to not allow themselves to have any help, no matter what."

Donna turned to him, and Jack needed every bit of brain power and backbone to not say, *Yes'm*, and do whatever she told him to do.

What was it with short women and him?

"People like Jack, here. And that's where you aren't as good — telling this kind of person, ones like Jack," she added, as if she hadn't been clear, "that they're going to get help whether they want it or not."

"I made a promise," Ed said softly.

"I figured you did. It was probably the only way to get Jack to be here at the Slash-C when he first came — ah, yes, I see from his face that it was."

What the hell she meant by that when he was damned sure not a muscle in his face had budged he didn't know.

"I'd never ask you to break a promise, Ed," she was saying. "The problem is that what Jack needed when he first came has become a burden now. It's like a puppy that you keep inside a fenced yard when it's young so it doesn't wander off, get hurt. But as it grows up, the yard is too small, the dog doesn't have the space it needs. Ah, I see you don't like being compared to a puppy, Jack."

"I didn't—"

"How about this analogy, then. I knew a dancer who hurt her leg. She had to protect it for quite a while so it could heal. But then the time came when the doctor said it was time to start using it. The first time she tried it hurt. It hurt a lot. So, instead of trying to do a little more on it each day, she went back to protecting it. And the muscles grew weaker and weaker. Until she could barely use those muscles at all.

"Whatever your injury, Jack, I know it was real. I know it was — and is — painful. You needed to protect yourself early on. All that's true. It's also true that you made a change some time back. So slow, so gradual, it was hard to spot. You surely didn't realize it at the time or I'm sure you'd've tried to undo it. Might not realize it even now, but we're not going to let you undo it. At the start, and for quite a while, you worked each day like it was a limbo to be endured, only to face the same thing the next day. You worked hard, but with no heart. What's changed is the heart. And that's meant you start a day looking forward to what it holds.

"But you're still standing back seeing what the day sends. You're not reaching out to grab hold of it. You're still in a cast."

For an instant he thought she'd said *past*. He made the mistake of meeting her gaze during that instant.

She didn't let up. "That's gone on too long. Now you've got to stop protecting your injury. You've got to risk some pain. Or you'll never be able to stand on both feet again."

She put one hand to his cheek.

"Ed made you a promise. I didn't. Not then, anyway. But I am making you one now. I'm going to do my best to push, prod, and order you into using those parts of you you've let weaken to such a dangerous level by trying to protect them. Starting by saying, yes, you *will* come to the party tomorrow. As part of your official duties as foreman of the Slash-C, as one of the representatives of the Slash-C, and as our friend."

She smiled that sweet smile at him, and if he wasn't numbed by the fact that she'd as good as threatened him, he might have smiled back.

"That includes escorting Valerie to the party. No — don't even try. Besides, it won't take all that much time, since she's staying in the office again tonight. Don't forget the spare bulbs for the colored lights, Ed," she added before walking away as calmly as ever.

Ed clapped one hand to his shoulder, and said with a blend of compassion and humor, "You're in for it now, son."

Chapter Nineteen

Valerie unhooked the office's screen door, pushed it open to let Addie outside. But not wide enough that she'd have to see him standing on the porch calling for her, as Donna had ordered.

From behind the door, Val said, "I'll be ready in a minute. Will you keep an eye on Addie? Donna will be here anytime to pick her up. Okay?"

She'd let the door swing closed while her daughter made for the flower box on the north side of the porch. But now she opened it up again, stepped out and said, "Will you keep an eye on her?"

It seemed an unnecessary question. "I'm looking at her," he pointed out. Better to focus on the daughter than the mother anyhow. Especially since he'd seen she was wearing a dress. How could someone so short have legs that looked like that?

"Not the same thing. And I'm not risking something happening to her because I thought you were watching her and you didn't hear me or otherwise know you were supposed to be looking out for her."

"Okay, okay. I'm watching."

"Okay." She pivoted, swung the door wide, and marched inside. Each motion swung the material of that dress, hinting at a slightly different combination of muscles, bones, sinew and flesh working together. The combinations gave him a fresh appreciation for the formation of her bottom and legs that had his throat working long after the door slapped closed.

This was bad.

He had to get his mind — and other parts of him — to stop fixating on her backside. Or any other parts of her.

He dropped down to sit on the porch, twisting sideways to lean against the post, and putting one boot on the porch floor, the other down a step, letting the bent leg cover the tightness in his jeans.

Addie straightened from the flower bed, then brushed her hands against each other in a gesture that was so like her mother that he looked away. He kept listening, however, tracking her footsteps on the wooden porch.

So he wasn't entirely surprised when the toe of first one pint-sized shoe, then another entered the limited field of vision allowed by his lowered cowboy hat.

"Whatcha doing, Jack?"

Instead of answering, he huhed in disapproval. "You've got a shoelace untied. Step on that and you'll go down on your nose."

"Dow' on 'er nose," she parroted.

"Or worse," he added, since she didn't seem to be taking it seriously. He took the trailing laces in his big hands and wondered if he'd be able to manipulate them. Amazing that the entire foot of this decidedly individual human being wasn't much longer than his thumb. "You shouldn't be wearing those flimsy things at all. You need boots if you're going to be walking around here."

"Boots like Brennan."

"That's right." He figured with the Trimarco females it was best to grab hold of anything resembling agreement whenever you had the chance. "Boots'll protect your feet better from rocks—"

"Rocks."

"—or twisting your ankle—" He pulled the loop through on the bow. "Ankle."

"—or snakes." A double knot should keep it more secure. Might as well do the other one, too.

"Snakes."

He shouldn't have said that one. "Don't worry, we wouldn't let you go where snakes are. But sometimes they can be where you don't expect them."

Like Valerie Trimarco was where he'd definitely never expected her.

Inside his head. Inside—.

"Why are they were you don't 'spect 'em?"

"Because they're sneaky. That's why you have to listen when I say no." Why wouldn't her mother listen when he said no? Why wouldn't any of them? He patted the top of her second shoe, signifying the complete of his double-knot there. "Understand?"

She didn't answer or repeat. Instead she dropped down into a squat in front of him, bringing her head under the brim of his hat, still lowered from his focus on her shoes.

Before he reacted to that she reached out and put her palms on either side of his face, forcing him to look at her.

Forcing him.

Ridiculous. As if she had the muscle to force him to do anything.

But she had the power.

The memory of Donna's one-handed version of this touch flashed through him.

He felt the rub of grit still on Addie's palms, proving her Valerie-like brushing off movement hadn't completely succeeded. Then, as he brought his gaze to her face, it felt as if the grit had transferred to his eyes and his throat.

Yes, she definitely had the power.

Forced or not, he was looking at her, just as she'd wanted.

He stared into this child's eyes. Open wide, hiding nothing. So ... safe. He didn't think he'd ever seen eyes exactly like that.

Her mother's eyes were similar, the melting color, the shape, the dark lashes. But with Val there was that zing between them that complicated things. Even when Val was determined to ignore the zing, the effort that took cast a shadow that proclaimed the existence of what it tried to deny.

With Addie it was simpler. Simpler than he could ever remember. Ever.

"Don't be scared, Jack," Addie said.

Lost in staring at her eyes, he struggled to absorb the words.

"Scared? I'm n—"

Donna Currick's voice cut across his. "Addie, are you ready? Time to come over to the main house."

Addie dropped her hold on Jack's face and skipped down the stairs without a care.

Leaving him suspended, still feeling her hold. On his cheeks and in a part of him so much deeper than his flesh.

Donna took Addie's offered hand at the bottom of the stairs and turned to start away, then turned back. "Sorry to interrupt, Jack, but I had to so you wouldn't lie to a child."

She was gone before he could protest.

Lie? What —

Oh. He'd been about to tell Addie he wasn't scared. Donna meant —

Before he could complete the thought, much less absorb the impact, the screen door squeaked open, then slapped closed. He came to his feet, needing to be on his feet, ready to move. It had nothing to do with avoiding a repeat of the moment at the Flying W foreman's house, looking up at her, feeling gravity shift.

Val stood in front of him, a tilted smile on her face. "Scary, isn't she?"

He thought she meant Addie. But Donna qualified, too, so maybe she meant both.

That thought might be what slowed his reactions enough that he didn't anticipate.

Before he knew it, Val had put her hands up to his cheeks, where Addie's had been. But the effect of this touch was not at all the same.

The grubbiness of Addie's contact had scratched down through layers of resistance in ways he hadn't realized until Val's palms — for all their cool smoothness — flowed heated balm into him.

"That girl of mine would have been branded a witch for sure if she'd been born three- or four-hundred years ago." Her soft palms brushed at the grit on one side, then the other. "Did you know there were women accused of witchcraft in Gloucester right around the same time as Salem? But none of ours were ever hanged. So there's probably witch blood flowing through—"

He stopped her words and her motion by grasping her wrists. His hands easily encircled the narrow juncture of delicate bones.

She looked up, and there were those eyes. Like her daughter's, not at all like her daughter's. Wide, and brown, and challenging, and warm ... heating.

Her breathing had picked up. Without looking away from her eyes, he was aware of her breasts rising and falling faster under the light fabric of that dress. Narrow straps were all that held it up.

"Have to go." His words were jerky.

She nodded. "You're right. We don't want to be late for the party."

That wasn't what he'd meant, but what choice did he have?

He released her wrists, and watched her descend the stairs in front of him. He sucked in a breath and followed her.

****

Val absently rubbed a wrist.

She'd caught herself doing that ever since they joined the people happily milling around the patio and into the main house. She did it absently while she greeted, helped, talked, laughed, shared, mingled with people she'd come to like a lot. She was having a good time, truly she was. Yet she was partially disconnected. Because, as she did all those things, a portion of her was still back in that moment.

He hadn't hurt her. Certainly hadn't left any bruises. But he had left an impression.

Many impressions, in fact.

Of the strength and weight of his hands.

Of the physical contact's effect on her hormones. Which had mostly been *He's touching me. Yay! Let's go for more!*

Of the struggle inside the man. The flex and release of his hold. Never enough to hurt, at least not to hurt *her*, but what about himself? It was as if that flex and release had been a barometer to emotions pulsing through him. And his emotions had had nothing to do with the Let's-party response of her hormones.

What it all came down to was that instinct had made him grasp her wrists. But then he hadn't known what to do with the grip he had on her.

Her heartbeat stuttered at broader implications of that thought.

He didn't know what to do with the grip he had on her.

That didn't bode well for her.

****

He'd done better than he usually did at parties.

Maybe with so many guests it was natural that he'd find a few — or they found him — to sit with at a table, interspersing widely separated comments into watching the swirl of people.

Ed came by, set a drink in front of him and clapped him on the shoulder with a "Good boy." Shane Garrison and his father came and sat for a while, talking with him about sports and the ranch. Matty brought him a plate of food that could have lasted a village a week. Lisa gave him a sisterly hug before being called away. Addie, Brennan and a half dozen other kids zipped around the table three times in some game of their own making. On the last pass Addie threw her arms around as much of him as she could, shouted, "Jack!" in his ear, then took off again. Taylor took the seat Shane had occupied earlier and asked about Phantom, then listened when Cal showed up and the talk turned to cattle. While they were at it, Donna stood at the far side of the table, smiled beatifically and gave him a nod of approval that would have warmed him if he'd let it.

Val kept her distance.

That was okay. In fact it was good. The dress was worse than that damned white blouse. If he'd had to see it up close…

Between her keeping her distance, the size of the crowd, and the blue of the dress blending in more than her blouse had Thursday night, especially once it got full dark, it was harder to keep track of her. That was good, too.

Until he didn't spot her at all. As much as half an hour since he'd last seen her for sure. Back when Addie had been over there on the porch swing with some other kids, being read a story by Shane's mother, and Val had been nearby.

He stood to look over the section of patio filled with dancing couples. No Valerie.

Maybe she was putting Addie to bed in one of the rooms used as kids' dorms. He'd seen how that worked at other parties. They stacked 'em up side by side like firewood and the kids slept like they'd been knocked out — maybe they had, from the combination of excitement, food, exercise, and stimulation. But they recovered fast, waking up early, ready for the next adventure while the parents, some of whom had stayed up dancing most of the night, could only groan.

He sat back down and waited as long as he thought it might take to put a kid to bed, plus two minutes. He didn't waste the time, using it to scan the crowd more carefully. No Valerie Prudence Trimarco.

Time was up.

She was gone. Missing.

He made himself breathe slowly. She wasn't missing. Zoe Parisi had said Angi Pilson was on her way back to Minnesota, and certainly no one here presented a danger to Val.

He stood, excused himself.

He'd brought her here, even if it was only a hundred feet from the ranch office. He'd find her.

He took a deliberate route from his table's back corner, though the maze of other tables, around the dancers, past a spattering of couples along the corral fence. One couple slipped into the barn, but the female wore jeans, not a blue dress, and had blonde hair, not dark curls.

By now he was in the open area between the main house and the other buildings. As he kept walking, he looked at the rows of parked vehicles, but few had left. He saw a female figure among them … then recognized the minister's wife returning to the party with a sweater.

A dim light showed from the office, but it was hard to tell if it was inside or the reflection of landscaping and party lights. He angled closer to it.

Enough light showed inside that he saw the temporary ladder set up to reach the loft, now that the staircase was down for the week.

Movement.

On the ladder.

He was across the space, up the steps, in the screen door before he knew it.

"What the hell, Valerie—"

She looked over her shoulder, which was damned stupid, since she only had one hand holding the side of the ladder, while the other held a stack of books. "Oh. Hi, Jack."

As he swung the main door closed behind him, he controlled his voice. If she slipped— "What do you think you're doing?"

"Coming down the ladder." She suited action to word. Down one rung, then the next.

He refused to let his eyes notice the way the skirt moved around her legs. Or how much of her legs he could see.

"Everybody said I could borrow as many books as I wanted any time. They said there are lots about old-time cowboys like you'd talked about. I found some that look really interesting. Cowboys from back in the late 1800s writing about their lives—" she hitched a shoulder to indicate the books she held. "—and I thought I'd like to read them, so I — ah."

"What the—"

But she'd righted herself before he was to the ladder. He wasn't worried about the sturdiness of the ladder. He'd built it to hold his weight. But she had on flat-soled sandals that could have had a layer of ice permanently attached to their bottoms, judging by the way they slid across the rung. The armful of books didn't help.

"You're going to break your neck wearing those shoes. Give me the books."

She handed down the books, which he tossed on the seat of an overstuffed chair nearby.

"They are a little slippery. The shoes, not the books."

Smiling, she turned to look at him as she said that, and the soles of her sandals slid across the rung again.

"A little," he grumbled. He grabbed at her, and got a fistful of skirt with one hand, while the other was spread wide, cupping the curve of her butt cheek through the fabric.

"Oh!"

She squeaked that, as if he'd pinched her, when he was doing his damnedest not to close his fingers around her flesh the way they wanted to, in a squeeze that —

"Oh," she said again. In an entirely different tone that was like a jolt of electricity to the nerves in his fingers. Judging from her voice she had looked over her shoulder. For some reason that sent another zing to his nerves, and in places a good distance from his fingers.

He felt the rise and drop of his chest, was aware of the sound that made, aware of her breathing hard, too. Once, twice, three times.

"If you'll, uh, just steady me here for a second..." She faced forward again, proving her recovery time was faster than his. Damn it. "Then I can get my feet back under me and..."

But her feet slid again and he found himself with his arms stretched up, now each hand cupping a butt cheek and his head tipped back to observe the operation, but also taking in the sweet roundedness of her posterior above him.

He muttered curses. It worked when a horse stepped on his foot. A good long string of curses, the regular ones and some creative ones put together on the spot, would distract his mind from what his body was experiencing.

Only he was only able to think of a few curses now, so he had to keep repeating them, muttered or in his head, and it wasn't working. Wasn't distracting his mind. Or his body.

"Good," she said.

"Good?" *Good?* Was she crazy?

"Yeah," she said, though he didn't think it was in response to his mental question. "With that support I can..."

He felt more than saw the shift as she extended her leg, reaching, searching for the next rung down.

As first one foot then the other found a perch on that lower rung, he transferred the corresponding hand to her waist.

That had to better. Right?

No.

Now she was low enough that he could smell her hair.

How bad would it be to bury his face in that scent? He'd have to climb up one rung. He could do that, and his body would trap her, keep her safe, so—.

Bad. It would be bad.

As bad as squeezing her butt? Close call. Maybe —

"Okay, I'm hopping down now."

Hopping?

The sound of the syllables conveyed no meaning at all to brain circuitry occupied with something else entirely.

Then she was turning toward him at the same time she jumped.

God, she was jumping. He'd had to release one side of her waist. But his other arm encircled her, scooping her toward him, while his newly freed arm went around her back.

She brushed against him as she descended. The contact of her breasts down his chest like a butterfly of flame. Her hands touched lightly on his shoulders, then followed that trail of fire blazed by her breasts.

He forced his arms to loosen as he pounded logic into his brain. She'd brushed against him. So what. Barely touched him... Oh, *hell. Barely.*

Barely.

Bare.

Her. Him. Bare.

"Thanks, Jack." She smiled up at him.

"What in damnation were you doing?"

She blinked, but her smile didn't disappear. "I told you. Getting books on cowboys. Maybe I'll find out the whole story behind what you said about cowboys leaving. Selling their saddle."

He rubbed his face. "Okay. So you've got your books. You can leave now."

"Leave? No, I'm sleeping here. I thought I'd read some before going to sleep."

"What?"

She tipped her head toward the couch in the alcove. His sluggish brain took in that the back cushions were stacked on a chair and the seat cushions had been partially covered in bedding. "Sleeping. Here. Me." She tapped her chest to emphasize the final word.

Damn, he wished she hadn't done that. The motion made the neckline of that dress dip for an instant. That was enough. No bra.

"I knew you got ready here. I didn't think…"

No. he didn't think. Couldn't think.

"Where do you think I've slept the past two nights? With you making such a big deal of me not being alone in the foreman's house, the Curricks have insisted Addie and I stay here. Addie's in with all the other kids in the old office in the main house. It looks like camp or something with kids tucked in practically every nook and cranny. I guess some folks will scoop up their kids and take them home tonight, but I understand others leave them to sleep peacefully and many won't be leaving until dawn anyway, so …"

His arms were around her again. She was here. Right here. Looking at him. Her mouth… that mouth he'd tasted two nights ago. He had to… He had to…

He kissed her, pressing her back against the ladder. But only for a moment, then her arms were around his neck, opening her mouth to him.

They were moving. He pushed something aside with his leg. They were turning, her feet off the ground, the sway of that rubbing her against him while their mouths never parted.

He'd had no consciousness of it, but he must have been aiming for the couch, because there it was. Perfect. Perfect.

He sat, taking her with him, the two of them cooperating to drape her over him, straddling.

"Oh," she breathed into his mouth, as their bodies aligned and she must have felt the change in his.

He released her mouth.

"It's okay. We won't..." One strap of her dress had slid of her shoulder, he drew down the material in the middle to kiss the top curves of her breasts. Lick it, kiss again. "We'll... But we're not going to..."

"No, no. Absolutely not. *Ah.*"

He'd pushed the other strap down, the top dropping. He stroked across her breasts, absorbing the peaked softness. Her breath came short, sharp.

She shifted an arm, he drew that strap down, freeing her on one side, the other.

"Just..."

"Yeah. But not ...

"No. None of that."

He put his mouth over her nipple and drew on her. His arms supported her as she arched into him with a cry.

"If you..." His hands on her waist drew her down tight against the bulge of his groin. They rocked against each other. The rhythm... "*There ... Oh, God.*"

"Jack," she whispered. "Jack."

He raised his head to kiss up her throat, one hand spread at the base of her skull as her head fell back.

"I could..." His other hand, under her skirt, brushed at the junction of her legs.

"But you. ..." She straightened, her hands on his zipper. His hands over hers meant to still her, but somehow they were helping. And he was free.

"Condom," he said. "We won't, but in case, maybe..."

"We won't." Was she repeating? Asking? Disputing?

"No. We won't."

Both hands under her skirt, down her back, under her panties, cupping her, holding her to him as he sucked again on her nipple. She rocked against him with the rhythm.

Their rhythm now.

Their rhythm.

She felt the end of his penis against the fabric separating them. Then at the edge of the fabric —.

"Condom," she said on a gasp. "In case."

His movements extracting it from his jeans pocket nearly pushed her over the edge. She kissed him with some vague thought of slowing… It didn't slow anything. Especially not when he paused while putting on the condom to kiss her back. She was shaking as he finished.

Her dress had risen back over a breast. He drew it down with a deliberate, slow motion that drew a long breath from her even before he touched her. He put his mouth on her and sucked.

Sucked harder, until she was rocking with the pleasure and the need. His hands at her waist kept her steady. Her hands in his hair held him to her.

If he touched her now… *Oh, please, please touch me now.*

But if she felt this way, he must, too. Her fingers stroked down his chest… *Huh, when had his shirt been opened.* …lower, lower, to touch him, to cup him.

His hips came off the couch with his groan.

With one hand he grabbed both of hers and pulled them up, away.

"Not unless you want to—"

"No, no," she assured him. Then the tip of his covered penis found an opening between flesh and fabric created by all the shifting and moving, and touched her. She felt herself opening, yearning to draw him inside her, wanting … "Yes," she whimpered.

His strong hands came to her waist, holding her tight. He would lift her up, away from her own temptation. He would end this. He would—

He brought her down as his hips thrust up.

"*Ah!*"

Their rhythm was there. In them, between them. She felt it rising in her, tipping, quick and bright, in a release of long abstinence. Without ever faltering, it built again, more, more. Fast and hard and complete. His arching strength beneath her, inside her. The shuddering collapse…

His forearms crossed at her back, her face buried into the top of his shoulder. His face turned, into her hair.

Her muscles were gone, useless, but every nerve thrummed.

And celebrated.

Chapter Twenty

They'd settled into boneless comfort without changing position. Eventually, he raised one hand and stroked her hair. It made her eyes sting.

He was so gentle. So … loving. To her, to Addie. When he'd let himself be. When one of them got under his guard. When his guard was lowered … as it was now.

"That must have been a doozy," she said against the side of his neck.

"What?"

"The end-of-relationship that's soured you on humanity. Because all your instincts are to, ah, enjoy the benefits of being connected to people, so something—"

"I'm not soured on humanity."

She raised her head and gave him a level look.

He twitched an eyebrow in barely-there-concession. "Just don't spend a whole lot of time with them."

"Especially online."

"That's hardly humanity."

"Sure it is. It's people online. And you want nothing to do with them. Why?"

"Experience."

Experience… The way he felt about the Internet… "So it was an online relationship?"

"No."

"Then why—"

"Was all this working up to getting me to a state where I'd spill my guts?"

She jolted upright, whacking the top of her head into his chin. He groaned, but no way was she going to be distracted now.

"You think this was all a big plan to *seduce* you in order to get you to talk, Jack Ralston?"

"I didn't—"

"Of course — it's so obvious. I came up with the plan to celebrate my child's unusual birth, set up everything ahead of time, traveled three-quarters of the way across the country, all so I could get you in the sack as a prelude to asking you questions. And I suppose I planned that you'd act like a jackass when I showed up, too? I'll tell you, I should be in the Pentagon with planning skills like that. They sure could use me looking that far ahead and—. Oh, wait, no. It wasn't only this summer."

She pushed at his chest to get herself more upright.

He *hmm*'ed in apparent pleasure. She raised herself more, severing the contact.

"Of *course*," she said with unsubtle sarcasm. "I planned the whole thing from the start. I got my car to break down at precisely the right spot at precisely the right moment, scoped out that no one else would be close enough to help, then went into labor on cue. All so you'd have to stay to deliver my baby, which was the secret weapon of my deep, dark plot to get you into bed — three-and-a-half years later — because you would be so enchanted with my gorgeous bod in labor and then the oh-so-glamorous act of giving birth, not to mention my calling you every name in the book while—"

"Not any book I've ever read." His tone and expression were relaxed.

Not hers. She still had a head of steam.

"—I did the bowling ball through a needle trick. That's such an old way to lure a guy to bed — three-and-a-half years later, mind you — that it's become a downright cliché. In fact, with a seducer like me you can't be sure I didn't get pregnant in the first place just so—"

"All right, all right. I give."

She heaved a couple more breaths, then pivoted away and flopped back against the seat beside him, but with a good foot between them.

"Jerk," she said.

He upped her with a self-aimed, "Jackass."

She huffed acceptance of that description.

They sat there for maybe a minute before he said, "Really should put some of the things you called me that day into a book. Very inventive."

"That's me. Inventive when terrified."

"You didn't act terrified. You had every right to be hysterical. You never lost your calm." He made a considering noise, then added, "Smart-ass, but calm. Impressive."

She gave another huff, "Thanks."

"It's the best thing I've done in my life."

She turned her head, still resting against the back of the couch, to look at him. Her eyes stung. "Me, too."

He mirrored her motion, meeting her look.

"Thank you, Jack." She had to clear her throat around the tears in it. "That's what I wanted to say to you at that party. Thank you for being there that day. Thank you for what you did. Thank you for my Addison Rose."

He brought his hand to her cheek, caught a tear she hadn't realized had slipped free. Then he leaned closer and kissed her.

Light and pure. Healing, she thought. Though she wasn't much of an expert on that. Better at bombardment than peace.

She drew in a deep breath and released it. Yeah, healing.

He lifted his head, looking in her eyes.

Then his look changed.

She gasped, even before his mouth met hers.

****

Through the darkest of the night there was little talking and less sleep.

She was on her side, his arm around her. She could see him staring straight up at the ceiling. The fact that it was visible was proof that the night was starting to lift.

"My girl friend disappeared."

Her breathing hitched. He had to have felt it, yet she fought to make her voice steady. "Disappeared?"

"I'm not telling you details. Not who or where or when. That clear?"

Very clear. He didn't trust her enough for that. But he trusted her enough for this. She'd take that for now. She nodded her understanding and acceptance of his terms.

"Went missing, they called it. The police, college officials, search groups. Like she had a choice in the matter."

Thoughts clicked through her brain too fast for her to grab onto them individually. "She's … she's never been found?"

"No."

The black hole was there. Right *there*. She felt it pulling at him.

"You were in college, and she was your girlfriend — how long had you been dating?"

"Almost three years."

"Three years. So you were serious."

He paused, then, "Yeah."

"Was she kidnapped?"

"That was one theory."

She sensed that answer edged them closer to the power of the black hole. "What were the other theories?"

"I'm not going to—"

He started to rise, she stretched her arm out across his chest, as if that could hold him.

"Okay. Tell me more about her." *I'm not telling you the details. Not who or where or when.* What did that leave? What could she ask him that would keep him talking, that would maintain this shadowy view into him? "How did you meet?"

His body remained tense, but he eased back. And some muscles around his mouth almost seemed to want to grin.

"She threw a football at my head."

"I've had the same temptation," she said before she could stop herself.

But his mouth did that same not-quite-a-twitch.

"Co-ed flag football. Dorm against dorm. Her side had a trick play going, handing it off to her, then she was throwing back to the quarterback. Instead, she reared back and hit me square in the side of the head as I played defense. Knocked me flat. Hayley kept saying she hadn't seen me."

Valerie remained absolutely still. Watching him, seeing flickers of a younger man. A man without so many defenses, without so much pain.

"She probably never would have seen me if it hadn't been for her throwing the ball at my head," he said at last.

He turned away, cleared his throat.

"So, you swept her off her feet by falling at her feet?" The feeble attempt at humor was mostly to give him time.

"Guess you could say that." He hitched one shoulder. "Had coffee after the game. Talked a while. That's how it started."

And nearly three years later it ended with her disappearance.

"It must have been good."

"It was. But …"

"But what, Jack?"

He shook his head.

She reached toward him.

He jackknifed up and stood. "This was a mistake." She tried to reach for him, but his movements as he dragged on his jeans, bundled up his other clothes, warded her off.

"Jack—"

"No. This was a mistake."

The door closed behind him.

****

Tears slid down her cheeks as she rooted in her tote for a t-shirt. Such pain. Such horrible pain.

He wanted her to leave his past alone. To leave him alone. But she couldn't. Not with that past shadowing his every moment. She couldn't.

She went to the bathroom, dashed cold water on her face, then roughly toweled it dry.

Then she turned on her laptop and began searching.

She pieced things together from a number of articles, spending the most time on one that provided a good recap.

The missing girl and her longtime boyfriend were both attending summer school at their Pennsylvania university. The boyfriend's account was that he'd last seen the missing girl the previous evening at the surprise birthday party she'd thrown for him in his apartment. He said she left shortly after the last of the partygoers for her own apartment, then he stayed up studying for a test.

After his test and another class the next day, he'd called her cell shortly before noon. A student with no connection to the missing girl or her boyfriend had answered, saying she'd heard the ringing and tracked it to a phone partway under a bush beside the sidewalk.

The boyfriend had gone to the missing girl's apartment. She wasn't there. Her roommate said Hayley had not returned the night before. He called campus police right then.

The search began.

It also started the questioning of Michael John Ralston as a person of interest in the still unsolved disappearance of Hayley Robertson eleven years ago.

Chapter Twenty-one

"Val? What're you doing?"

Jack's voice, and she felt her insides clench and her heart rate accelerate. Talk about a conditioned response. After one night together. "Washing my hands."

He'd stopped half a dozen feet from the pump outside the back door of the Flying W main house. "Do your dirty hands have anything to do with the flowers by the porch?"

She kept working at the dirt under her nails. Maybe he hadn't overtly avoided her in the thirty hours since he'd walked out of the ranch office, but he sure hadn't sought her out, either. Thirty hours while she'd read and re-read every scrap. Building a picture of the black hole of pain he'd fallen into eleven years ago, but only a partial picture. To truly know would require Jack talking to her, really talking to her.

"Yep. Matty and I thought perennials would do well there. They should come back every year without any effort from you. I wasn't expecting you here."

"Weren't you?"

She looked around. "No."

He was staring off and didn't appear to notice her shortness. "Where's Addie?"

"Taylor took her and Cassie to the library for the morning."

"Huh. And Matty just sent me over here."

"Did she?"

"Yeah. Some coincidence, huh? Taylor taking Addie, Matty sending me over here right after she found out I'd given Bryan work that'll keep him in a distant corner of the Slash-C all day."

At the change in his voice. she looked over her shoulder at him. "Did you?"

"I did." He came close behind her, not touching. "Val. Saturday night… Sorry. Sorry I took off like that. What happened between us was… True."

True. She closed her eyes. The word sliced right through thirty hours, bringing them right back to that couch.

He came up against her back, reaching around to cover her hands with his under the dwindling flow, washing first one of her hands then the other until the water ran clear.

She leaned back against him, watching as he slowly drew his wet hands up her arms to her shoulders. Water dripping from his hands made small round pools on her shirt, the fabric clinging to her skin.

He trailed his fingers up her throat, under her chin, his thumbs behind her ears, massaging in slow, even circles. Her gaze shifted, down to a new round of damp on her shirt. Her nipple tightened against the spot.

"Val."

At the choked version of her name, she turned to him.

He picked her up. She wrapped her legs around his waist.

"Inside," he said.

"Hurry."

But he took the time to bend his head, bringing her higher, so his mouth covered her damp breast through t-shirt and bra.

It felt… "Don't stop."

"If I don't—"

"Okay, okay. Stop. For now."

He gave a pained chuckle and started for the house while she bit softly at his neck.

"Val," he warned as he reached for the back door.

She sucked. That would show him she was not someone to be warned off.

He released the door, adjusted his hold, raising her higher, then pressed her against the wall.

"What are you—? *Ah.*" He'd taken advantage of the wall helping to support her to free his hands to pull down her top and bra together, covering one nipple with his mouth and the other with a hand.

She was panting. "I'm not going to—" His hands were at her shorts. He had them open. He was touching her.

"Yes, you are."

He had them off her almost before she realized her feet had touched the floor. Shorts and panties.

"Then you, too." She was at his belt, the snap and zipper.

"No. Me upstairs. You here."

He picked her back up. Reflexively, she wrapped her legs around him again.

"Val—"

She was pushing down the waist of his jeans.

"This can't—" he started, but his hands were helping. Moving, adjusting.

"Yes, it can."

It had to. Now. Now.

It did.

"Yes." She slid down him, so complete, so right. The only motion in the universe was the pulse of him inside her.

And then she wiggled.

And motion was everywhere. Around her, between them, and — oh, yes, oh, yes, oh, yes — inside her.

****

Lying on her stomach beside Jack in his bed, Val wallowed in boneless bliss.

Until he sat up abruptly and swore.

She turned her head toward him but as long as the world was still in one piece she didn't have the energy for more. "Hmm?"

"Your back." He swore again. "That outside wall. What the hell was I thinking?"

"Nothing," she said with lazy satisfaction. "No thinking at all."

"Does it hurt?"

"A little tender. But worth it."

"Val, why didn't you say—"

She laughed. A little laugh so it didn't move her much from this absolutely perfect position. "Wasn't thinking about my back."

He bent and pressed his lips lightly to her flesh.

"Now I am," she murmured.

201

"Hmm?"

"Thinking about my back," she explained. She started to turn.

His hand on her shoulder stopped her. "You are not lying on your back."

"I'm not?"

He kissed her back again, slid his leg under her, lifting her atop him. "You're not."

****

"I read about Hayley. You knew I would."

They were on their sides, facing each other. He squeezed his eyes closed. "Damned Internet. So, do you want to ask if I did it?"

"I know you didn't. You weren't ever a serious suspect. It's very clear you weren't."

But it explained so much. His tendency toward solitariness, encouraged by his upbringing, had been cemented by his loss and the investigation. Add in the media attention and the knowledge that the story, the suspicion, the doubt would last forever on the Internet…

His shoulder moved. Possibly a shrug. "That's what my lawyer said. It sure as hell felt like I was. Suspecting me made sense. I saw that. She had that damned party for my birthday even after I'd told her I had a big test. We fought some about that. People heard. Then when everybody'd finally gone, she wanted to fool around. I said no. She left in a huff, saying she was going back to her place. If I hadn't said no, if she'd stayed—"

"You can't know that, Jack."

"I can. I do. She never got back to her place. Somewhere between my place and hers… They wouldn't let me help search. Potential contamination of evidence." The last sentence was said so flatly it took her a couple times of re-running it through her head to recognize the implications. And how it must have felt to him then. "That was hard. But then her family came…"

She thought he'd stopped. She was afraid he had, because this might be her last chance to get him to talk.

But then he started again. "She took me home to meet her family that first Thanksgiving we were together. They welcomed me. Made me part of everything. All of them. I'd never known anything like that. Like them. I was part of it. Three years. And then they walked into that police station and I knew. I wasn't part of the family anymore. Even before…"

He shook his head. "How could I blame them? How could anybody? I'll never forget their faces when they arrived. What it did to them. But until you and Addie, maybe I didn't understand, not completely, what it meant to have their daughter missing."

Val felt as if her heart was simultaneously expanding and being squeezed.

"For almost a year there were searches and appeals for information and something would come up that looked like it might be a lead. But every damned one evaporated. Then her family sued me."

"*Sued* you? Why?"

"Wrongful death."

This had not been in the articles she'd read. "Oh, God, Jack—"

"They kept saying all they wanted was for me to tell everything I knew about that night. To not hold anything back, so they could find Hayley. They said the only reason they sued me was to find out everything I knew."

"But you'd told them. How could they—?"

"They didn't believe me. A couple years ago I started thinking … maybe they *couldn't* believe me, because believing me meant there was no answer. The answer of me killing her was better than no answer at all. But at the time… I wanted to give up. God, I wanted to give up. I thought about it."

Val made herself breath slowly, fighting back the terror that he'd considered suicide.

"My lawyer kept saying I *had* to keep on living and fighting for Hayley's sake. Because if I stopped living, everyone would think I'd killed her and they'd stop looking for her. Marion is a very smart woman."

She said a quick, silent thanks to the lawyer who'd given him a reason to keep living. "What happened, Jack?"

"I kept living and kept fighting, right through the suit. And then it was over and I'd won … *won*. Right. So there wasn't anything to fight for anymore. Nobody was really looking for her because there was nowhere to look, nowhere that made sense. She could be anywhere. Or nowhere. And then there wasn't anything to live for, either."

She heard the rasp of her own breath, holding back the tears. She would not cry. She would not add comforting her to all that this man already carried.

"So you started driving west."

"Driving, not necessarily west. Anywhere. When I wasn't driving, I was drinking. Oh, I didn't drive drunk. No way was I going to risk killing somebody else and coming through without a scratch myself."

She put her arms around his neck, drew his head to her shoulder. "You came west and you found the Curricks. So you were here to find me when Addie and I so desperately needed you."

There is so much for you to live for, Jack. If you'll just let yourself see it.

But she didn't say that to him. Not now.

She rocked him even after she knew he'd fallen asleep.

She couldn't imagine how exhausted he must be from all these years of carrying this, of never letting it out, of never having any support.

She couldn't imagine, either, the pain of Hayley's family, her parents. But dammit, how could they have known Jack and not known he couldn't possibly have hurt Hayley? How could they have turned away from him — really the only family he'd known — when he'd most needed them?

…The people I knew would love Addie no matter what. That's what home is. That's what it means.

I wouldn't know.

He'd turned to the people he'd thought would love him no matter what, and they'd not only not loved him, they'd suspected him — accused him — of murdering the woman he loved.

She refused to let the tears drop, because he'd feel them and she wanted him to sleep. But she held him a little tighter and rocked him more.

****

"How do you hold the reins, Addie?" Jack asked.

"Firm but light."

"Good girl."

Val wished he could see Addie beaming at his praise, but she was sitting in front of him in the saddle on Buster, so he couldn't see her face.

Jack had resumed overseeing her horseback-riding education, including hands-on instruction of how to get into the saddle from the ground. So hands-on that it took three tries to complete the lesson. She'd added to her store of knowledge that a roll in the hay was scratchy and sneezy and so highly uncomfortable that she would have avoided it if it hadn't meant doing without Jack for the three minutes it would have taken to get inside.

This was the fourth lesson he'd given Addie, once sitting on a saddle with no horse under it, twice on Bo with Jack holding her on while Matty led the horse, and now the two of them in the saddle on Buster with Matty joining Val outside the fence, along with Taylor, Dave, and Bryan. Even Taylor's dog Sin and the Curricks' Vegas were in enthusiastic attendance.

"She's doing great," Taylor said. Cassie's old helmet had been adjusted to a perfect fit for Addie.

Cassie's helmet, Brennan's boots, Dave's horse, Bryan's volunteer labor preparing the horses, the big saddle Donna and Ed had taught their children on — it took a whole ranch community to bring this smile to Addie's face. But most of all it took Jack.

"Don't worry. Buster's an old hand at this," Matty said.

"I'm not worried." Jack wouldn't let anything happen to Addie or to anyone or anything else in his care. They'd come here to the Slash-C for this lesson on Buster because he didn't think Bo should carry his weight.

Taylor cut her a look that Val didn't return.

There'd been an unspoken conspiracy in the weeks since the party for Lisa and Shane, participated in by every one of the people here, along with Donna and Ed, Cal Ruskoff, Lisa and Shane before they left, and who knew how many else. She wouldn't put it past the stool-sitters down at the café to somehow have a hand in the plot to maximize the time she and Jack had together. A fair amount of it alone.

As their equally unspoken part of the conspiracy they'd accepted unusual work assignments for Jack, abundant sleepovers for the kids, you've-gotta-see trips requiring Jack's escort for her. Unspoken to the others or to each other. They talked of her past, but never his. They talked of Addie's future, but never their own. They talked of making love, but never of being in love.

These weeks had been the best, the worst, the strangest, and the most natural of her life. And now they were coming to an end.

Four more days.

Ninety-six hours. No, ninety-three.

"Next step will be out on the trail," Matty said easily.

There would be no lesson on the trail for Addie, because this was the last lesson.

Chapter Twenty-two

"Anybody home?" Matty's voice came from the back door.

"C'mon in," Val invited. She might not want company, but how could she refuse when Matty owned the place?

"You were kind of quiet at Addie's riding lesson yesterday and I wanted to see if—" Matty stopped at the open double doorway to the bedroom. "What are you doing? You're packing."

She'd answered her own question with an accusation.

Val kept her hands moving and her voice steady. "I am. Addie and I have accumulated so much extra that I'm sure it won't all fit in the suitcases. So I'm shipping a couple boxes home."

"But… Jack?"

"What about him?"

"Oh, Val."

"It's okay, Matty. *I'm* okay. I will be okay."

"He hasn't said…?"

"No."

Matty moved around to the far side of the bed and waited until she looked up. "Have you?

****

The clock moved on, unmentioned.

She and Jack had a full night together when Addie had a final sleepover at the Slash-C. Val slept little that night, storing up the sensations of being in his arms, making love with him, watching him.

The day before their ticketed flight back to Boston, she drove to the Slash-C, choosing a time when she knew Jack, Dave, and Matty wouldn't be there. She rather hoped no one would be there, but Donna and Ed were sitting on the porch of their little house, side by side, holding hands and looking out to the horizon.

She left a box of things — kitchen supplies, towels, toys, and more — that had migrated from the Slash-C main house to the Flying W foreman's house over the past seven and a half weeks, along with her note of heartfelt thanks by the main house's back door.

Then she headed toward Donna and Ed, carrying the boots she'd borrowed.

She produced a smile along with her words of thanks and appreciation as she set them on the porch.

"Don't say good-bye now," Ed ordered, interrupting her farewell. "It's already decided, we're taking you to the airport tomorrow. Unless…?"

She answered the question by not answering it. "There's no need for you to come. I have to turn in the rental car, so I have to drive. I sure am going to miss seeing the mountains." She turned in that direction quickly, putting her back to the couple. "Jack says you have to respect the mountains. I understand that. You have to respect the ocean, too, or you get in trouble fast."

"That's true. All of it," Ed said. "There's something more, though. The mountains — the ocean, too, I'd expect — can build a man's self-respect. Not by ever respecting you back, mind you. But when you work with or against something that demands that you respect it day after day, you can't help feeling that being able to rise to that level makes you worthwhile, too. Does that make se— Hey, what's that all about? You okay, Valerie?"

She blinked back tears. "I'm okay, Ed. I'm just so grateful Jack found you all those years ago."

"We're glad he came to work for us, too. Works hard. And smart. That's a rare combination."

"That's not what she means, Ed," Donna said quietly.

"Oh. You mean…" He turned from his wife to her. "Give the boy time, Valerie. Time and space. This land can bring a man answers that nothing else can."

She considered that. Then she shook her head. "No. If all the years since he came here haven't been enough, if all the space of Wyoming, not to mention the space he's put between himself and other people haven't been enough, then, no. If time and space were going to do the trick, it would be done by now. And it hasn't. No more time. No more space."

"Valerie, I know you and Jack went through something extraordinary when Addie was born, but you don't really know—"

"She's right, Ed."

"Donna—"

She placed a hand on his arm and his protest stopped. When she spoke, she looked only at her husband, but Val felt the words striking deep in her.

"Jack's had plenty of time and plenty of space. If anything, he's dug himself deeper into the pit of aloneness he keeps himself in. You know that. You've seen it. If it doesn't stop — if it doesn't stop now, there'll just be a husk for the world to see, and no way to reach what's inside him. It's past time to try something new, before time and space eat him alive."

Her husband obviously was considering her words, but he also was frowning. "So, what do you propose? You can't demand that a man open up his soul to the world."

Donna abruptly beamed at him, kissed him on the lips, then turned to Val, still beaming.

Val blinked at her. "What?"

"*You* can."

She was lost. "Can what?"

"Demand that he open up his soul to the world. And do it before time and space eat him alive."

"I don't—" Bam. There it was, clear and simple. "Oh. Yes. I see." It would take nerve. Not to mention worrying whether it would backfire horribly. "I don't know…"

She met Donna Currick's eyes, and the other woman patted her arm.

"Everything worth doing is worth risking everything — or everyone — for," she said with another pat. "You have to be brave."

****

She pulled the car to the side of the road, stopping short of sliding into the ditch this time.

She wouldn't have found the spot on her own, but Donna and Ed knew it, and their directions had been clear.

Odd that she hadn't returned to this spot until now. She got out and looked around. She remembered the road as narrower, the ditch as deeper and wider, the surroundings as a white blur.

Now, mountains provided a horizon of rambling glory. The foothills lifted and folded in unpatterned peace. Wildflowers softened the sides of the ditch … yellow wildflowers with red markings. Yellow monkeyflowers, blooming in this ditch of all ditches. Then she saw that the water was mostly gone. The blooms were drooping.

She propped her butt against the side of the car and remembered.

Adventures and accomplishments.

Mistakes, and how she'd gotten past them, most often with the help of friends and family. Often in the form of tough love.

The hours here with Jack on Addie's birth day.

These past three-and-a-half years of joy and occasional terror as Addie's mother.

And these past weeks with Jack.

You and me … Everything's going to be okay.

She pushed her hair back one-handed as she reached for her phone with the other. Only when she had it on did she remember that there'd been no service here three and a half years ago.

But whaddya know? Cell service had stretched to this spot in Wyoming. At least when it wasn't the middle of a blizzard.

"The Fishwife," came the voice on the other end of the phone.

"El?"

"Val! You haven't changed your plans, have you? You're coming home tomorrow?"

"I don't know. I think… I have to try something."

"Are you okay, Val?"

"No."

****

"You're leaving."

"Yes."

She gave him time as she continued layering Addie's t-shirts into the suitcase sitting on the bed, aware of him behind her in the doorway. Aware, too, of Addie on the porch. The front door was open so she could hear and see her daughter through the small living room. But Jack had come in the back door, quiet enough that Addie hadn't heard him.

"You could stay a little longer." His voice was harsh, strained.

"No, I can't."

"Val."

"I can't. It would be wrong. For me, for Addie. Even for you. Not *a little longer.*"

"You know—"

She spun toward him, clutching Addie's Rope a Lobster shirt to her chest. "I know you think you can't risk loving again. But I also know what you said about Storm and Phantom and the other horses you've worked with. Tough things, wrong things have happened to them. They responded in ways that became habits, so now they don't think, they just react. But they need to think again. To think through the situations and to find a new response. That's what you teach them. That's what you need to do for yourself, Jack. That's—"

"I can't."

"Won't. This is a choice—"

"I was going under. Do you understand? Going under for sure. I found a rope to hold on to and it's all that's kept me from drowning."

"Cutting yourself off from people? Not letting yourself feel? That's a rope all right. A rope—"

"I'd be a fool to let it go. A fool who'd deserve to go under."

"—you've wrapped around your neck, and now you're all tangled up in it, so it's pulling tighter and tight. Choking you." This was coming out too fast, too jumbled.

"What do you want from me?"

"Everything."

His eyes went dark with pain and struggle. She wanted to take his face between her hands, she wanted to wrap herself around him.

She held still.

"I need you to talk to me about Hayley and everything that happened. How you felt about her, how you felt when her family—"

"I told you."

"Drops. Squeezed out of a stone. I need a gusher."

"I can't." He turned, took two steps. With his back to her, he stopped. "Maybe it's can't, maybe your right and it's won't. But either way—"

"No, don't say it, Jack. Don't close that door in your own head. Keep the possibility open. Someone else might come along who—" She swallowed tears and heartbreak, pulled in air and the strength to fight for him even after she was gone. "I know you care about me. And Addie. I know you do. But if this just isn't strong enough, something else — someone else — might be. I hope so. I pray so. Because you're a wonderful man, Jack Ralston. You deserve all the love and friendship and camaraderie that's all around you, waiting for the moment you stop denying yourself. So I'll hope that someone comes along who can make you take the risk of living again. Of loving again."

He didn't move.

Her breaths rasped in and out, fighting to get past the emotion jamming her throat. Was there anything else she could say, anything she could do that might make him see—?

"There won't be anyone else, Val. You and Addie are more than any man deserves. There won't be anyone."

Holding the door knob, he turned his head, looking over his shoulder toward her, while every other part of him still aimed for the exit.

She crossed the space, stretched up, kissed him on the cheek and said, "Goodbye, Jack. I love you."

He walked out.

Her heart shattered once to know he did love her and Addie.

It shattered again to know that he would not let himself know their love.

****

Even in the dawn light, he'd spotted and recognized the rider from well off. So he had no need to turn to check out the approach when the horse's easy hoofbeats drew near.

The rider brought his horse to a stop beside Storm.

"Jack," Cal Ruskoff said in a neutral greeting.

When he said no more, Jack knew this wasn't about ranch business. He hadn't held out a lot of hope that it was, since Cal was no longer foreman of the neighboring Flying W, instead starting his own place farther north. Far enough that it was highly unlikely he'd ridden all this way.

Especially since he was on a Flying W horse.

That meant he had arrived by vehicle at the Flying W and mounted up there. And that meant—

"Not you, too," he grumbled.

Cal looked out across the valley, taking his time, dry humor in his tone. "You're acquainted with your boss' wife Matty? And my wife Taylor?"

Jack grumbled a curse word, but the fire went out of him. "Why didn't they send Dave?"

"Wish I could tell you he's being saved as reinforcements. Might make my mission easier. But the truth is, he told Matty he'd talked to you once and he wasn't doing it again. Wish I'd thought of that," Cal said dryly. Then his tone turned serious. "We don't know each other real well, Jack. But you might as well accept it that we have people we care about in common. You've painted walls in my house, for which I thank you." A smile shifted across the other man's face, then was gone as he continued. "And we've worked together some. Get to know a fair amount about a man when you work together. Stuff that no amount of talking tells."

Jack grunted an acknowledgment — not only of Cal's words, but that their work together had bred mutual respect. Wasn't like they were buddies, but there was a recognition of a fellow man who worked hard and well and smart. Maybe even a kind of understanding.

"There's also sense in their sending me. Don't know how much you know, but I've got some experience doing my best — or worst — to leave behind some people and some history."

He knew a little. Enough to know Cal Ruskoff had had good choices, and chose Wyoming — and Taylor. Jack didn't have choices.

"The hell of it is," Cal said, "you only think you're leaving those things behind."

He'd heard enough. He cut off the other man. "They come right along with you — I've heard it. Anywhere you go, there you are."

Cal nodded. "Sure. But it's more than that. Not only do those things come with you, they're driving you. You might think you're in charge, but you're like the poor, dumb cow that thinks it's making all the decisions, when it's actually been sent down a route all fixed up by the cowboy who's back there quietly directing the whole drive."

The other man cut him a look. Jack didn't return it, continuing to stare down at the valley. But whatever he saw must have satisfied Ruskoff, because he nodded again.

"Wasn't until I dealt with the history that I found a path I wanted to follow instead of only avoiding one I didn't."

"You don't know — nobody—"

He hadn't meant to say that much. Wished he could pull it back.

But Cal didn't try to push into the opening. Not much, anyway. "No, I don't know. Nobody knows, unless you tell them."

Jack appreciated that it was an invitation, not a demand.

Appreciation didn't mean he'd accept it.

They sat in silence for several minutes before Cal said, "I'll talk to you more, any time, Jack. Or listen, if that's what you're after. But I won't hound you, either. Just know you're not alone in this. Not unless you want to be."

Cal turned his horse a quarter turn, then stopped, twisting to face him, one hand propped on the back of the saddle.

"What you said about nobody knowing? The thing is, I thought that, too. Only, somehow, Taylor did know. Not what, I don't mean that. But me, I guess." His mouth didn't move, but the lines around his eyes lifted and his focus softened. "No matter the shell I tried to crawl into, she knew me in ways I didn't know myself. I'm not saying Val's doing that with you. After all, Taylor's an extraordinary woman. Extraordinary."

And Val's not? Is that what you're saying, Ruskoff? The hell she's not. The hot words flashed through his mind, but the guard on his tongue clamped down.

The other man shifted in the saddle. "Just saying that what you're thinking nobody can know might not be what really needs knowing."

Cal lowered the brim of his hat in farewell, turned his horse and headed away.

And Jack was alone again.

That's where he was when he watched the dust kicked up by the caravan leaving the Flying W mid-morning, led by Val's little rental car, heading for the airport.

****

Addie cried from the moment at the airport when she realized Brennan wasn't coming with them, through the landing in Denver.

Great, gulping sobs that had most of the passengers' looks divided between pity for Addie and pity for themselves. A small minority — all women — looked their pity toward the sufferer's mother.

The worst for her was when Addie started crying for Jack. "Jack'll fix it. Jack'll fix everything," she cried over and over.

213

Addie slept much of the leg from Denver to Boston. And was all smiles when she saw her grandparents waiting for them at Logan Airport.

Late that night, with Addie finally asleep — on Wyoming time — El poured each of them a glass of wine, tugged her arm to make her sit beside her on the couch and said, "Okay, tell me everything."

That's when Val cried.

Chapter Twenty-Three

Jack sat up from the office couch. He rested his forearms on his thighs, his head dropped down.

He wasn't asleep anymore, but wouldn't call himself awake either. Wasn't thinking anything, wasn't feeling anything. Didn't want to.

He'd been working on the accounts. Couldn't keep his eyes open. Even stretching out on this couch, remembering, hadn't kept him awake.

Slowly, he got up. Went to the bathroom. Came out. Stood in the middle of the room and stared at nothing.

A sound came from outside. Didn't interest him much, but he started walking toward the door, as automatic as going to the bathroom had been.

His head felt numb, wobbly. But as long as he didn't move the rest of him much, it might stay attached.

He opened the door slow.

Donna Currick sat on one of the rockers. Not rocking, just sitting.

He knew she turned to look at him, but he didn't return the favor. He took the other chair and, even slower, he sat.

"Donna," he said, moving his mouth the least to let the word out.

"Good nap?"

He gave a negative grunt. He couldn't remember the last time he'd slept during the daytime. No wonder, considering how he felt now.

"The way you've looked this past week you're sure not getting any sleep at night," she said.

And then he did remember the last time he'd slept during the daytime.

It was that little motel in Nebraska. He'd come out feeling just the way he did now. Then the guy with his arm in a cast, struggling with the divider gate on his cattle truck.

He'd helped. The man had asked if he wanted a job for the day.

He'd wanted to sit and stare at nothing just the way he was staring now. But the man had needed help, so he'd gone.

There'd been another job. Another. And another. Until his path crossed Ed Currick's.

"You used to do this a lot," Donna said.

He grunted a not very interested *huh*. He'd sit here and breathe. That was as much as he could ask of himself in this moment.

"When you first came to the Slash-C," she added. "This thousand-yard stare."

"Was asleep," he mumbled.

"Yes, you were. Truly sleep-walking through your life. For quite a while. Then half asleep for years after that. Until Val came. Val and Addie."

Inside his numbness, something squeezed hard. It hurt. A lot. But, oddly, as the squeeze released, something else flowed over the pain.

Val and Addie.

"And now they've been gone a full week."

"Her choice. Nothing I can do."

She spurted out a short, exasperated sound and poked a finger in his chest. "You've loved two women in your life, Jack Ralston. You lost one through no fault of your own, yet you acted like it was. And now you could lose the other, entirely through your fault, and you're acting like it's none of your doing."

"How do you—? Val told you—"

"Nothing. Val told me none of your secrets. But I'm not stupid. You had to have loved a woman before or you wouldn't be so wounded. If it had been your fault you lost her… I know you, Jack Ralston, and you'd never have trusted yourself again. Instead, it's other people you don't trust."

She waved away his past. "But forget that. Forget all of that. What matters now is Valerie Trimarco and what you're going to do."

****

There was nothing he could do.

Goodbye, Jack. I love you.

Did that make any kind of sense in any world? Even Val's? No. Dammit, it didn't.

Nearly a month had gone by and now that she wasn't in front of him, crying, he was ticked at her.

Some.

He missed her.

Physically, but not just in the sexual way he might have expected. There was something weird going on with his hands. It was like they'd been burnt, and now they were raw and stiff, awkward at the most mundane task. Storm had turned his head and stared at him this morning while he was saddling up, and Jack didn't blame him. He'd been more awkward than a first-timer.

The fence he'd repaired yesterday had to be redone today because it was a mess. He'd been so distracted, he'd been out a couple hours on Storm before Bryan called asking where he was. Only then did he remember he was supposed to drive the truck over to the Morton Creek with some pipe first thing.

He'd left Bryan idling, while he tended Phantom before he headed back out in the truck. At least that was taken care of now, Bryan's questioning looks behind him, and he'd get on with his afternoon of redoing fence.

Since that run-in with Donna a week after Val and Addie left, he'd kept himself away from the home ranch from first hint to last glow of light. That meant eating something he had with him or skipping lunch. But he kept forgetting to bring anything. Yesterday he'd eaten the last power bar and final trail mix he in his utility. He generally resorted to those only in emergencies, which added staleness to their other charms. Now, even those were gone, though he had the bag with him with a vague notion of restocking it.

He just needed enough to tide him over this afternoon. It didn't need to be much. Sure didn't need to be good.

He dug into an inside pocket of the bag he rarely messed with. Pulled out matches, army knife, a space blanket in a tiny square. Also some fishing line and ... what was this? A blob of something dark, mashed, and slightly shiny.

He poked at the mystery blob. That provided no answers. He picked it up for a closer look and realized the slightly shiny was plastic wrap. Slowly, he peeled back a corner.

And then he knew.

He held what had once been a chocolate brownie. His birthday brownie.

He peeled back more plastic wrap. The scent of chocolate wafted up, standing out from the scents of sun-heated dust, cattle, and his own sweat.

He held it close to his nose, his eyes drifting closed as he took in the aroma. And, damned if his olfactory senses didn't think they'd picked up the cool smoke of a certain dark-haired woman, and even the residual talcum powder and sunblock of a little girl, all mixed in with the chocolate.

His mouth watered and his stomach growled. That gave him the excuse to ignore the ache in his heart.

He studied the mashed brownie for signs of mold. None. No scent or sign of anything wrong with it.

What the hell. He bit into it.

He focused on the sweetness in his mouth, the calories flowing into his system. His hand tightened around the plastic wrap.

Val, smiling at him. Holding him.

Addie, with full faith he could rope a lobster. "Don't be scared, Jack."

Laughter.

Love.

"Jack?"

Dave's face was there looking at him. It took a moment to realize Dave was driving another Slash-C truck, and had stopped beside him, open driver window to open driver window.

What bothered Jack was he didn't remember turning off the truck. Yet here he sat, middle of the ranch road, engine off.

"You okay, Jack?"

"Yeah. Fine."

"Okay," Dave said, drawing out the two syllables to about ten. "Look, Jack, I don't want to pry into your life, but ... maybe I recognize the symptoms because Matty and I had a rocky time, before we got married and after. And I know what that does to you. So, if you want to take some time off..."

"No. Thanks, no. But… Dave, there's something I've got to tell you. You and the others. Can we talk tonight?"

****

"We're here," Val called, as she opened the door into the Inn's private living quarters.

"We're here," echoed Addie with far more enthusiasm.

Addie was always happy to go to the Inn. It meant seeing her cousin Sam, as well as El, Cahill, and Cahill's brother, Kiernan.

Valerie was less happy about it tonight. She would have preferred staying home. El had insisted she and Cahill were taking her out for dinner, while Kiernan watched the kids.

"Good timing," El called. "We're back in the kitchen."

Addie headed toward voices coming from the playroom off the living area. Val went to the slice of private kitchen that connected to the Inn's commercial kitchen.

"Cahill's upstairs changing his shirt," El said as she came in.

Cahill's younger brother, a hottie if ever there was one, gave her a cheeky grin and said in his wonderful Irish accent, "And El's been instructing me on the proper actions for any contingency from a national emergency to not having enough ice cream to go around, which would surely start a riot."

"There's plenty of ice cream if you give them a reasonable amount instead of— Oh, you." El swatted her brother-in-law's shoulder as he completed a gesture of having hooked her and reeled her in. "Go ahead and laugh you two—"

Though Val wasn't sure her sound qualified as a laugh.

"—But I do have one more thing to say. If you turn on the TV, do avoid the news stations. That horrible story's all over."

"What horrible story?" Kiernan asked.

Instead of answering him, El turned toward her, her eyes glinting with mischief. How could it be so good to see her cousin so happy while she felt so bad for herself? "You know, Kiernan doesn't have time for such paltry things as news these days. Not since he met *her*."

"Her who?" she asked, playing along, even as Kiernan groaned.

"That's exactly what Cahill and I have been asking, but he's been all mysterious about this one, unlike the dozens and dozens of others."

Val knew her role. She propped her hands on her hips, facing Kiernan.

"So what's she like, this woman you're being so mysterious about?"

"She's smart and lovely and intriguing—"

"Intriguing," repeated Eleanor. "In other words she doesn't fall over in a faint at your feet?"

He pointedly ignored his sister-in-law, instead addressing her cousin. "Just because I'm not running my mouth—"

Val interrupted. "The way you usually do about your conquests."

An arrested look came into his eyes. It was gone before she could examine it as he slipped behind a cloak of overdone dignity.

"If we leave behind the sordid world of gossip — not to mention the outright abuse of himself—" He spoke the insert in a broad brogue before returning to pompous TV announcer intonations. "—And return to the topic of today's important news."

El sobered instantly. "It is truly horrible. They've arrested a man in Pennsylvania. They've found all these poor girls buried in his mother's basement, including his own cousin, who went missing from her college right after her boyfriend's birthday party years ago."

Pennsylvania…. Missing from college… her boyfriend's birthday party. Val grabbed El by the shoulders. "What's her name? The cousin who went missing—what's her name?"

"I don't know. I don't remember. Why? What's—?"

"The killer. What's his name?"

"Robbins? Robinson? Or Roberts, I think—no. Robertson."

"Oh, my God. Oh, my God."

Val was only peripherally aware of El asking her what was wrong or of heading for the TV in the living area or hearing El ordering Kiernan to keep the kids in the playroom as Val turned on the TV and sat on the edge of the coffee table in front of it, wildly flipping through channels.

A strong male hand took the remote. "It's the news you're wanting then?"

Cahill McRae found CNN, keeping the volume too low to be heard in the other room.

She was aware of Cahill and El conferring behind her, but she was too focused on the screen, too intent to bother with what they might be saying.

When a commercial came on, Cahill took the remote again and muted the set.

Val was already reaching for her phone. "I have to get there. I have to get there right now."

"Val, what is this about?"

"I have to get to Jack. Please, will you take care of Addie? Will you help me?"

Cahill gripped her shoulders gently, crouching down so they were face to face. "We'll move heaven and earth for you Val, but you must be telling us what this is about."

"Jack was that girl's boyfriend when she disappeared — the cousin of the man who had all the bodies buried. The prosecutor wouldn't try him criminally. Her parents took him to civil court for wrongful death. They lost. Because there was nothing. But for Jack, the questions, the media, the trial, all of it. Coming on top of losing the girl he loved and having her parents accuse him… It nearly killed him. It did ruin him. In so many ways. He can't— And now … Oh, God. I have to get back there."

El hugged her, but Val backed out of the embrace. "I can't… I can't cry. There's too much to do. I need to fly back. A car there. As fast as I can. After the first wave of the story, they'll remember him. They'll look for him. They'll find him."

Would he leave? Would he cut ties from the place and people he loved — yes, he did love them, no matter what he said. And he needed them. If he were ever to believe that he could love again, he needed them all desperately.

He had to stay in Knighton. He had to.

"Addie will be fine. Don't worry about her. Flights?" El looked at her husband. He nodded, taking out his phone and heading toward the kitchen. "And we'll go get you packed now."

"Yes. Thank you. Thank you both. But first I have to call…" She had her phone out, hearing it ring as El led her out to her car, gesturing for the keys so she could drive.

"Slash-C," said the familiar voice.

"Oh, thank God. Donna. It's Val. Jack needs your help."

Chapter Twenty-Four

She slowed at the sight of three trucks, two news vans, and a rare passenger car pulled over near the main entrance to the Slash-C. It was the first time she'd seen the gate closed. A clot of people were by the gate, but a few had stayed back by the vehicles. They looked at her closely as she went by, but appeared to dismiss her when they saw a woman they didn't recognize.

"Give it up. No interviews," one called to her, apparently taking her for a fellow journalist.

As she slowly rolled closer, she heard one say to the men behind the gate, "Why are you blocking this road?"

"Because it's a private road, and the people who own it want to keep it private," said Hugh Moski. He appear to be the leader of the four men she recognized as stool-sitters from the Knighton Café.

"Ralston has been completely exonerated. You'd think he'd want to celebrate."

"We don't need no reporters saying he's been exonerated in order to know the man he is. Where were you all when he was getting a rum deal? Not so interested in the real story then, were you?"

Val suspected at least a couple of the reporters had been in high school at the time, but she wasn't about to raise that point.

"We just want to ask him a few questions."

"He don't want to answer your questions, and that's what matters to us — us and the folks who own this ranch and these roads. Oh, and a couple more folks, too. The sheriff's department of Clark County. Hey there, Val. Good to see you back. C'mon through."

"Why're you letting her in?" demanded indignant voices.

"She's a friend."

He winked as she passed through the gate he'd opened for her.

****

Jack must have seen her coming. He straightened slowly from the open back of the horse trailer where he'd been stashing things in a saddlebag and faced her.

She'd worried that being near him again would weaken her resolve, but seeing him packing took care of that.

"You aren't leaving," she said. An order.

"Val. What are you doing here? I have to—" His gaze did a quick scan around, then came back to her face. "Where's Addie?"

"El and Cahill are looking after her," she said, because she saw real concern. But he wasn't getting out of this that easily. "You—"

"Are you okay?"

His interruption surprised her enough to stop her. "*Me?*" She started again. "I'm here to help you, Jack." And tear anyone who tried to hurt him apart with her bare hands. "You are not leaving this ranch, do you understand me, Jack Ralston?"

He considered her an instant, then tugged down the brim of his hat. "Richard John Ralston. Don't you listen to the news?"

"Yeah, you're back in the news. And, yeah, there are reporters and cameras outside the gates dying to dig into your life and ask you questions. Your worst nightmare. I know. But you are *not* leaving the Slash-C. Because you do love it, whether you'll admit it or not. You love the life here. And there are people here who love you, whether you'll admit *that* or not. So you're not going to run, thinking that will make you feel better. Because it won't."

"Like when you ran away from Gloucester to Washington State, then realized it didn't make you feel better and you wanted to be home to have your baby."

"*Exactly.*" Her flash of triumph evaporated as she tried to absorb that he was agreeing with her.

"What about your leaving here?" he asked. "You like it here, too.

Don't you?"

"Of course I do. It's amazing and the people are— But that's not the point. I wasn't running away from here. I was going home. Totally different thing."

"Is it? Or could it have been a little bit of something else?"

"I don't know what you're—"

"You do, Valerie. You do."

"I wasn't running away." This time she left off the "from here" because they both knew that wasn't the issue. "I'd pushed you and pushed you and you didn't—"

"I was all tangled up with my thoughts. It's like I told you with the horses, sometimes you've got to push so they stop reacting from habit and start thinking."

She sucked in air between parted lips. Fighting hope, holding on to sense. "Like *you* told *me*, huh?"

"Yeah. Like I told you. After you spent most of this summer hammering away at me, in ways above and —" He gave her a significant look. "—below the belt." Then he grinned. "Somebody I know told me to quit choking myself with the rope I'd wrapped around my own neck."

She propped her hands on her hips. Partly because they were shaking. Partly because if she didn't hold onto herself she was either going to drum her fists against his chest or fling her arms around his neck. Neither seemed like a good idea until they had this straight.

"Just like that? You're finally going to listen to sense just like that? Oh." Her hands dropped. "No. It's not that. I'm so tired and so worried, I'm not thinking straight. It's not that you've decided you deserve a life and love. Of course, not. It's from the news. From knowing—"

He moved so fast that even at her best she couldn't have avoided him clasping her shoulders and drawing her close enough that she had to tilt her head way back to keep looking into his eyes.

"No. It's not. You're wrong. The news— I'd be lying if I didn't say it wasn't a relief. It is. It lifts… To know what happened. To know the Robertsons know. To know Hayley can be mourned now. And I can remember her — just *her* — separate from what followed. But you have to know…"

His hands tightened on her then eased.

He started again. "After you called Donna about the news breaking, there was a lot of talking. It was decided this is a good time to start trailing cattle down from the mountains to get ready for roundup. By the time those people at the gate figure out other ways to get to me I'll be gone up the mountains."

"Oh." For the first time, she took in that Storm and Buster were loaded on the trailer. If he'd been leaving, he might have taken Storm, but not Buster. She should have realized that. But she'd been too tired, too scared, too happy to see him that she hadn't taken the time for logic. "But if they find out you're up there alone—"

"Won't be alone. Takes a fair number of hands to bring the cattle down. Even if some reporter could find his way to where we are ... well, these are all people who wouldn't approve of my privacy being disturbed. Not to mention our cattle drive being disrupted."

He grinned a little, but she didn't return it.

That's when he started worrying.

"Thank God," she said. "So Dave and Ed are going with you?"

"And Matty and Bryan and Cal and half a dozen others. It'll take a few days. Those folks at the front gate will get bored by then. So when I get back, we'll talk."

She shook her head. "I have to go."

"Go where? Oh, you mean the Flying W? The foreman's house. Okay, but reporters might—"

"Gloucester."

"You're leaving again?"

"Yes." Her voice was strained, with tears and more. "If I don't, you'll never know what you want."

"I know I want you."

"I know you do. That's not enough. It would have been more than enough for me before. But not now, not with Addie. Now I have to have more. I have to have what you've denied yourself for more than a decade — a future. And for me to know we're going to have that with you, to be sure, you need to come to us." She looked up at him, the motion making the tears spill down her cheeks. He didn't realize he'd started to reach for her until her raised hand stopped him. "*I need* you to come to us."

"It's going to be roundup soon. No way can I leave. Wouldn't do that to the Curricks, wouldn't be able to hold my head up."

"I understand."

"Good. It's more practical if you stay here. Well, go get Addie, bring her back, then stay here. That'll work."

"What works and what's practical are your problem. I came to be sure you're okay now that everyone knows what happened to Hayley. You are — or you will be. But that's separate from—" She waggled her hand back and forth between them. "—us. That doesn't depend on practical or convenient. Addie and I deserve the grand gesture."

"Grand gesture? What kind of grand gesture?"

"That's your problem, too."

"I don't—"

"Jack." Dave shouted from the driver's seat of the trailer. "Sorry, Val, but we've gotta go now. Hugh called and says they're talking about coming around from the south on county roads. If we don't get out ahead of them…"

"Go," she said.

Jack tried, "If you stay until I get back—"

"No."

"Damn it, Val—"

She stretched up and kissed him on the lips. "Good-bye, Jack. I love you."

Again? *Again?* He would have been ticked at her if her shoulders hadn't been shaking as she walked away.

He swore and swung into the trailer.

****

It was too dark to see it, but the sound and the smell of the ocean were with him as he rang the doorbell on Great-Aunt Susan's house on the beach in Gloucester, Massachusetts.

"Just a minute!" Val called from inside. The sound of her voice swelled his heart until he thought it might burst.

The door swung open and she was there. All he could do was stand and stare at her.

She was doing the same — standing and staring.

"Jack."

The wavery way she said it, sent a bolt through him like Wyoming lightning, so he felt awed and powerful and privileged.

She reached for him. He dropped the saddle he'd held so he could reach back, turning with her into the entryway beside a set of stairs disappearing into a dark second story.

Then, even as her hands grabbed onto his shirt, and he started to put his arms around her, she pushed against his chest. Hard. Pushing him away.

"You didn't. You couldn't have. How could you? I can't believe you. No, no, no."

Her words came too fast. Too fast for a man dog-tired from roundup, followed by a long trip toting a saddle. Too fast for a man who'd done a damned good job ignoring the possibilities of disaster until the last hundred feet to her front door. Too fast for a man who'd been away from her too long.

"What?" was all he could get out.

"Storm? The Curricks. The Slash-C. No, you couldn't have."

Unshed tears were like a layer of glass between her eyes and him. But the glass hid nothing of the pain she was feeling. For him. She felt that pain for *him*.

Then the tears started to fall, the glass shattering into shards that sliced through any guard he had left.

"Val. Val. Don't cry."

He tightened his arms around her, and her elbows bent. He caught her to him, feeling the wetness of her tears at the open V of his shirt.

"I love you. You and Addie. I love you."

"I know you do, you big lug. And we love you. That's why we can't let you do it."

His head was spinning. "Do what?"

"Sell up. Leave the Slash-C and the Curricks and everybody else and Wyoming. It would be too much like before. We can't let you do that. We can't."

"I haven't."

"But your saddle —?" Her head jerked up, the top of it cracking against the underside of his chin. "Sorry. Sorry. I — why are you grinning? That had to hurt. I heard the *clunk*, and your eyes are tearing . . ."

"It did hurt. It *does* hurt. Like hell. Reason I'm grinning is it makes it all feel real now. Seeing you. Holding you. Wouldn't feel real without you or Addie half cracking my head open. But the tears in my eyes aren't from pain, not all of them."

"Oh, Jack."

He bent for her mouth, but before he reached it, she stiff-armed him again. "The saddle. Explain the saddle."

"Val—"

"Explain the saddle."

He stepped back outside, got a hold of it, and swung it around to land beside her in the hallway. "It's my grand gesture."

She looked up at him, unvoiced laughter abruptly lighting her face. "Showing up at my door was pretty grand to start."

"Glad you feel that way, because I was thinking maybe I could stay here a while. Then you and Addie could come back to Wyoming with me in the spring with enough lead-time so I can be on top of things for calfing season."

"You mean you haven't quit the Curricks?"

"No."

"Still have Storm?"

"Yes."

"And you've thought out this whole schedule?"

"Yes."

"So the saddle..."

"It's sort of a symbol, see."

"Ralston," she warned.

"Taking it off Storm when we finished up roundup this morning. Carrying it from Wyoming to here, toting it through airports, getting it in a taxi and—"

"You took a taxi from Logan to Gloucester? That's crazy. You—"

"Focus, Valerie. Grand gesture, here."

"Sorry."

"Anyway, toting it through airports, getting it in a taxi, hauling it across the sand — it's all to say that without you and Addie, I might as well sell up. Because without you, I don't have a home. Don't have a heart. Don't have tomorrow. It's all—"

"Oh, Jack."

"Don't stop me now. I've memorized the whole speech and I'm not stopping until it's done."

"Go right ahead," she said, tears slipping down her cheeks, with a smile lighting those wonderful eyes.

He encircled her with his arms. "Hell, I don't remember a word of it now. But you've got to know this, Valerie Trimarco. It was you. It was all you, and what I feel for you. And it happened before the news broke about Hayley. I've got Donna Currick as my witness. Matty, too, if it comes to that. And Dave. Ed and Taylor and Cal."

"Good heavens, was there a party?"

"It was the night before the news broke. I told them … about Hayley, the trial. Not a lot, but enough. Then I said I was going after you as soon as roundup was over. Donna she said it was about time, but Dave should let me go right then. I said no. And then Cal — did I say he and Taylor were there? And Lisa and Shane on the computer when I said it. So I told them all. Taylor and Matty had it in their heads I should bring you monkeyflower, but I stuck to the saddle. But I had to stay through roundup."

"Poor baby. Not only talking, but about feelings, and in front of all those people.

"You've got a smart mouth, you know that?" He swiped a thumb across her lips, then returned his hand to her shoulder, drawing her closer.

"I've been told that a time or two."

"Don't you want to know what I told all those people?"

"You think it's something I'll want to hear?"

"It's something I need to say." He dropped a quick, hungry kiss on her mouth. Then pulled back just enough to say. "I love you, Valerie Prudence Trimarco. I love you and Addison Rose. You're my home. You're my heart. I'm here to give you and Addie every last thing I have. Every last thing I am."

She reached up, her hands at his face drawing him down to her.

"That's all I've ever wanted."

Epilogue

Gloucester, Massachusetts

"Spring's coming," Val announced as she stepped inside El and Cahill's home.

Cahill, in the act of helping her take off a winter coat studded with icy crystals said, "It's snowing."

"Spring snow," she said. "Couple weeks, and the crocus will be up."

"And we'll be back in Wyoming," Jack added from behind her.

"Not yet," protested El, coming out of her office tucked under the main stairs.

Val grinned. "That's the deal — returning to Wyoming each spring."

"Like monkeyflower," Addie said abruptly. "The lady said. It comes back to Wyoming every year and it spreads if it's happy. Us, too. Like monkeyflower."

"The woman in that little flower shop in Jefferson did say that, didn't she?"

"Monkeyflower? I think I've heard of that somewhere," El lightly teased. She reached out for Addie. Jack held on. She exchanged a smiling look with Val before she added, "Just so you can get your jacket off, Jack. Then I promise to give her back."

With the grownups' jackets hung up and the procedure of divesting Addie of all her necessary outer garments in progress, El and Cahill's son Sam came riding in on his Uncle Kiernan's shoulders. Kiernan swung him to the floor with a flourish. After that, there was no question of Addie going back into Jack's arms. She wanted down to play with Sam.

When Kiernan started after them, Sam gave him the stop sign hand.

"No," that masterful personality said. "Just kids. You're a grownup."

"It's stricken to the heart I am." He thumped a dramatic hand to his heart.

It didn't melt Sam. Worse, it made Addie giggle as the two little ones departed, hand in hand.

"Don't worry," El said, patting his arm. "There are compensations to being a grownup. We're going in by the fire and having Maria's taquitas before dinner."

"Ah, compensation, indeed."

"Now you've done it," Cahill grumbled good-naturedly. "There'll be none for the rest of us. I thought they quit eating like this when they graduated college."

"You work up a hunger learning the cattle business in Wyoming," his younger brother proclaimed.

He'd been helping Jack with updating the Slash-C's software in addition to work full-time for a Boston tech company.

Over the winter, Jack had kept up with the ranch's ordering, record-keeping, and breeding statistics by computer and phone. He'd done more by visiting half a dozen top producers on the East Coast. Encouraged by Ed, he and Dave had settled on introducing a new bloodline to a portion of the Slash C herd.

"You know," Kiernan added, "I'd like to see this ranch behind all the data we've been crunching. Maybe I'll come out summer."

"We'd love to have you visit," Val said as they moved into the living room where a fire crackled. "And so would the women of Knighton."

"No, not you, too, Kiernan," Eleanor protested. "Deserter."

He slung an arm around his sister-in-law's shoulders and kissed the top of her head. "Console yourself with knowing you could rent out my room." Then he reached for two of the taquitas on the platter on the coffee table.

"You should come out, too," Jack invited.

"It's so hard to get away in the summer," Eleanor said. "It's our busy season."

And it would be even busier, since El and Cahill would oversee renting out Great-Aunt Susan's house this summer while Val and Addie were in Wyoming with Jack.

"Our busy season, too," Jack said with his amazing smile.

Winter had been the right time for him to get to know Gloucester. Despite being nearly overrun with Trimarco relatives, first, wanting to check him out, then, wanting to hang around because they liked him, they'd both found peace walking the winterscape beach.

But now the Curricks wanted him back. Infinitely more important to Val, he wanted to return to the Slash-C.

"Ah, but it's far too long before you'll be back here," Cahill complained.

"Maybe you'll *have* to come to Wyoming," Jack said. "If she says yes."

"You've asked her — you're getting married? That's wonderful. When—"

"Whoa, whoa, El," Val protested. She gave Jack a stern stare. "I thought we agreed not to tell anyone."

"You said that. I'm telling everyone. Need all the help I can get with your answer."

"You said *no*?" El demanded.

"I haven't said no. Haven't said yes, either. I've told him that we'll see how we do in Wyoming. Then we'll decide."

Cahill groaned. "All the way to the fall? Marry the man, Val."

Jack faced Valerie, with *See?* spread all over his face.

"I'm not going to rush you—"

Cahill and Jack groaned in unison.

"—or let you rush me. I'm not."

"So you're the holdup, since *he's* already decided," El said, reasonable as ever.

"I'm trying to be patient," said the saintly martyr who'd possessed Jack for the moment. "Until she comes around, I'm appreciating all that I have, especially my two girls."

Val tipped her head. "Maybe three girls. Or two girls and a boy."

A beat of silence followed, giving way to a burst of exclamations and hugs.

"Well, now you'll *have* to come home during the summer," Eleanor declared. "For the wedding, and again for the baby to be born here at home."

"We have two homes. And two families."

"We know the Curricks and all the rest you've talked about in Wyoming have been wonderful to you, but we're your ... we're your first family, aren't we?"

"Oh, El—" Val started, knowing she'd hurt her cousin.

But there was one who looked out for Eleanor first and always. "You'll marry from this house or you'll answer to me," Cahill told Val. As if he were big and scary, instead of big and lovable.

His wife hugged him.

"I'd like to see you take on my mom over that one, Cahill."

He grinned. "Ah, and you think I'm not knowing how to get around Aunt Lucy?"

Val laughed. His brogue came out strongest when he was most intent on charming, and darned if the man wouldn't manage to charm her mother if he set his mind to it.

"Everyone from Wyoming would be more than welcome. We could block out a couple weeks, both here and at your house. The wedding at the church, then the reception here. And—"

El was happily organizing and planning with Cahill's encouragement, while Val tried to slow down the wedding express.

But not all her attention was devoted to that.

Jack had his arm around her and she had a hand on his chest. Under her palm, she felt the beat. Strong, solid, and true. Jack's heart.

****

Knighton, Wyoming

"...so, what do you think? Put an addition on the foreman's house or renovate the main house at the Flying W, or build a new place here on the Slash-C?"

The Curricks — Dave and Matty, Ed and Donna — had made the offer in what had been billed as an organizational meeting for the coming season, but had felt more like a welcome home brunch. Before making a decision, Jack had asked for some time for the two of them to discuss it, and suggested a walk.

Val tightened her jacket around her. She'd opted for their walk to take them inside the barn, where not only did she get to rub some familiar noses, but there was some warmth to be had. Neither of her homes seemed to quite get the idea of *spring*.

She burrowed against Jack, for his warmth and for the wonderful feel of him. His arms came around her as she looked up to say, "I have one requirement — wherever we live I get to plant monkeyflower. Beyond that, we have my family home in Gloucester, so you should get to pick here. Besides, what does it matter as long as it's you and me, Jack Ralston."

"You and me," he confirmed. Then he smiled. That smile that gave her a view into not only who he was now, but so much better, who he was becoming each day. "You and me and Addie and the baby and maybe a few more."

"I can live with that. Oh, wait — as long as they're not born in the back of a station wagon." She considered. "Or a truck. Or a hay wagon. Or anywhere else uncomfortable and not sanitary."

"Okay. What about the conceiving? Any requirements about that?"

"That," she said with satisfaction, "is open to discussion."

He began the discussion by taking her mouth with his, long and firm and deep.

"Jack?" she said after a while, breathless and decidedly warmer.

"Hmm."

"I was wrong about one thing."

"I'm amazed."

She high-mindedly ignored that. "Likening you to those horses you rehabilitate."

"You mean comparing the training I do with those horses to how you've set about rehabilitating me, whether I liked it or not?"

She flipped her hand, conceding however he wanted to term it. "What it's really been more like is that day you got the steer out of the bog hole. Wading in to the muck, prying your stubborn rear up, trying to avoid getting kicked in the head for my pains, then giving you a good, firm push while circumstances dragged you — protesting and fighting every inch — into a better place."

For a long moment he didn't react.

Then, slowly, lines fanned from the corners of his eyes, his mouth stretched into a grin, he tipped his head back and roared out a laugh.

****

From just outside the doors at the far end of the barn, Donna Currick heard the sound. Her eyes filled with tears.

"Now what are you crying about woman," scolded Ed, as he gently pulled her into his arms. "Sounds to me like they're getting along fine."

"Tears of happiness, my darling husband," she said against his strong, comforting, achingly familiar chest. "Pure happiness."

-THE END-

I hope that reading Val and Jack's story has been
as much a pleasure for you as writing it was for
me, and that you'll share that experience with fellow
readers by leaving a review. They'll thank you, and so do I.

For news about upcoming books, subscribe
to Patricia McLinn's free newsletter.
www.PatriciaMcLinn.com/newsletter

Wyoming Wildflowers series

Donna and Ed's lives are worlds apart.
Can they ever bridge the distance . . .
Wyoming Wildflowers: The Beginning

Dave Currick has everything he wants,
except the woman he loves . . .
Almost a Bride

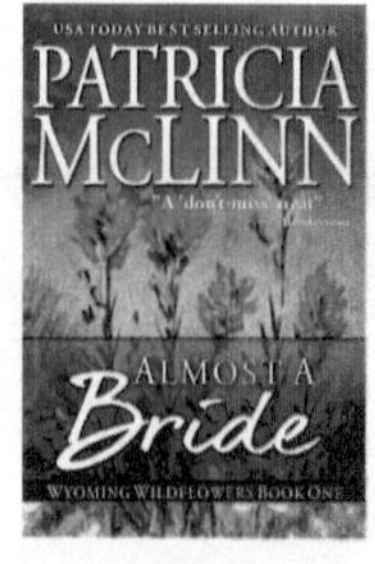

Cal and Taylor can spark a wildfire,
but will they come together in . . .
Match Made in Wyoming

Lisa Currick's carried a secret
in her heart for years—
and he just hit town
My Heart Remembers

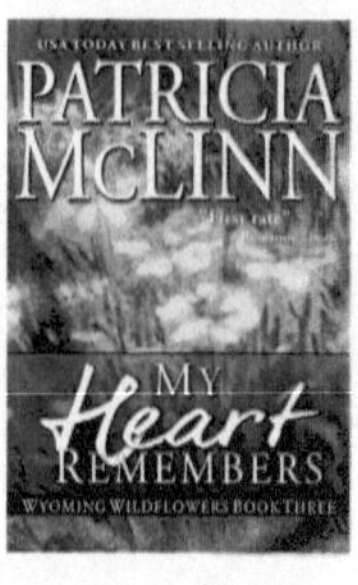

Or read the three books for one great price in the
Wyoming Wildflowers boxed set . . .
Wyoming Wildflowers Trilogy Boxed Set, 3 Books in 1

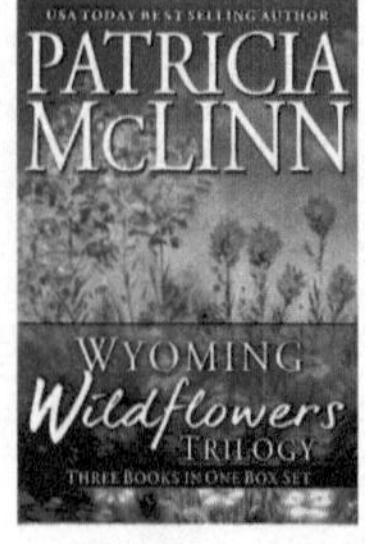

If you particularly enjoy connected books – as I do! – try these:
A Place Called Home Trilogy
Bardville, Wyoming Trilogy
The Wedding Series
Find a complete list of Patricia's books
at www.PatriciaMcLinn.com.

About the Author:

USA Today bestselling author Patricia McLinn's novels — cited by reviewers for warmth, wit and vivid characterization – have won numerous regional and national awards and been on national bestseller lists.

In addition to her romance and women's fiction books, Patricia is the author of the "Caught Dead in Wyoming" mystery series, which adds a touch of humor and romance to figuring out whodunit.

Patricia received BA and MSJ degrees from Northwestern University. She was a sports writer (Rockford, Ill.), assistant sports editor (Charlotte, N.C.) and — for 20-plus years — an editor at the Washington Post. She has spoken about writing from Honolulu to Washington, D.C., including being a guest-speaker at the Smithsonian Institute.

She is now living in Northern Kentucky, and writing full-time. Patricia loves to hear from readers through her website, Facebook and Twitter.

www.PatriciaMcLinn.com

www.ingramcontent.com/pod-product-compliance
Lightning Source LLC
Chambersburg PA
CBHW050516190726
48284CB00003B/821